House of Cads

ELIZABETH KINGSTON

Other books by Elizabeth Kingston
A FALLEN LADY
THE KING'S MAN
FAIR, BRIGHT, AND TERRIBLE

In collaboration with Susanna Malcolm:
THE MISADVENTURES OF A TITIAN-HAIRED
GODDESS AND AN OUTRAGEOUS HELLION

ISBN: 1986254860

ISBN-13: 978-1986254861

For Caitie

❦

You deserve laughter and adventure and,
above all,
to be loved as well as you deserve.

Chapter One

Marie-Anne de Vauteuil was in the midst of navigating a mud-puddle that stretched inconveniently across her path when she admitted to herself that she had just been jilted for the first time in her life. So galling was this reality that her fingers lost their grip on her skirt. This caused her hem to skim the surface of the dirty water and, immediately snatching it up out of harm's way, she discovered to her astonishment that she could not remember a single appropriate curse word. She would dearly like to use one, preferably a very grand one that would encompass the jilting, the muddy hem, and the fact that she did not have enough bread in her cupboard to suit her dismal mood. Sadly, all the curses seemed to have been wiped from her memory and replaced with the names of men she herself had politely abandoned over the years.

"Oh, vex," she said testily, deciding on the spot, as she often did, that this English word served her purpose well enough. She had learned that, stated with sufficient feeling, most words could easily become epithets. And that one had a pleasing v at its beginning, and an x at its end that was quite satisfactory to land on.

She grasped a sturdy branch of the yew tree that hung in an advantageous spot, and hauled herself up and over the puddle. It did not spare her boots entirely, but at least the leather wasn't soaked through. Heaven knew she would prefer to avoid a trip the shoemaker for a while, as he was the one who had jilted her.

But really, she thought with a scowl as she walked toward the village, was *jilted* the right word? It seemed to be used most often in the context of a betrothal, not an illicit liaison such as she and Jeremy had shared. She did not know another word for it, though. *Declined*, perhaps –like a delicacy that no longer appealed to the palate, because one had already had one's fill of it. Yes, that was a perfect word, whether it was used this way among the English or not.

Certainly she herself had *declined* the continued affections of many men in her day. Perhaps this was her reward for those casual dismissals of her youth. For instance there had been Martin, the lover she had politely declined after Napoleon abdicated and just before she left France for England – an excellent moment to end things, she had thought. Poor Martin had not agreed.

"Before that was Gurvan," she confided to John Turner's goat, who stuck his nose out from the gate to greet her as she passed. Marie-Anne pulled up some leaves from a withered cowslip and offered them to the grateful animal. "Gurvan could not believe when I *declined* to live in Nantes with him and raise goats. I hope you will not take offense, *mon ami*, it was not the goats but the man I did not want. And of course before that, there was Maurice, Antoine, Flavio... But they were very agreeable when I *declined* to continue with them." The goat looked at her without blinking. "Do not judge, monsieur goat, they were just barely more than flirtations. And all of them were forgotten when I met my Richard."

She said goodbye to the goat and moved along the lane, hoping it would stay empty until she reached the bakery so that she would not be forced into genial conversation. She much preferred to be left alone to think of her Richard, who was the only man she had never considered declining in any sense, at any time.

Her Richard would never have jilted her. He would never have even considered parting from her, had a fever not forced him into an early grave. How very unjust, that he was taken from her too soon. And how selfish of her to think it a further injustice that because of it, she had been reduced to seek the affections of an inferior man. A man who made shoes and who now preferred the arms of another woman. The arms, she must acknowledge, of a woman he would wed.

She told herself it was perfectly acceptable that Jeremy preferred a wife to a lover. Not that he had used those words. He was terribly kind about it. He was so sheepishly happy that she had congratulated him and meant it most sincerely. And it was very sweet, how he had made it obvious he was grateful to her and would miss their little trysts, and would always think of her warmly.

Oh the swine, to deprive her of even the pleasure

of calling him a scoundrel.

"Bread, Monsieur Higgins!" she called, allowing herself to be as French as she could manage while still being understood by the baker. Higgins was charmed by her Frenchness, and she used it ruthlessly to her advantage. He had closed up the bakeshop, but she applied her fist to the door anyway, knowing he was still within. "*Je t'en prie, mon ami,* you cannot imagine my need. It is enormous."

"Miss Marie-Anne," came his faintly exasperated voice from behind the door, "You were in this morning and had my best loaf. How can you need more already?"

"That was a loaf to fill my belly, monsieur, and now I have need of a loaf to bandage a wound to my soul."

She said it in the most dramatic, throbbing tones available to her. All bakers were, in her view, poets who expressed themselves in flour and fat: yearnings rendered in yeasty interiors, insights offered in golden brown crust. Mr. Higgins was no different, and that was why she knew that upon hearing her declaration, he now paused in sweeping the crumbs from his floor. He only hesitated because he was irritable from rising even earlier than usual, to meet the increased demands of the villagers during this festival week. The sounds of his muttering reached her barely, which she was certain he intended. Who grumbled so loudly if not to be heard?

"Please, Mr. Higgins," she said softly through the door. She was alarmed to discover a lump in her throat. "I will much prefer your bread to sop my tears than a flavorless handkerchief."

The door opened on the squat little man. He held

the broom in his hand, and his full-faced frown did not conceal the soft concern in his eyes. How eloquent he was, this silent poet.

"There's naught but three buns left, and them gone half-stale," he grunted.

Gratitude and affection must have made her smile quite dazzling, for he seemed to soften for a moment before scowling even more ferociously. He thrust the broom into her hands and turned to take the bread from a basket on the counter. When he took the buns to the oven, she protested faintly. "No, no, my friend, you do not need to heat them for me."

"Oven's still warm," he muttered.

"But that means you baked a second batch later in the morning. How busy you have been! You must be very fatigued, Monsieur Higgins, you must not trouble yourself."

Another grunt was his only answer, a clear opinion on the notion of handing her cold, hard bread. This was his way with her, for all the six years she had lived in Bartle. He was gruff and frowning and never said a sweet word to her or anyone, as far as she could tell. But he always kept the fattest loaf aside for her, and never turned her away if she came late to his door, and frowned reproachfully at her if she skipped her regular visits to his shop. This past winter he had even sent the blacksmith's boy to her house with a basket of bread and a jar of delicious hot soup when she was so ill, and would not let her pay him for it.

For all these things, Marie-Anne called him friend. But there was a limit to this friendship. Many limits, in fact.

She pulled off her muddy boots and stepped inside. She was careful to leave the door open, so that no one could accuse them of impropriety. There was no escaping her reputation. Even if the villagers did generally like and approve of her, she still carried a whiff of the scandalous. It left no room for error and rather hampered friendship with entirely respectable people.

While he added the bread to the oven, she applied the broom to his floor and imagined what the conversation might be, without the limitations placed upon them. *I am so very lonely*, she might confess to the baker if she were allowed such intimacy, *and so unbearably bored*. She supposed that even in a better world, she probably would not tell him of Jeremy and the jilting. Jilting Jeremy! What a perfect sobriquet. That is what she and Helen would have named him immediately, if Helen were still here to laugh with.

Mr. Higgins crossed the floor and took the broom from her with an irritated clucking of his tongue. Like so many of the villagers, he considered her too fine a lady for such work. He recommenced the sweeping and looked down at the floor as he asked, "What word from Maggie, then?"

Marie-Anne sighed a little. No Helen and no Maggie. No wonder she was so sad to lose her perfectly adequate shoemaker lover.

"I have had no letter from her since last I told you. But it was happy news that she sent, you remember. She will marry her Irish lad."

"Happy news," Mr. Higgins nodded. "What's his name, then?"

"Niall," she said and heard the mournful note in her own voice, which made her nearly stamp her foot in irritation at herself. It *was* happy news, and she had grown so pitiful that her feelings were not joy for her friend but sadness that it meant Maggie would never return to England now.

"And the little girl who was her cousin, the one who went to America, what word from her?"

"I have not heard from Katie since Christmas time." Oh how childish, that wistful note in her voice.

"No word of her through Miss Helen?" he asked. "Lady Summerdale, I mean to say."

Now she did stamp her foot a little, only to gasp a faint *ow* when she felt the rough boards beneath her stocking feet. She'd forgotten she had removed her boots. Higgins heard it and looked over his shoulder at her. She lowered her brows at him, annoyed that he did not politely ignore her ridiculousness.

"You are intent on reminding me of all my friends who are not here to comfort me." She crossed her arms with a delicate huff of indignation. "It makes me quite unhappy to think of it. They have all moved on and moved out and changed entirely. It's only me who remains here. And I am the same as ever."

It was as close as she could come to saying she was bored silly by her life here without her friends to entertain her. She held the tasseled ends of her shawl tight between her fingers and gradually came to realize that her face was arranged in a pout. She hoped it did not seem a coquettish expression to Higgins. She certainly didn't intend it as such. Try as she might, she could not wipe it from her face. She wanted to pout. She might even like to stamp her foot again. Perhaps she would throw herself on the floor and howl and hope that some kindly passerby would bring her a sweet to soothe her.

All the while, Higgins just looked at her. Finally he said, "Bread."

He went to retrieve the buns from the oven, and put them in a little sack. She sighed, and stepped to the door to put her boots on again. They were very nice, these boots. Jeremy had made them so they could be laced quickly and easily. He'd insisted to her that sometimes, no matter how much she might disagree, practicality was preferable to being fashionable. She must admit that in this particular matter he'd been correct. It took only a moment to get them on and when she rose, Mr. Higgins held out the bread to her. They stood for a little moment on the threshold with her hand on the sack. She did not want to say goodbye.

"What is the word when a lover leaves you, Mr. Higgins?" she asked, very softly. "I can only think of jilting, but that is used for a serious beau, when there are clear intentions, is it not?"

He didn't answer her, so she sighed a little again and held the warmed bread against her chest. It was a very unseemly thing to have asked, she knew, but she was not known for her adherence to convention. Nevertheless, she should not torment Higgins with impudent questions, even if they were sincere. She blinked, composed her expression, and lifted her chin to look at him with a polite and inquiring smile.

"Or perhaps there is a word for the person who does the leaving?" she asked.

He jerked his head, a firm nod. "A rare oaf is what I'd call him, Miss Marie-Anne."

Oh. Oh, the dear man. In the midst of her brilliant smile, he turned away and closed the door. The sun was beginning to set now, and he must get to his bed so he could bake a pile of loaves tomorrow before it rose again. She had no doubt that all the while, the scowl would remain on his dear, grumpy face.

"*Merci*, Monsieur Higgins, my friend," she said to the door between them, before taking a warm bun from the bag and stuffing it unceremoniously into her face.

~

Bread was for lonely and despairing times, and pastries or cakes were for happy times. This was Marie-Anne's philosophy, and she was fully aware that she called it a philosophy even though it was only the well-known preference of her mouth and belly. If her friends could see her now, walking through the village street at twilight with a mouth full of bread, they would ask what had happened. Alas, her friends were not here, and so she took another bite of the bun.

She was quite fortunate that she had always had mostly happy times in her life, and that until recently she had never had the means to indulge herself in as many cakes as she had felt herself entitled to. "Of course," she said to the second bun as she pulled it out of the bag and opened her front door, "if I do not cheer up soon, I shall grow bigger than Mr. Worster's sow." Her financial situation had improved lately, and her nearest friend was the village baker. A bout of melancholy could too easily spell disaster for her figure.

The thought that immediately followed – that she may as well let her figure go since she was likely never to have a lover again – was so uncharacteristically dismal that it had the same effect as a friendly slap across the face. Really. *A little self-respect, Marie-Anne,* she told herself. Even immediately after Richard had died, even after she had miscarried their child, she had never fallen into sadness for too long. It had been horrid, never a worse time in her life – but though she had wallowed in her grief for some months she had not lingered overlong in that dejected state. It was simply not in her nature. "Endeavour to live a life where you laugh at least twice as hard as you cry," Aurélie had said to her once when she was very young, and Marie-Anne had taken it to heart.

Standing over the table in her kitchen, she shook the last bun out of the bag. With it came a ball of fabric, a torn bit of an old, thin towel wrapped around something. She unfurled it to find a little cake, iced and smelling deliciously of lemon. Oh the dear man. It made her a bit teary even as it made her smile.

In her philosophy, as Higgins well knew, sweets were for happy times but also for the absolute worst of the worst times. If she reached for a sweet in her sadness, then things were truly dire. Oh, she must have looked horribly sad for him to have given her a cake, for him to think she should have a sweet in reserve. It was terribly tempting, sitting there on her table. She was sure it had bits of candied lemon peel in it, though she had learned not to hope he'd be so adventurous as to include a layer of cream or liqueur. He was a simple man, for all that he had the heart of a romantic. It seemed to her to be meant as both comfort and hope at once: comfort in case she grew despondent in the night, but also hope that she would return to a happier state before the cake grew stale.

Well. She sniffed and banished the tears – she would take it as hope. How very maudlin she had become. And over Jeremy! He was merely a dear friend, not some grand love. Once her grief for her darling Richard had faded to a tolerable level, she had made a point of finding a lover, and found Jeremy. It had been for purely practical reasons. One could not neglect the necessary bodily functions, including the more erotic ones. It simply was not healthy, like failing to bathe or clean one's teeth. So – to lose a utilitarian lover was no great tragedy, it was merely an inconvenience. Eventually she would find another. No need to give up.

In the meantime, she must really try to cheer herself or that cake would go to waste. She suddenly remembered the letter that had come this afternoon just as she was leaving to meet Jeremy. She hadn't even stopped to see who it was from, assuming that since it had come from London it must be Helen. A letter from her friend would be the perfect antidote to this absurd mood.

But to her amazement, it was not from her friend. It was from Hyacinth Shipley – *Lady* Shipley, as she was ever quick to remind anyone who forgot it – the woman who had come within days of being her mother-in-law. It was without a doubt the most cordial communication she'd ever received from her.

With the season in high swing, Lady Shipley wondered if Marie-Anne would have occasion to find herself in London at all and, if so, Lady Shipley hoped most earnestly that she would come to call on them. Indeed, she wrote, they would love nothing more than that Marie-Anne would see fit to stay with them for the duration of the season, and there was a room waiting for her should she be so kind as to take full advantage of their hospitality.

"*Mon dieu,*" breathed Marie-Anne as she read, and

nearly crossed herself. Had the poor woman had some sort of apoplexy? Perhaps one that had caused her to lose her memory, if not her entire dreadful personality? She had not thought Lady Shipley was terribly old, but it was possible that the many and varied beauty treatments she employed had actually worked to disguise her true age. It could be that the woman was positively elderly and had begun to lose her mind. That would explain it.

Lady Shipley was Richard's mother, and had never been more appalled than when her son announced he would make Marie-Anne his wife. True, they had made it a bit more appalling by putting off marriage until Marie-Anne was pregnant, but her Richard had been so busy in his comings and goings with the military that it really could not be helped. Nevertheless, upon hearing of their engagement Lady Shipley had begun a series of screeches and swoons that had lasted until, just a week before the wedding, poor Richard had fallen ill. At which point, Lady Shipley had subsided into woeful moans and hissed recriminations. Sir Gordon Shipley, Richard's father, had been no less disgusted by the connection though he was considerably less voluble.

When her Richard had died so suddenly, they had barred Marie-Anne from the funeral. Ten days later, she had miscarried the child and eventually sent a note to let Sir Gordon know that Richard had not left an heir. She vividly remembered debating over whether to write *heir* or *bastard*, and had decided that Richard's intentions mattered more than the cruel reality. It hardly made a difference, though. Her note was answered with the briefest of messages, which read only: *Thank God.* She had heard nothing from the

Shipley family since.

The letter she held from Lady Shipley now referred to none of this. There was no apology, not even an attempt to wave it away by referring to a "misunderstanding." It was written as though none of it had ever happened. Marie-Anne tried to think if Richard had ever said there was madness in his family. It was the only explanation she could think of, until she noticed another, smaller note wedged down at the bottom of the envelope.

It was from Amarantha, the eldest Shipley daughter. *Marie-Anne, it is unforgivable of me to write to you now when I have so sadly neglected you for all these years,* it began. Oh sweet Amy, who had been barely fourteen when it had all happened. Marie-Anne wouldn't dream of faulting the girl for following her parents' example – indeed, the whole of Society's example – in shunning her. She ran her fingers over the writing with affection, and wondered if Amy always wrote in such a cramped style or if she'd merely been trying to make the smallest note possible, to ensure it could be slipped into the envelope without her mother's noticing.

Please come, Amy wrote. *I am newly engaged and D and P will ruin all my hopes through their actions. They will listen to you, if you will be so kind as to come, though I am sure none of us deserve it.*

Oh well this was very interesting. D and P could only be Amy's younger sisters, Dahlia and Phyllida, who had from birth been quite a trial to anyone's patience. They would be seventeen and eighteen now, and were apparently having an eventful season. At their darling older sister's expense.

What a family. Not for the first time, Marie-Anne

wondered how such a gathering of awful people could have produced her dear Richard. The arrogant father, the grasping mother, the silly and spoiled sisters. Well not Amy, though, she was the best of the lot now that Richard was gone. Oh and the brother, Percy, who was so priggish that she used to joke he was destined to be the oldest virgin in Europe one day, even if one included every priest on the continent in the final score.

Marie-Anne began to giggle. It was not at all a refined sound, rather more of a tittering that grew into snorting laughter. Oh heavens, what must they be up to, to make their mother desperate enough to invite scandalous Marie-Anne de Vauteuil to stay at their precious townhouse, at the height of the season? Of course she felt sorry for poor Amy, but there was no denying that there must be a delightful spectacle waiting to be viewed in London.

It really was a perfect answer to the desperate boredom she'd begun to feel in Bartle. And she could visit Helen! Oh what a lovely prospect, to help Amy while watching the antics of her sisters *and* the acute distress of the more horrid members of the Shipley family. And to be able to laugh with her dearest friend about it all as it happened! Except that Helen had mentioned a trip – a holiday somewhere Nordic – or would that be later in the summer? No matter, so long as she had a little time with her.

Yes, she would accept this most unlikely invitation. How could she possibly resist? She must write back without delay, and send a note to dear Helen too.

Marie-Anne went back to the kitchen and popped the little lemon cake into her mouth. It was delicious.

The cake, the letters, the entertainment that was promised in London: it was all *most* delicious.

Chapter Two

"Watch out for that one," said Freddy with a nod toward the newly arrived guests who had been announced with some pomp.

"Summerdale, was that it?" asked Mason, looking toward the aristocrat. Not just an aristocrat, he immediately noticed, but very aristocratic. God, they really knew how to breed them here. Centuries in the making, and this Summerdale was a perfect specimen: impeccably dressed, ramrod straight posture, oozing circumspection, and with just the slightest superiority as he scanned the room. Of course, all those things really just made him the perfect specimen of what the aristocracy *supposed* themselves to be. Mason had seen enough in his brief time in England to know that most of them fell far short of this ideal – and that most did so gleefully.

"Earl of, old boy," emphasized Freddy. "A bit elevated for this company, I'd think, but perhaps he owes Huntingdon a favor and is paying up by making an appearance."

They were at the Right Honorable Lord Huntingdon's ball, given in honor of his niece's recent engagement to the third son of the Marquess of…he'd have to check his notes. Mason never felt more American than when he struggled to remember the many names, titles, ranks, and honorifics that all Englishmen seemed to have printed on the insides of their eyelids. But Huntingdon was a baron, which was definitely below an earl, which he thought was below a marquess. Possibly not below the third son of a marquess, though. He'd have asked Freddy to clarify if his head wasn't already close to busting with spare bits of the high society minutia.

Besides, he'd just spied the woman who'd come in with Summerdale and he really didn't relish looking at Freddy when she was there to be looked at instead.

"No surprise he's brought the wife, I hear they're inseparable. She was a scandal in her day," Freddy was saying. "But best to pretend she was never anything but spotless, around Summerdale. He'll take us both down without batting an eye if we give him half a reason, remember that. But she's old news, who's that with them? Damn, I wasn't listening."

Mason made himself absorb all this information but didn't ask any of the questions he normally would have. He just didn't feel like working now that the pretty, lively Lady Summerdale was there to be looked at. He could believe she had scandal in her past. It took next to nothing for these people to consider a woman scandalous, and she looked like a merry ball of mischief all packaged up in a blue-eyed, blonde-haired, fashion plate of a woman.

Crying shame, that she was married. She looked

like the type that might be up for it anyway, but he had his own scruples. Not many, but he had them. Besides, if Freddy said her husband could cut them off at the knees, then best to listen.

As Mason watched her, she tilted her head up to better hear her friend, a very elegant, dark-haired woman who exuded as much reserve as the blonde woman exuded exuberance. The dark-haired woman was so graceful in her movement that Mason found himself momentarily distracted by her form. She possessed an outrageously perfect figure, one that made him want to study her at length until his pencil captured her exact proportions. It even made him think for a moment that he should try his hand at sculpture. She seemed far more suited to the Earl of Summerdale than the lively, petite blonde.

"Hey, Fred," he hissed, grasping the other man's cuff as the thought occurred to him. Freddy had started to slink away. "Which one is Mrs. Summerdale?"

"*Lady* Summerdale, Mason, do try to keep it in your head when it's one of the higher ranks."

"Right. Lady, I knew that. Just forgot it for a second. Which one?"

"Dark hair, tall and lovely. Don't know who short-and-lovely is, try to find out, won't you? I just saw Bilson head for the card room."

Bilson was the main reason they'd come to this thing. Well really, they'd come because Mason had been invited. Freddy had managed to slip in because the Huntingdon staff was notoriously easy to bribe. Bilson was a lawyer, the most indiscreet one of those who worked for a certain marquess. That marquess was considering divorce, and a divorce trial would sell a lot of papers, and so here they were in the hopes Bilson couldn't resist the opportunity to share the latest gossip. Freddy would skulk around and maybe ply Bilson with drink, hoping to get something they could use. But first he warned Mason once more to be careful of the Earl of Summerdale.

"Don't make him curious about you or it's the end of us," said Freddy, and headed to the card room.

Finding out who the pretty blonde fashion plate was while avoiding Summerdale would require some creativity. He noticed a few people looking her way and surreptitiously whispering to each other, but they were careful not to be too obvious about it. He certainly couldn't overhear them. The hostess was the answer, he supposed, and fortunately for Mason, this particular hostess was Lady Huntingdon. She loved nothing more than to educate him as to who was who on the London scene, and to include all sorts of inside information.

Lady Huntingdon was moving toward Summerdale's party and her demeanor made him pause. On second thought maybe she *wouldn't* tell Mason anything more than the woman's name. The trio of women met with genuine joy and affection, the warm greeting of true friends and not the usual fake delight. Which meant the blonde mystery was an actual friend to both a baroness and an earl's wife.

What was an earl's wife called? It was the odd one, not like duchess or viscountess. There was no earlesse, a fact that he'd fortunately learned by misspeaking to Freddy and not through any more embarrassing experience. But in any case, if she was dear friends with these people, she was probably pretty elevated herself.

He heard the music change, the dance winding down to a close. As the next dance started up, he watched Lord Summerdale escort the petite blonde to the dancefloor, leaving Lady Summerdale behind to talk with the hostess. Mason moved toward the women, finding a spot between a well-placed fern and a majestically proportioned matron with a plumed headdress that would hide a frigate – a perfect place where Mason might hear their conversation without being seen.

"Norway!" Lady Huntingdon exclaimed, loudly enough so that Mason could hear it. "But my dear, you could go anywhere at all, why do you let him drag you to Norway of all places!"

"I assure you I am the one doing the dragging, Joyce." Lady Summerdale was laughing. It was a wonderful sound, all gurgling and burbling like a brook, and didn't seem to match her elegant exterior. She seemed aware of it and quickly swallowed the sound. "There is so much I want to see there, but we will have only a few months. I'll tell you all about it when we return. Now in the meantime you must..."

Here her voice wound down to a more discreet volume and she brought her fan up to shield her lips as she spoke to her friend. He watched them, unable to hear anything they said but enjoying this rare display of real friendship at a high society event. He also enjoyed the line of Lady Summerdale's back and how perfectly the ice blue dress suited her. Not that she'd relish hearing it, or that he'd ever dare to say it, but she would make the most enviable artist's model.

He looked to the dancefloor, where the women were watching Lord Summerdale and the pretty blonde dancing. Her movements were out of step with the other dancers and she didn't seem so very graceful. In fact, he thought she must have stepped on the earl's toes once or twice. This was evident not by any grimace on the earl's face, but on her own – a little apologetic cringing amid all the laughter she was valiantly holding in. The earl never missed a step, of course, and he wore the same expression of suppressed mirth. It was a shared joke, obvious in the way the earl slid a look toward his wife from time to time while he guided the other woman through the steps and they both tried not to laugh.

When the music stopped, the earl whisked her off the dancefloor and back to where Ladies Summerdale and Huntingdon stood. As soon as they were within steps of the other ladies, the mystery woman let her smile open up to her friends, though she seemed determined not to laugh aloud.

"Oh what a disgrace I am!" she cried.

"On the contrary, madame, you are the most delightful dance partner any man could hope for. It has been not only an honor but a very great pleasure."

Lord Summerdale said it all quite smoothly while making an elegant bow over her hand. Mason wondered how long it took to perfect that move. He'd tried it himself a few times but nothing could convince him he didn't look like a complete ass.

"It has been nothing but cruelty to your well-trained toes, my lord, and your wife will not forgive me if I have ruined you for more dancing tonight."

She had an accent – French, he thought, though he'd like to hear more before judging, and he wasn't sure he could count on the matron with the elaborate headdress to continue to create his perfect hiding spot much longer. Fortunately, Lord Summerdale's toes weren't so damaged that he couldn't dance immediately. He murmured something that made the ladies laugh prettily and then offered his hand to his wife. She gave the Frenchwoman a questioning look.

"Go, go, you have done your duty." She shooed at them fondly with her fan, and they glided away into the moving mass of dancers.

This was Mason's chance, and since he had no idea how long the music would keep playing, he wasted no time in presenting himself to his hostess. Being a graceful fellow, he nearly toppled the fern and somehow managed to get his mouth full of ostrich plume as he freed himself from his secluded little spot. He thought he felt the feather snap as he shoved it aside, but ignored that in favor of moving speedily away from the site of his destruction. He let the unsuspecting woman tend to her headdress while he surreptitiously spat out bits of it before he was spotted by the ladies. Naturally, that took no time at all – one of the inconveniences of having flaming red hair.

"Oh Mr. Mason!" Lady Huntingdon called as he swallowed a bit of ostrich plume. She waved him over the last few steps. "What a shame, you've just missed Lady Summerdale and I particularly wanted her to meet you. But here, this is our dear friend newly arrived from the country, Miss – that is, Madame Marie-Anne de Vauteuil."

He remembered he was supposed to be a very important and wealthy American gentleman, which helped him to square his shoulders and look sufficiently confident as he gave a small, restrained bow. "Madame, a pleasure."

"Monsieur," she said with a graceful dip of her

knees, and then looked up at him. She might have said more but he was distracted by the perfect blue of her eyes. He knew that color, exactly. On a clear fall evening at twilight, just before the light was completely gone, that was the blue of the sky above the layers of orange and pink. When you faced northwest, anyway, and stood on the Kentucky side of the Ohio River.

It took an awfully long time for him to realize that the blue was framed by an expression that was half dubious, half laughing.

"It is possible Mr. Mason believes I will be insulted if he does not ask me to dance," she said, never looking away from him. "Shall we give him assurance that I will only be very relieved?"

"There's no need for that at all, my dear. Mr. Mason knows very well that he is the only gentleman in attendance who is entirely excused from asking ladies to dance," explained Lady Huntingdon.

"Because he is American?" asked the perfect blue eyes.

"Because I'm the worst dancer on this side of the Atlantic, ma'am. The man who held the title before I arrived is probably dancing for joy. Poorly."

Her lips held in laughter. Her eyes crinkled at the edges with it. "What coincidence, we must alert the papers to this momentous occasion! For I am your female counterpart, monsieur. Such luck for our dear hostess. If the evening becomes too boring, she can invite us to partner a waltz. The spectacle will make her ball the talk of the season."

"No waltzing even in jest, Marie-Anne," Lady Huntingdon corrected her. "Something less daring, for our purpose."

The Frenchwoman's smile dimmed a bit, which Mason found he didn't like at all.

"I'd propose a quadrille, ma'am, so we could share the burden of celebrity with three other couples."

"I would protest this," she said, her lips curving up again. "They will never forgive me, these three other couples, for marching all over their toes for the length of a quadrille."

"No, you're right about that," he agreed.

It was an actual, physical relief to see her smile back in place. It was clear she had the sort of sense of humor that was discouraged in fine company such as this. Could he bring it out? Could he resist trying? Of course he couldn't.

"Here's an idea – I went to see the menagerie in the Tower of London this week. If it's a spectacle you want, we could select a couple of animals to take our place in the set. We'd get all the same entertainment but they'd get the blame for the destruction."

"What an excellent idea. Perhaps there is a pair of monkeys?" She said it with a perfectly straight face.

"Too agile, to represent me. They had some red gazelles…?"

"That is far too graceful for *me*. Are there any water oxen?"

He shook his head. "None that I recall, but there were some kangaroos. They'd make a good show."

Her eyes lit up. "No, it is a real word? Kanga – kanga-ruse." She looked to her friend to verify, mouthing the word again. "Well it must be these, of course."

"I daresay they would be kinder to my floors than the water oxen," Lady Huntingdon interjected.

"But we must consider the cakes. You are very

resourceful, monsieur, and I'm sure you have already considered that they might eat all the cakes if we let them in. I cannot allow that."

"Well, they're city beasts, ma'am. They've learned their manners."

She liked that. She was trying very hard not to laugh. Who needed dancing? He could do this all night, with her.

"What a marvelous plan! But you wouldn't mind, Lady Huntingdon, if it gave you the reputation for eccentricity?" She turned to their hostess, but he noticed she kept her eyes on him for as long as possible as her head turned, as though reluctant to look away. "You see Mr. Mason and I invent the latest craze. We are very clever, aren't we?"

Lady Huntingdon looked between Mason and Madame de Vauteuil with an unmistakable look of satisfaction before answering. "Indeed, I believe you are a perfectly suited pair for such devilry. I'm sure I should shudder to leave you alone. Alas, I see Mrs. Linwood has damaged her monstrous fine headdress and is very distressed over it, the poor dear. I'll take her to the retiring room where we may repair it. I leave my dear friend in your care, Mr. Mason. I won't return to find a pair of ocelots in evening dress, I trust?"

From the way Lady Huntingdon looked at him, he realized abruptly that he had been forgetting to play his part. He hadn't done or said anything incriminating, though, and he didn't think there was any harm in letting Lady Huntingdon see he was capable of absurd humor. He assured her he would not abandon Madame de Vauteuil to stand alone, nor replace her with any jungle animals, and their hostess fluttered off to attend to Mrs. Linwood and her broken ostrich plume.

There was an awkward little silence. He was suddenly shy to be left alone with these perfect blue eyes and the shiny waves of hair with the velvet ribbon woven through. She was so pretty and polished. He was wearing the finest clothes he'd ever owned, yet he felt like he was barefoot and grubby, dressed again in the remnants of a flour sack. He became convinced there was dirt behind his ears, even.

"You have been in London long, Mr. Mason?" Marie-Anne de Vauteuil asked him politely.

It snapped him out of his scrutiny of her gown, a dusky pink moiré beneath a diaphanous golden overlay. He was wondering how much just the overlay would cost, and how many hours it must have taken some nameless woman to make the embroidered pattern on it. Obviously he hadn't been here long enough to grow accustomed to the riches.

"Barely two months, ma'am. Or Miss." He was fumbling now, because her eyes were dangerous. "Or Madame? I'm sorry, my manners have also been here for barely two months. Just long enough to learn how bad it is to bungle a title."

"Oh there are worse things to bungle with these people, I assure you, though not many." She said it like it was a secret between them, and her heavily accented voice reminded him that despite her appearance, she was also an outsider. "There are not many that have the same good humor as Lady Huntingdon. But these English can be quite forgiving, if one is hopelessly foreign and very, very charming."

"And if *two* are hopelessly foreign, with no

Englishmen involved?"

"Then one of these two must be very, very, *very* charming," she answered with a full and unrestrained smile that put a deep dimple into her right cheek.

He smiled back at her, because it was impossible not to – and because he had a very similar dimple deep in his left cheek. He saw her notice it and widen her own smile even further. They stood there gazing at each other like a couple of sapheads, mirror-image smiles of delight plastered on their faces.

Coup de foudre, he thought out of nowhere. It was one of the very few bits of French he knew: lightning strike. That's what it felt like, standing there smiling with her.

Lord almighty, this was not good. And lord almighty, he did not care.

"Well one of us is definitely that charming, Miss Marie-Anne de Vauteuil," he finally said, and his voice was low and slow and full of Kentucky. Not at all who he was supposed to be. "Or Madame. Which is it?"

She broke the gaze at last, a little look down as she busied herself by tugging up her gloves. "I prefer to be called just Marie-Anne, but it seems that is not allowed. Between us, I believe I am properly a Miss Marie-Anne, for I have never been a Mrs. Anything. But here in London I am called madame, for very tiresome reasons. Would you like to hear them?"

"I'd rather hear you tell me why you've come to London from the country, and where in the country, and where you are staying and if you'd like to go for a drive in the park with me tomorrow. I hear that's an acceptable thing to do here." Not at all acceptable for him, though. What was he thinking?

Probably because he was being so obvious, she seemed to suddenly become conscious that they were standing in a very well-populated ball room. Her eyes still twinkled at him and her mouth still held its curve of amusement, but she took the tiniest step back from him before turning to look out at the dancers.

"This is rather a lot of questions, Mr. Mason. But it must be that you see how I am flooded with young suitors who fall over themselves to beg I will dance with them." She gestured eloquently with her fan at the empty space around them. "How heroic you are, to save me from it with your conversation! But I shall only answer if you will do the same."

"Agreed," he said. What a shame. He'd have to lie to her. "Where in the country were you, before you came to London?"

"It is a town called Bartle, in Herefordshire. That is north and west from London," she explained. "Its proper name is Bartle-on-the-Glen, though no one has ever been able to explain to me why. Glens are Scottish, I thought, and we are nowhere near Scotland."

"Is there a glen, though?"

"Oh yes, a very pretty one."

"Perhaps a Scotsman first lived there?"

"Or a Scotswoman." She smiled again, but kept her eyes on the dancers. "Now it is your turn, Mr. Mason. From where in America do you come to us?"

Here he could be truthful, thankfully.

"New York City. But I'm not from there. I was born and raised in a place called Kentucky. Have you heard of it?"

"Kentucky," she said, trying out the syllables. Her mouth liked the feel of them, he could tell. "It is a province?"

"We call them states."

"Yes of course. Kentucky," she said again in that adorable way. She actually made him feel nostalgic for the place. "The name of your village?"

"Skillman." Less poetic – or so he thought, until she repeated it.

"Skeel-man. Perhaps a very skilled man first lived there!" She seemed delighted with herself for thinking of that, and turned her smile to him again. "But now you must say why you have come to London. You are first, this time."

"Business, ma'am."

She gave a pretty little scowl. "Well that is my answer too, if we are allowed to be so very vague."

"The lumber business. Or timber, I should say." Before he got to London, he had considered saying the fur trade, because he knew it better. But there was too much American fur decorating London's finest citizens. Inventing a fur-trading enterprise would invite too many questions and inevitably lead to an unsustainable load of deceit. Lumber was boring, and these people cared more about the riches he said it had brought him than they did the actual product. "It's also very tiresome, but I would not want to be vague. And your business in London?"

She opened her mouth and took a breath to say something, then stopped. She was thinking very hard. Was she lying too? Now that was an intriguing proposition.

"Social restitution," she finally said, with a note of triumph.

"That's not tiresome at all. What does it mean?"

She gave an impish grin, very satisfied with herself.

"That is not in your original set of questions, monsieur, and I decline to answer you."

The music was stopping, and he saw her friends coming toward them. God, he'd have to deal with Summerdale, who probably could spot Madame de Vauteuil flirting with a red-headed American across a dozen ball rooms and might be just the sort to ask all sorts of uncomfortable questions about Mason's fictitious business. No time to waste.

"Your direction," he said hurriedly. "Where may I call on you, madame?"

She looked slightly taken aback. "I have not said you may call on me."

The smile sliding so abruptly from his face wasn't nearly as embarrassing as the flush that replaced it. It was purple, and it mostly stayed in his neck but crept just a little up the sides of his face when he least wanted it to – like now.

"Of course. My apologies."

"Oh, monsieur, you must not think–"

"I see your friends are returning. I'll leave you in their care." He gave a quick, taut bow. "It's been a pleasure, madame."

He beat a hasty retreat and told himself he was lucky. He couldn't call on her, and a drive in the park with Marie-Anne de Vauteuil was out of the question. London society was very different from the world he knew, but it wasn't *that* different. He couldn't flirt shamelessly with a woman and then drive through the park with her while his fiancée cooled her heels at home.

Chapter Three

Marie-Anne came down to breakfast to find Lord Summerdale sipping coffee and talking with Collins, the butler. He rose swiftly as she entered and greeted her, then returned to his conversation as she filled her plate at the sideboard. It was lovely, the heaps and heaps of food. There were servants, and a carriage if she wanted to go anywhere, and when it was cold all the fires were lit without any worry of running out of fuel. She had been here for six days, doing the social rounds necessary to discreetly announce she was in the good graces of the most respectable Earl of Summerdale and so must therefore be acceptable to everyone who mattered. At the end of a week, her reputation seemed largely rehabilitated and she was becoming accustomed to living a bit extravagantly.

Marie-Anne's allowance had never permitted any luxuries, and when Helen had lived in Bartle too, her own allowance had been even less. Now that marriage had brought a change in fortunes, Helen had insisted on sharing the wealth with Marie-Anne, who regularly found herself accepting deliveries of gifts large and small: great huge hampers of food, new stockings that Helen said were not her preferred length but were perfect for Marie-Anne, a box of bed linens that had languished unused in a cupboard at the Summerdale estate and should not go to waste, piles of the latest fashion magazines – "because you love them," read the accompanying note.

The result was that Marie-Anne now lived quite comfortably at her little cottage in Bartle. But it was nothing like the luxury at the Summerdale London townhouse, and she was enjoying being so pampered.

"Have you abducted my wife, madame?" asked Lord Summerdale when she sat down at the table with her plate. "She has completely disappeared after announcing she would say goodnight to you last evening. I suppose she fell asleep talking with you into the night?"

"Oh *mon pauvre*," she murmured with a smile as she spread jam on her toast. "To sleep in a cold bed, to wake up alone! You will never invite me to visit again if you are deprived of her embrace one night of every six. It is very disagreeable of me."

Lord Summerdale was nearly as easy to discomfit as his wife was, though he was far better at hiding his chagrin. He did not give her a repressive look, but merely cleared his throat and quietly asked the butler to check on the progress of the servants who were loading baggage into the carriage. The footman who stood attendance while they ate went with the butler because Summerdale had, by some impossible to discern signal, clearly indicated he wished a moment of privacy.

Abashed, Marie-Anne put down her toast.

"I am here so many days and still I forget that I must not say outrageous things before the servants. Forgive me, my lord. I will try very hard not to bring you disgrace, and undo all the work you have invested in repairing my standing."

"Good God, Marie-Anne, if you will become so meek and serious, I will undo the work myself."

He actually shocked her a bit. Taking the lord's name in vain was one thing, but calling her by her first name was entirely contrary to his ingrained sense of propriety. She blinked at him, confounded into silence for a moment before gasping in delight.

"Oh! May I call you Stephen now, my lord?" She gave a gleeful little clap of her hands when he grinned – reluctantly, she knew. The un-stiffening of Stephen Hampton was an ongoing and delightful process to watch. "Only in private, of course, among friends. But I cannot say I will remember in front of the servants, so perhaps you should not give me such liberties."

"There is no need to worry about our servants in the matter of these small details, I assure you. All of them, and most especially Collins, have developed the greatest affection for Helen. They cannot help but forgive her little eccentricities and they have been warned they may expect similar from you."

Marie-Anne supposed by "eccentricities" he must mean Helen's genuine interest in the servants' welfare, opinions, and feelings. Marie-Anne knew she herself was likely to be even more over-familiar with the staff. Well, it was what they *called* over-familiar, but Marie-Anne only called it amiable. She felt fraudulent, putting herself above them, trying to keep a calculated distance at all times from the people who were there when she dressed and washed and ate. She always had. The circumstances in which she herself had been raised were far less elevated than these people who were employed as servants.

"In the matter of your reputation," Stephen continued, "I don't believe there's anything you're likely to do that could possibly damage us in any way. Even if you did so, you can be confident that Helen and I would far rather have you as an acquaintance than anyone who would condemn you."

"Even if it would cause havoc for your many business interests?" she asked, knowing that this was virtually the only reason he cared at all for society's opinions of him now.

"Even then," he agreed. "The Summerdale fortune is hardly at stake. So you must feel free to be your natural self, which I'm sure will attract a great number of admirers. You may break as many hearts as you like."

She bit into her toast, considering. It was true that he was unlikely to suffer if she caused a scandal, but any bad behavior was sure to reflect poorly on Helen.

"Well, perhaps not *many* hearts," she said after swallowing. "Just one or two, and I will make sure they do not belong to very prominent men."

"Ah, and we arrive at the matter of Mr. Mason," he said smoothly, politely ignoring how she choked on a fresh bite of toast. "I'm sorry to say I've not met him, though I heard only last week that Sir George Whipple was considering an investment in Mr. Mason's business. I had intended to look further into it but other affairs have taken precedence. I will be happy to leave instruction with my secretary, however, to inquire after his reputation and background in my absence."

She wanted to protest that she was indifferent to Mr. Mason's background and reputation, but curiosity got the better of her.

"You think he could be an adventurer?" she asked.

"I think if he *were* an adventurer, Whipple is a perfect dupe. But there is no reason to think Mr. Mason is a fraud."

"Mr. Mason is a fraud?" Helen was entering, a stricken look on her face as she caught the last words. "No! But he looked so very kind!"

"Yes, my love, charlatans specialize in looking harmless." Stephen rose and went to the sideboard to pour coffee for her. "Come, you've had a late start and you must eat quickly or our schedule will be ruined."

"I had to dress, and I was rearranging which books to take in my small valise, and how can I eat when you tell me a charlatan has been flirting with my dearest friend!" But she said it as she reached for a plate. She and Marie-Anne had indeed fallen asleep while talking, and the talk had largely centered on how very handsome and charming Mr. Mason was.

"I was saying there's no reason to think ill of him." Stephen assured her. "If he were an adventurer, half the moneyed men of our acquaintance would have been approached already."

"What if he approaches them while we are on the other side of the North Sea? However shall we protect Marie-Anne from it?"

"I believe I am protected by my lack of money, *mon amie*," Marie-Anne said. "And of course my lack

35

of interest in timber. Now, if his business was to import the shawls of Kashmir, it would be a different matter. I would sell off your silver so I might invest. But trees? No, I am very safe."

Helen sat and, dear friend that she was, transferred an extra piece of toast onto Marie-Anne's plate from her own, followed by a slice of seed cake. "Well, you must keep it in mind if you meet him again, and watch very carefully for any deceit." She sipped at her coffee but did not pick up her fork. She was frowning. "You did say he was so very charming. It would be dreadful if he sought to gain your trust for criminal reasons."

Marie-Anne opened her mouth to distract Helen from her worry with some amusing nonsense about the charms of American men, but she was not the only one who looked to soothe her anxious friend.

"I'll have a quick word with my secretary and ask him to look out for any news of Mr. Mason that might be cause for alarm," said Stephen, and relief immediately came over Helen's face. She cast a grateful look at her husband. "But there will be no time to consult with him," he said with a pointed look at Helen's plate, "if we linger at breakfast."

Helen smiled and began to eat. Between bites, she told Marie-Anne that she must stay at the townhouse however long she liked, that she had two more dresses that she insisted were not to her liking and the modiste would make arrangements to alter them to Marie-Anne's measurements, and that Marie-Anne must not be shy with Collins because he would take care of her "as well as if you are Lady Summerdale yourself." As though he only waited for this declaration, the butler reappeared and informed them that the baggage was loaded and the carriage ready and waiting to whisk them away to Norway.

"I do wish you'd come with us," she said to Marie-Anne as she put on her bonnet. "The Shipleys do not deserve you. Odious people. If they are horrible to you again, I'll…I'll…"

"You will what?" asked Marie-Anne, curious.

"I'm sure I'll think of something. No, I'll have Stephen think of something, he always does."

Marie-Anne helped her to button her gloves, saying, "I am sure I can think of something as well, but I do not believe they will be bad to me. They need me, after all." She reached up and re-tied the ribbon under Helen's chin so it laid more prettily. "Now you will go and see your fjords, and then we will all meet again in Bartle in the fall where your husband will pretend to care about the hunting. I promise to save you all the best stories from my summer in London, *ma chérie.*"

As they embraced, Helen whispered, "I hope some of them are about the American, if he deserves it – or at least someone else who puts stars in your eyes as he has."

How alarming, to learn that he'd managed to put so many stars in her eyes that her friends felt compelled to remark upon it. And it had only taken a few minutes of conversation. She *had* enjoyed talking to him, more than she'd enjoyed any man for years, and there was no denying that when Stephen had invited her to break a few hearts, her imagination immediately went to Mr. Mason.

Perhaps she should seek him out again while she had the chance. But first she would learn what mysterious task the Shipleys had in store for her.

༄ঙ

Amarantha Shipley looked very well, if one disregarded her considerable distress. The poor girl was very emotional, which was quite out of character. Or at least Marie-Anne had always known her as a very steady girl, the eldest of the three Shipley daughters and the only one of them who could ever have been described as steady. Even as a very small child, Amarantha considered her own name frivolous and wholly unsuited to her personality, and declared that she would only answer to "Amy" – an act that her mother took as personal insult. And though Marie-Anne did not dislike the nickname, she did privately think it a poor match for the girl's nature. An Amy should be less serious, and should be able to laugh more at life.

Alas, this Shipley daughter found no humor in her situation at all.

"Amy, *ma petite*," Marie-Anne soothed, laying a hand reassuringly on her arm. "You must know you can tell me of your sisters' behavior without any fear that I will judge you by it. If I was inclined to hold your family's sins against you, would I come to London for you? No, and if this Mr. Harner truly loves you as you say, then he will never let the silliness of your sisters stop him from marrying you."

"It isn't Mr. Harner who is bothered by it," Amy explained. She chewed briefly on her bottom lip and looked around the little morning room in the Summerdale house where they sat. It was decorated in a cheery yellow, and the elegance of the décor could only bring to mind the far less refined taste on display in the Shipley's home. "Indeed, he is more tolerant of their nonsense than I am, but he is at the mercy of an uncle who is a very superior sort. If his uncle disapproves of the connection, he will not grant Mr. Harner the living of the parsonage, you see. We'll not be able to marry."

Marie-Anne almost asked if Amy's marriage portion was so very small before she remembered that of course it would be. The Shipley family were comfortable, but they had three daughters and no great wealth. Even if they could settle a large sum on one of their girls, they would never do so in order for her marry a church man. And though Amy was not as grasping as her mother, she also could not imagine living on such a very reduced income. Not everyone, Marie-Anne reminded herself, was practiced at mending clothes until they were more patches than petticoat.

"Oh I know it's selfish, truly I do," Amy said. "But I cannot believe either Phyllida or Dahlia will be anything but mortified by their own actions in future. I think they too will regret the consequences. They are so impulsive."

"And very accomplished, I think, to have found something that unites you and your mother against them – and makes even me welcome in the Shipley home again!" Marie-Anne set her teacup down on the little table, in case she should spill it in shock. "Now tell me, please, what do they do that is so very bad?"

"They have both gotten themselves engaged to the most unsuitable men. Or I suppose not properly engaged. Nothing has been formalized or announced yet because mother is desperately attempting to change their minds."

"Ah, and the disapproval of the mother makes these unsuitable men much more desirable, of course. But are they so disastrous, these men?"

Amy furrowed her brow, giving the question due consideration. "Well, in Dahlia's case, I think the match is not an unfortunate one. And I only say he is unsuitable because they seem so very ill-suited to each other. But really, it's her behavior that is so objectionable. You see, it seemed to everyone early on in the season that Lord Releford would offer for her any minute. He's the heir to the Duke of Morely."

Marie-Anne could not help but gasp. "Oh *mon dieu*, your mother must have been in raptures!" All Lady Shipley had ever wanted – with an intensity that was deeply uncomfortable to witness – was better social connections, to climb higher and higher in society. Heir to a dukedom!

Amy rolled her eyes slightly and nodded. When she was young, she and Marie-Anne had joked often about her mother's more ridiculous ambitions. How unlikely, that she had nearly realized one of them at last.

"Yes, she was jubilant when we were all certain he would propose. But then something happened. Dahlia won't say what it was, but suddenly she began to...well, to welcome the attentions of other men, while virtually ignoring Releford. It was all anyone could talk about, how she flirted with every man who crossed her path. I suppose it's better now that she's settled on one she says she will marry, and he's a very good sort even if he'll never be a duke. But now instead of flirting so very obviously, she takes every opportunity to speak loudly and at length about his wealth and his good looks. It's so very vulgar! I have overheard many of our acquaintance remark on it a number of times. Our housekeeper told me even the butcher has commented on it. The *butcher*."

Marie-Anne bit her lips together to prevent herself saying, *Heaven forbid, that the butcher have a poor opinion of your family!* It would be cruel to say it to Amy, who would think Marie-Anne was mocking her. But she did not mock Amy. She mocked the mannered little world in which the girl was caught up. She knew from personal experience exactly how exuberant behavior and loud, public delight was condemned. There were few sins greater than the dread vulgarity.

Instead, she asked what trouble the last Shipley sister had gotten into.

"So Dahlia is telling everyone about the money she will marry, I see. And Phyllida? She has refused another duke, perhaps?"

"Oh no, a duke is not nearly romantic enough for Phyll," said Amy, who suddenly looked very cross. "She has settled for nothing less than an impoverished poet who thinks himself the next Byron, and spends more time arranging his hair than in writing any sort of verse. I should not mind any of that in the least, even though he is very tedious, but he has worked so diligently at creating a reputation for himself as a libertine that he has actually succeeded at it. No decent girl should be seen in his company at all, much less making calf eyes at him."

Marie-Anne picked up her tea again and sipped at it before it grew cold, considering. Well, she *had* been drawn to London by the promise of a spectacle, after all. And this certainly qualified as entertainment. A libertine poet, a future duke thrown over in favor of a wealthy suitor, two young girls determined to make very public fools of themselves, and a mother who was no doubt tearing at her coiffure regularly over it all. Oh, and a very proper uncle who had the power to withhold a living from Amy's fiancé. And now, of course, right on cue: Enter the scandalous Frenchwoman.

"Set it to music and put it on stage, it will make for a most charming opera," she mused.

"Music?" asked Amy, who had only half-heard.

She looked pale and so very anxious. She must really be quite in love with this would-be vicar. Marie-Anne finished off her tea and waved aside her flippant remark. An opera was too grand, in any case. This was more suited to a ha'penny puppet play.

"What I want to know is why you have called me here. How is it that I can help this situation? I think my presence can only make it worse."

"Oh no, you must understand how very much both Dahlia and Phyllida admire you," protested Amy, and Marie-Anne only looked at her in confusion. "They have such fond memories of you, and they loved Richard so very much. We all did. And he loved you in defiance of our parents, whose disapproval has only commended you to girls of such spirit, and with everything that happened back then... Well, it seems you've become something of a romantic figure to them."

"A romantic figure," echoed Marie-Anne. She was immediately visited by the romantic memory of the chilblains on her fingers that first winter in Bartle, and having to choose between wearing her only pair of wool socks on her feet or on her hands.

"It must seem terrible. I'm so sorry. But you know what young girls are."

"Yes, they do love a tragedy." Try as she might, Marie-Anne could not quite produce a lighthearted smile. Nevertheless, her lip curled upwards. "A forbidden love affair, a scandal, a lover who dies young. A miscarriage and a banishment. I may even have declared that I would never love again, when they said he would not live. Such a drama it was, of course they would make me a heroine."

"They have taken to heart the notion that you gave up everything for love." Amy said it like an apology. Her cheeks were turning a delicate pink.

What very silly girls. But then, how could they know that Marie-Anne had had nothing to give up? Being with her Richard, in any capacity, could only have given her more, not taken anything away. It *had* given her more, for the little time they were together.

"They would like to vex your mother, then? And so they think to be like me." Marie-Anne began to regain her humor at the idea. "It is a perfect chance for me to make some mischief, your mother must see that. And yet she has said she also wants me here. Ah, this explains why she invited me to stay in your home – to make me feel obliged, I think?"

That was what she said, but what she thought was: *to try to win me over, to try to write over the old story of animosity with new flattery.* She did laugh a little at that, to herself. Lady Shipley probably could not conceive that one could resist flattery, since she herself was so susceptible to it.

Amy cleared her throat, and the delicate pink on her cheeks turned a little darker and spread to her ears. "She agrees that Dahlia and Phyllida will listen to you and follow your advice. But I must confess now to what you will surely understand after only the briefest conversation with my mother – that her opinion of your character has quite radically changed since she learned of your close friendship with the Earl and Countess of Summerdale."

Marie-Anne's mouth slowly dropped open in amazed discovery. "*Mais bien sûr*," she breathed. "I am her golden goose!"

"Her beanstalk, I would rather say," replied Amy in a muffled voice.

Marie-Anne hooted with laughter. "She will climb me! To reach giants!"

It was too perfect. There was really no other response than to laugh – and laugh, and laugh, until even Amy could not help but join the inelegant guffaws. It could only be this funny with Amy – oh, and her Richard, of course, who she liked to imagine was chuckling somewhere in Heaven. That Lady Shipley's greatest ambitions could only be realized through Marie-Anne, of all people, whom she had described as "that brazen French hussy" who was destined to "ensure generations of disrepute for the Shipley name!"

"You should have seen her face when she heard your name in connection with Summerdale," giggled Amy, who had been such a tender age when she reported the Brazen French Hussy remark. "It brought on an acute attack of dyspepsia that lasted days."

Marie-Anne caught her breath and willed herself to stop laughing. If only she could have been there for the moment that Lady Shipley had swallowed that bitter pill.

"One can only imagine she recovered by pretending she always liked me," she said. This was how Richard's mother had always gone about her life: convincing herself of a new reality every time the old one was inconvenient or uncomfortable. "Well, she is lucky I like you more than I dislike her. Which means I like you very, very much. Now, if I have so much power over these silly romantic girls, I must know how you want me to use it. Phyllie must end the infatuation with this libertine poet, true?"

"Oh, if you could only make her see him for what he truly is, Marie-Anne! Phyll is not entirely brainless, she's only been taken in by his affectations."

"He is very handsome?"

"I suppose, if you like that sort," said Amy, wrinkling her nose a bit. "Dark eyes and pale skin, and he does have quite good hair. But he's forever bursting into verse about the lambent light in Phyll's eyes or how her cheek is the rosy hue of dawn's first rays. And he has a bit of a limp, though he's quite heroic about walking in spite of it."

Marie-Anne blinked in the face of this breezy nonchalance.

"What?" Amy was nonplussed.

Marie-Anne stared at her, willing her to hear herself. But sweet, practical Amy seemed utterly uncomprehending, which forced Marie-Anne to an irritated bluntness.

"You know, of course, that I am not a virgin."

"Pardon me?" Amy asked faintly.

"Forgive me, you are not Catholic and you do not know it is very rare that a saint is not a virgin. So I think it is unlikely I can perform miracles."

"Oh," Amy frowned, struggling to keep up. "Do you think it will be so very difficult?"

Marie-Anne turned her eyes up to the ceiling but

refrained from crossing herself in her silent prayer for patience.

"Dark eyes, beautiful hair, young and handsome, making poems to her cheeks!" Amy only looked blankly at her. "Penniless!" she continued insistently. "A limp!"

"But I am sure if you say you find him unappealing, she will agree," Amy said earnestly.

"And will I convince her that puppies are not adorable, too? It is so simple, I will do it just after I make many loaves and fishes appear." Marie-Anne sighed at Amy's stricken look. "Oh, *ma petite*, you are so very much *not* fanciful that you will never see his appeal. But of course I will try. I will meet him and we will see if I can find something unattractive enough to aid our cause. So that is Phyllida. Now tell me what you think I must do for Dahlia. Push her into the arms of this son of a duke, this Releford man?"

"Oh, if you could persuade her to return Lord Releford's affections, Mother would kiss you!"

"I would rather kiss the ass of an ass, so another solution is preferred." Marie-Anne tapped thoughtfully on her chin. "It is only that she is so vulgar about this rich man she has chosen, *non*? You do not mind the man himself?"

"Not at all. Though I don't think their characters are well-suited, I like Mr. Mason very well indeed. Mother and Father do not like that he is American, that is their greatest objection. Of course they would so much prefer her to have Releford, but—"

"Mason, you say?" Marie-Anne felt her eyebrows raising with the pitch of her voice. "American?" Higher still, and Amy nodded. "Handsome and prosperous?"

She stopped before she began chirping. Already she wore the most idiotic expression of bright inquisitiveness, her head tilted just the slightest bit in perfect imitation of a bird. Like a bird wit. Bird brain. Birds of a feather. Birds and the bees.

Oh *mon dieu*, this was not good at all.

"I suppose he is handsome if one does not object to red hair," Amy was saying. "He's not at all refined in looks or manner, but he seems a very fine American gentleman nonetheless. Though Father says we should not call him a gentleman, but a businessman. He deals in all kinds of wood. Timber, you know. Marie-Anne?"

Marie-Anne tore herself away from a fervent contemplation of brioche, and made herself say, "But I met him only last night at Lady Huntingdon's ball."

"Did you? He's a very good sort, isn't he?"

"Yes, he was…very agreeable."

Amy went on about her mother's horror of passing up a future duke in favor of an American – "If he distinguished himself in politics and appeared favorably in the papers, she might be persuaded to think well of him" – but Marie-Anne returned to her deep longing for brioche. Probably Helen's cook could make some. She'd like to soak it in some kind of sauce, a good, thick kind of gravy. Or maybe soup? Men were very disappointing. Or soda bread would be good too, Maggie had used to make it sometimes, served with butter and honey. It had only been a few minutes of conversation. She had thought she would not see him again anyway. Perhaps there was some toast left over from breakfast. A great deal of butter was called for.

"Would you like to come with me?" Amy asked.

"I'm so sorry," said Marie-Anne, "I was lost in my thoughts. It is a great deal to think about. Come where?"

"To Gunter's. I've said I would meet Dahlia and Mr. Mason there so I can ride home in the carriage. I knew Dahlia would insist on coming with me today if they knew I was calling on you, so you'll be a surprise. If you want to, of course, the walk is not far at all."

"A surprise," she repeated. She thought back to this morning, her friend's worry that Mr. Mason was a charlatan of some sort. Well, if he would flirt with her and put stars in her eyes while his...his *unofficial* fiancée was not looking, he was certainly at least a little false. "He does not know of me? My history with your family, I mean to say."

"Oh no, I shouldn't think so. One doesn't speak of such family scandals, you know. Phyll might have mentioned you to the poet. It's the sort of thing you tell a poet, isn't it? But Dahlia has some sense of things and wouldn't be so daring, though I cannot imagine Mr. Mason would care."

Well, then. There were things more interesting to be done than to sit in splendor, eating bread and feeling sorry for herself. It would be amusing, and possibly enlightening, to see how he reacted to Marie-Anne appearing on his future sister-in-law's arm. It might even be so amusing that she would celebrate with some of Gunter's finest confections.

"I'll wear my best bonnet," she smiled, "and we shall surprise them in style."

Chapter Four

Mason was feigning a polite interest in Dahlia's confused recounting of a novel she had recently read when Marie-Anne de Vauteuil and her perfect blue eyes walked back into his life. He was stupid enough to actually feel nothing but excitement at the sight of her until, at the sound of his accidental fiancée's voice, his happy smile again slid abruptly from his face.

"Oh but this is wonderful, Amy, you are bad to keep such a secret, we were so hoping you would come to town, isn't it just wonderful?" Dahlia was gushing. It was genuine and artless emotion, Mason realized with surprise. He was not used to that, from Dahlia.

Before he was ready for it, Marie-Anne was looking directly into his eyes, expectant and faintly amused, while Dahlia clutched at her hands and turned to Mason to say, "This is Mr. Spencer Mason, recently come all the way from New York."

He watched the Frenchwoman's eyebrows lift slightly at the announcement of his full, false name. She must know. Amy would have told her that he and Dahlia had an understanding, as they said here. The slightest smile curved Marie-Anne's lips and drew his attention. It made the whole situation feel absurdly dangerous, like she knew his game and would call his bluff right here outside the confectioner's shop. Instead of putting him on alert, it gave him a little thrill.

"Mason," said Dahlia breathlessly, "This is—"

"Madame de Vautueil," he said with a bow. "It's a pleasure to see you again."

Her expression told him he'd passed a test – she'd thought he might pretend not to know him. God, he liked her more and more.

"You've met?" Dahlia was bewildered.

"At Lady Huntingdon's ball last night," he explained. Dahlia had not been invited, so he hadn't told her that he was. She would be annoyed, but he'd make a point of telling her it was a last-minute invitation and that she had said more than once that she was tired of attending balls when he would not dance with her. "But I had no idea you were acquainted."

"Here's the carriage," said Dahlia. "Marie-Anne, won't you join us for a drive through the park?"

"A drive in the park?" Marie-Anne asked it as though she had never heard of anything so profoundly innovative. "What a delightful idea, a drive together in the park. Don't you think so, Mr. Mason?" she asked, and directed her dazzling smile squarely at him, daring him to answer.

"You must not think she really means to go to the

park yet," Amy interjected. "We'll get in the carriage and sit in the shade here in the square as a waiter brings ices to us."

"It is a ritual of London I remember very well, because it was always my favorite. I shall leave the driving in the park to you, after we have our treat." And with that, Marie-Anne tucked her hand into Dahlia's elbow, leaned in close as though to share confidences, and set off across the road to where the carriage awaited.

It was left to Mason to fall in step beside Amy and try to act naturally. Last night, Freddy had said he'd never heard of Madame de Vauteuil and planned to ask around. But maybe Mason could learn something on his own this afternoon. He wouldn't even pretend to himself it was for any reason other than to satisfy his own burning curiosity about her.

"They seem like old friends," he observed to Amy. "Strange how your sister has never mentioned her."

"Madame de Vauteuil was very nearly our sister-in-law. She was to marry our brother Richard."

Amy kept her voice low. They always spoke in hushed tones about this deceased brother Richard, he noticed, though the subject was not raised often. No one had ever mentioned a grieving almost-bride.

"I hope you'll pardon my ignorance. If they were never married, why is she called Madame instead of Mademoiselle?"

"Because of my very advanced age," Marie-Anne answered him. They had reached the carriage, and she had overheard him as Dahlia waited for him to hand her up the step. As he did so, Marie-Anne continued, "And because I am so much more like a widow than a mademoiselle."

"It was so cruel," said Dahlia, settling into the landau as he handed up the other ladies. "To think that the wedding was just days away. Everything would have turned out so differently, if only..."

Marie-Anne made a soft tutting noise and shook her head gently at Dahlia. "No sadness and no 'if only', *petit chou*." Dahlia's face lit up at the endearment. "You were not a melancholy child and I will not let you be one now. Do you think I have done nothing but weep and mourn for all these years? No, because your brother would hate that, from me as well as you. So! What flavor of ice will you take?"

Mason tried to use the opportunity, as the ladies chatted amongst themselves, to look at the other well-heeled citizens putting themselves on display in the park. It was a perfect place to watch all kinds of little dramas unfold, the kind he could take back to Freddy who would then pull the details together and make a story of it for the paper. But even if there were no tidbits to take back to Freddy, there was no shortage of information to take in for his own purposes. The way they dressed, and preened, and were so obvious in how they watched each other while pretending that they didn't have a care in the world.

He took it all in, and later he would pull the visual details together to make a picture to go with Freddy's stories. It was so far a very entertaining and very lucrative endeavor.

But his eyes kept straying back to the carriage to watch Marie-Anne de Vauteuil lick at her spoon. Advanced age, she'd said, the most precious piece of nonsense he'd ever heard. He couldn't know her age exactly, but he was more practiced than most at guessing. She was in perfect prime – not a baby-faced debutante nor a fading beauty, in possession of a face that showed plenty of life experience but none of the cynicism or bitterness that age so often brought. And she was clever. And funny. And she ate iced cream in a way that was sure to give him some of the most erotic dreams of his life.

"Mr. Mason sells as much timber in a week as exists in all of England, isn't that right, Mr. Mason?"

Dahlia was determined to impress everyone she could with his wealth, so he'd gotten used to this. For the first time, though, she made it *not* sound like a boast, or like it was something that proved her own superiority. She seemed hopeful, which meant she very much cared that Marie-Anne de Vauteuil approved of the match.

Which meant that maybe if Marie-Anne didn't approve, he could get out of this mess.

"It's not difficult to do when there's so much of the stuff back home," he answered. He made sure to sound bored, hoping a little surliness would contribute to the impression that he was bad husband material. If nothing else, he hoped to discourage them from talking about this business he'd invented. A few days ago Dahlia had gone on about it to a naval officer, who immediately launched into a discourse on the pressing need for a new supplier of ship's masts. That was the last thing he needed, to get the Royal Navy involved.

"Is your business here in London to do with finding investors?" asked Marie-Anne. "What is the word – speculation?"

That did put him on alert, but he was well practiced at not showing it.

"Timber, speculation, social restitution," he

smiled, recalling her words last night. "I didn't expect ladies would want to speak of such tiresome subjects."

"But of course you are right," she smiled back, cool as anything. "Of what shall we speak, then?"

"Mason is very interested in art," offered Dahlia. It was the first time he'd ever heard her mention this fact about him, and she was downright eager. "Paintings and sculptures and so forth. It is a passion of his."

"Is that so?" Marie-Anne looked politely perplexed. "You must have learned to appreciate art, Dahlia? I remember how you loathed your lessons in painting. Once, you threatened to drink the watercolor to put yourself out of your misery."

"And you told me it would not be fatal and I would only turn green and be very sick, so it was not worth the bother. I confess I never learned to like it."

"But you must wish to show Mr. Mason the Academy's exhibition this summer. It begins soon, I think?"

"This week, in fact." Mason put in. He had wanted to go yesterday, and today, but an exhibition was not where Dahlia wanted to be. She insisted they must been seen here and in the park, all part of a social strategy he couldn't hope to understand.

"I am sure with an escort who has a passion for art, it would be most fascinating." There was something of a challenge in Marie-Anne's voice. Was it his imagination, or was she daring Dahlia to say she wasn't interested? "I can think of nothing more enjoyable than to see the art with someone who knows the subject very well."

Dahlia looked uncertain, glancing between Mason

and Marie-Anne. He knew she wanted to laugh and say that nothing was less appealing to her than a stroll past the paintings, but it was obvious Marie-Anne would disapprove of that. Then Dahlia's face lit up, announcing that she'd suddenly had a bright idea.

"Then you must let Mr. Mason escort you, Marie-Anne, as soon as possible! You will so enjoy it, I remember how well you love to look at paintings. Tomorrow?"

"Tomorrow?" Marie-Anne's slightly suspicious look landed on him. "But Mr. Mason, I am sure he has his business affairs—"

"Not at all," he chimed in. He politely pretended not to notice the urgent and pleading look Dahlia was giving her. For some mysterious reason, she desperately wanted Marie-Anne to spend an afternoon looking at art with him, and he was not about to disagree with the plan. "I can't think of anything more important than properly entertaining Miss Shipley's dear friend. Your direction, madame? Where may I call on you?"

Her eyes met his in an arrested look, and he knew she was holding back a startled laugh. It felt disproportionately wonderful, to share this tiny memory with her, this little secret, even if it did recall his own embarrassment.

"There you see, it's all settled," said Dahlia with satisfaction.

"Is it indeed," murmured Marie-Anne, still looking at him. Then she blinked the amusement out of her perfect blue eyes and told him he could call on her at Summerdale House.

Mason had never seen homes as elegant as the ones he glimpsed in London, and Summerdale House was so far the most elegant of them all. He admired the placement of some lilies in the foyer, how the size and color of them were the exact touch needed for the space, and wondered which of the servants had the artistic eye. He also wondered how much money the Earl of Summerdale must have, to keep a London house full of servants up and running for the sake of a single guest while he and his wife took a jaunt across the sea.

It was a very brief thought, though, and it did little to distract him from his nerves as he waited for a painfully dignified butler to open the door to a room of perfect proportions and graceful lines. In the center of it stood Marie-Anne de Vauteuil in her sprigged muslin and upswept hair. He almost said that he would paint her like that if she'd let him: the warm golds of the room a lovely backdrop to her cornflower blue dress, her form outlined by the white marble of the fireplace, strands of hair the color of honey artfully framing her face. He could never do it justice, but he'd like to try to preserve the image. It was so pretty.

"Mr. Mason, you are a cad," she announced quite cordially by way of greeting. "Would you like tea, or shall we go and pretend to look at art now?"

He sucked in a deep breath. She really was something entirely new in his experience. "Is tea one of these circumlocutions they're so fond of here? A polite way of saying pistols at dawn, or something like that?"

"No, of course not," she said, but then she looked

a little uncertain. Her own brows furrowed. "If it is, I have never heard it used that way. Have you?"

"I haven't, but I don't often hear of ladies offering tea to cads in the home of an earl. I'm a little out of my depth."

She looked beyond him and called, "Collins, is offering tea a way to declare dark intentions toward a guest?"

"No, madame," came the butler's reply from just outside the door where he had stationed himself. He appeared immediately at the doorway. "It is my experience that an invitation to tea is rarely more than an expression of hospitality."

"Except when it is Lord Summerdale's mother who offers it, I understand," she said with a sudden spark of humor in her eye. The butler maintained his impassive expression but – a slight triumph for her – ever so faintly cleared his throat. She let loose with a little smile. "We must thank all the saints she is not here. Will you ask the kitchen to prepare a tray for us, please?"

"Of course, madame." The butler gave a brief bow and disappeared again.

She watched his retreating form, her smile fading to thoughtfulness. "Later I will have to hear a very polite little lecture on how to use a bell pull. But I will explain that you do not deserve the finest manners of this house, no matter how prosperous and good-looking you are. Because you are a cad."

He tucked away the delightful knowledge that she found him good-looking – he could savor that later. For now, if she was going to be so wonderfully forthright, he decided the best way to proceed was for him to do the same. Within reason, of course.

"I suppose I am a cad," he allowed. "What made you decide that? If you don't mind being specific."

"Sir, let us not play games."

"Ma'am, I would dearly love to play all kinds of games with you."

"Ah! There it is, you answer your own question." He couldn't tell if she was annoyed or amused. Probably both. "And at the ball as well, you flirt with me and charmed me absolutely–"

"It worked?"

"Of course it worked, I am a living and breathing woman, do not be stupid." She was definitely annoyed, and he was definitely enjoying honesty. "Then you ask to call on me and to drive with me through the park, and all the time you are engaged!" She paused and he just looked at her. "To be married! To Dahlia!"

"Yes, well, I forgot," he said simply. "Momentarily. Because you're so–"

"Oh no, I beg you do not say it," she said in exasperated warning, and held a palm up to silence him. "You will save the compliments for your fiancée, please, who does not deserve this treatment. It is obvious she arranges this afternoon so that I will know you better and approve of you. Already you make it impossible."

"Wait." Mason began to feel the first stirrings of a great hope. "Do you mean you'll tell her you don't approve of me?"

"It is not my place to approve or not approve–"

"Because I can keep flirting," he assured her. "I'll ply you with roses, I'll ogle your ankles, I'll ravish you if you let me. Right here on the divan, the butler can be a witness to my depravity, where's that bell pull?"

"Mr. Mason!" She looked more surprised than scandalized. She blinked at him once, and then gave a sputter of laughter. Her hand came to her mouth to hide it, but it was too late. He realized he enjoyed her laughter as much as he enjoyed acting entirely like himself, without the faintest veneer of civility, for the first time since he'd come to London. He felt entirely at ease with her, which was as welcome as it was unexpected.

A parlor maid chose that moment to enter with a tray of tea. As she put it down, Marie-Anne said, with a smile still tugging at her lips. "Thank you, Susan, and will you thank Mrs. Chapman for the little cakes, too? You must take one for yourself so that I do not grow plump all alone, and please tell everyone that Mr. Mason is only making a joke."

The blushing girl bobbed a curtsy and hurried out of the room.

"Everyone?" he asked.

"The servants. They hear everything," Marie-Anne said, and sat. She began to pour the tea. "And Collins is just outside that door. To prevent any ravishing, you know."

Mason sat across from her and accepted a cup of tea that he had no intention of drinking. "I suppose ravishing even a willing woman would make me a pariah in this town, and I'm trying to avoid that."

She gave a shrug that was a hair too careless.

"You assume I would be willing."

"I assumed we were still not playing games."

She looked up then, caught him in her very blue eyes for a moment before her gaze slipped down to his lips. He gripped the tea cup like it was a talisman, a reminder of civilization that could keep him from leaning across the tea tray and kissing her silly.

"Well," she said in a very soft voice, and lifted her eyes to look directly into his again "There are games and there are games, *monsieur*. We will not play, you and I." She said it with a gentle finality, and he hoped it was only because he'd gotten himself engaged. She picked up her tea and assumed a more business-like demeanor. "Now you will tell me, please, how you have promised to marry someone you so obviously do not want?"

He hadn't planned on making her his confidante, but he couldn't see what he had to lose. It was all heading toward a bad end anyway. Maybe she could help it to be a little less disastrous, since she wasn't going to play any lovely games with him. He put down his tea and prepared to tell her the sordid truth, praying he would not flush too purple.

"I didn't mean to," he began. "It was an accident."

"How does one become accidentally engaged?" She furrowed her lovely brow, waiting in vain for him to say something. Finally, she gave an encouraging little nod and said, "Please continue, I am alive with curiosity."

Already the flush was beginning. He could feel it on his neck. But she was going to laugh loud and long, he was sure, so he may as well brace himself and get it over with.

"I never really asked her to marry me," he admitted. "She just misunderstood. I was asking about customs here, how long a betrothal is, do they read the banns out in church, that sort of thing. And then suddenly she was saying how it was endearing that I was so shy and I needn't come out and say it, she perfectly understood and would love to be my bride. And that was it. We were engaged."

Rather than laughing, she only looked stupefied. "I..." She took a breath. She set her cup in its saucer and cocked her head to the side, looking hard at him as if she had never heard anything so asinine. "What?"

It was even more mortifying than when he'd told Freddy about it. Now he said the same thing to her as he'd said then: "I was hoping she'd confide in me about Lord Releford. There was some speculation that he'd proposed and they planned to wed in secret, and I was... curious." What he'd hoped for was a tantalizing story that would sell papers, but he'd wound up with a fiancée instead. Not that he was prepared to tell all that to Marie-Anne de Vauteuil. "I never thought she'd take it as a declaration of my affections."

"So you just *agreed?*" She looked like she could not believe her own ears. "You cannot be so much an idiot!"

"It was a choice between idiot or cad," he said, a little rankled by her insults, no matter how accurate they were. "I couldn't fit a word in edgewise before she was telling her sister. And then they were crying tears of joy and talking about a double wedding and saying I was the most gallant man on earth while her father nearly swallowed his tongue in congratulating me. What was I supposed to do? Say that the last thing I meant to imply was that I'd ever want to marry her?"

"No of course not, but surely you could have found some way..." She frowned down at the little cake on her plate, like it would offer some opinion on what he could have done to prevent the disaster.

After a moment's contemplation, she seemed to give up and gave a very French kind of shrug. "Well who am I to judge? Once I ate blackberry preserves for three years because I was too polite to say I did not want seventy-two jars of it. But I like blackberries, and at least it only *felt* like a lifetime. I think yours will feel like several."

His relief that she was not laughing at him was the only thing that kept him from loudly doubting that she could ever be so polite about jam. She was so outright in her opinions and deft in her speech that he couldn't imagine her meekly accepting anything just to avoid some social awkwardness. But maybe that was long ago. She certainly seemed perfectly willing now to leave convention aside and come at a thing bluntly, so he felt free to do the same.

"Will you help me get out of it?" he asked. She looked startled at the proposition and paused in the act of taking a bite of cake. "Please?"

From the deepest reaches of his old bag of tricks, he dredged up his most pitiful, pleading look. It had a thick coat of dust but was perfectly functional. He watched her heart melt right before his eyes and, cad that he was, felt no remorse. It was always an immediate and involuntary reaction in women, related to the way they couldn't help cooing at the sight of baby shoes, and he'd learned at a young age how to solicit it. The smarter they were, the more quickly they recovered, so he was surprised that Marie-Anne maintained her soft look past the first instant.

"Oh Mr. Mason," she murmured, a sweet but faint note of compassion in her voice. "Of course it is very unfair to you, that so many women have let you believe this puppy dog look will always work." She clucked her tongue consolingly. "You poor man."

Oh, he liked her. He gave a smile so broad that it brought out his dimple. He was pretty sure that would work better on her anyway, and it had the added advantage of being completely sincere. "I'm out of practice, haven't done that since I wore short trousers. Needs a lighter touch. But will you help me anyway?"

She tried to hide it, but all the humor was back in her now. It tugged at her mouth and made itself known around her eyes. She gave a sigh, relenting a little.

"You are in great good luck, Mr. Mason, because already I have been thinking Dahlia should not marry you. Oh no, do not look so relieved yet. Right now she thinks very well of me, but mostly this is because her mother and I have always been on opposite sides. If I tell her you are not worthy of her, I align myself with her mother and become just another meddlesome old woman who has no notion of true love." Here, she cast him a slightly apologetic look. "She does not love you, that is plain, but she loves a romance very much. And her pride is in it now, I think. So it will require more than only a word from me, even if I was to tell her you are a cad who never truly meant to marry her."

Mason refrained from saying that he didn't necessarily want her to be so blunt about him. It would banish him from the Shipleys' good graces and they were far too valuable to him as a reliable source of society gossip. He needed the game to go on for another few months at least, until he had enough money in the bank to move on. If he could extricate himself from this marriage business without actually leaving Dahlia at the altar and socially ruining the girl, all the better.

What a relief to have a co-conspirator.

He said, "I've been trying to think of a way to get Dahlia to believe it's *her* idea to call the whole thing off." He'd been trying to push her in that direction since it happened, but had nothing to show for weeks of effort.

"Yes exactly," Marie-Anne said, pleasantly surprised he'd come to that conclusion. "It must be her who ends the engagement, or she may never recover from the humiliation."

"I've been trying for weeks and it's only shown me how dedicated she is to the plan. Didn't you just say I was in great good luck?" he asked. "I'm struggling to see where the luck is."

She put the bite of cake in her mouth at last, and reminded him so much of a cat with cream that he half expected her to purr. She swallowed and licked her lips, which was such a delicious sight that he nearly asked her to do it again, just for him.

"The luck is that I am immensely talented in matters of the heart, and I have a plan that will allow Dahlia to marry the man she wants. And *you* are not the man she wants." She gave a cheerful smile, as though nothing in the world could be more joy-giving than this little fact. "Naturally I will need your help in this. Will we go see the art now? I will tell you, as we gaze at uninspired portraits, how we can make her a duchess."

Chapter Five

Marie-Anne very, very much wanted to kiss Mr. Mason. It was quite troubling.

She questioned him about how and when Dahlia's interest in him began, to confirm her suspicion it was all an attempt to make Lord Releford jealous. He said he believed she was right and detailed the many incidences that had made him think it, while the carriage carried them to the exhibition and she thought of kissing him. When she suggested they try to make Dahlia's mother disapprove of Releford so as to make Dahlia determined to pursue him again, he laughed and laughed at the impossibility of it, and she did too – and she thought of tasting his tongue with hers.

He looked at most of the paintings with disinterest until he found one that absorbed all his attention. She watched his face go still as his eyes took it in, how he looked with interest and a little wonder and a faint but distinct longing – the same way he looked at her, in fact – and she wanted nothing more than to take his face in her hands and press her lips to his and never care that they were in the midst of a crowd of onlookers.

Of course she wanted to do much more than kiss him, but that did not trouble her. It was only natural, when he was so attractive and she was currently without a lover. In her bed that night, she happily allowed herself to imagine all the other things she'd like to do with him, but it always came back to the kissing. Her mouth burned for his and, judging by the way he watched her when she licked her spoon or ate her cake, he very obviously had similar thoughts.

Oh this was not good at all.

They were partners now in this scheme to convince Dahlia to break the engagement. They shared a secret; perhaps that was why she wanted also to share kisses?

"You invent a sweet illusion," she chided herself as she pulled on her stockings the next morning. It had nothing to do with sharing a secret. "You wanted to kiss him the moment he said kangaroo. Sooner!"

And she must stop thinking of it, because it would show on her face. She never could hide it when she liked a man very much. Bad enough that he saw it so clearly, but today she would call on the Shipleys and if *they* saw it – well, she would be no use at all if she only added to the shameful romantic spectacles in that house. Poor Amy would never marry her vicar.

The vicar. Here was something there that made her worry. She had brought up Amy's suitor yesterday as they looked at a particularly lifeless portrait of a bishop. Did Mr. Mason think him anything like this stern-looking man in the portrait?

"More than you might think," he'd answered. Upon further pressing, he explained. "He's one of those who never disagrees with her, but somehow he's constantly correcting her. It's always pleasant, you can't say he ever criticizes her, really." He shrugged. "You'll see. Maybe it's all my imagination. I just can't say I like him."

He called it a simple clash of personalities, but Marie-Anne thought he was being too humble to suggest it was only imagination. He was very observant.

He'd also surprised her by saying he mostly liked Phyllida's libertine poet, who had the ridiculous name of Aloysius St. James. "I'd bet you he's hiding something," he had said, "but I'd also bet anything it's harmless, whatever it is." She wanted to bet him a kiss, win or lose, and had to bite her tongue against saying it. Really, he had the most absurd effect on her. She blamed his red hair and his very young and handsome face.

In the end, she had managed to maintain a coherent train of thought as they discussed matters. He'd agreed to help her in the attempt to curb Phyllida Shipley's affections for the poet in return for her help in ridding him of Dahlia.

So they were in this together, she told herself as she rode through the streets of London towards the Shipley townhouse. It was comforting to feel like she had someone on her side as she entered this den of madness, and he would be there today. He'd said so when they parted ways after the exhibition, just after he'd asked her to call him Mason. Just Mason, without the Mister. "It's what friends call me, back home," he had said, with a little sheepish embarrassment that was not at all an act. Or at least she didn't think it was an act. Not that she could think very much beyond the wish that he was not engaged to another woman.

But as the carriage delivered her to the London home of the Shipleys, all her casually lustful thoughts were swept away and replaced with very different feelings. She vividly remembered the first time she had come here, all those years ago. She had had her Richard at her side then, and she felt his presence now as she looked at the home where he had introduced her to his family, where he had announced they would be married, and where he had drawn his last breath.

Richard was often in her thoughts, but now it felt like he hovered just outside her vision, waiting to take her hand and assure her she would survive an hour in his parents' presence. It fortified her to think of it. Of course he was here in spirit. He was there in his sisters, too, whom he had loved very much. He would never have wanted their prospects to have been tarnished by his indiscretion with Marie-Anne. Since he could not set things right, it was Marie-Anne's duty to do everything she could to help the girls now.

"*Je te promis, Richard,*" she said under her breath after the footman handed her down. A promise. She would not let Amy's heart be broken. She would not allow Dahlia to marry a man who did not want her, nor Phyllida to make a fool of herself with a libertine poet. It would not matter to Richard if his sisters made brilliant matches, so long as they were safe and cared for – and if Marie-Anne could not manage that, she at least believed she could prevent these imminent disasters.

She could not, however, prevent herself from embracing Phyllida tightly when the girl shoved aside the butler and barreled into Marie-Anne's arms.

"How I've missed you!" breathed little Phyllie, squeezing her so tightly that Marie-Anne nearly groaned. "I've written a hundred letters since I saw you last but I never knew where to send them. Mama was so hateful, she refused to tell me where you were. I was on the brink of running off to Scotland to elope but then Amy said you were invited to come and...and, oh I'm so glad to see you!"

"*Ma poupée*," said Marie-Anne when she got her breath back. It came to her as suddenly as Phyllie's enthusiastic greeting: she had used to call her *poupée*, just as she had always called Dahlia *petit chou*. Saying it caused the girl to go all dewy-eyed and throw her arms around Marie-Anne again. "You are as good as a tight corset string, how you squeeze me. Oh no, do not stop, my waistline will be the envy of London!"

It was all very undignified and improper, this conspicuous emotion, and it suited Marie-Anne perfectly. Such expression was her natural disposition, though she rarely had the chance to indulge it among these absurd British. Thank goodness the other Shipley brother, Percy, was touring the continent instead of standing here, sour-faced. One less Shipley to deal with. Over Phyllida's shoulder, she saw Lady Shipley's valiant attempt to conceal her unease with what she would certainly call a very vulgar display. It was plain she would not object to anything Marie-Anne did, though. Her ties to the Summerdales was far too valuable. Oh, this was all going to be very amusing.

Sir Gordon Shipley was there too, undoubtedly

forced by his wife and daughters to muster some cordiality for the occasion. They all engaged in the expected mummery: Sir Gordon was gratified to know she had managed so well for herself after Richard's death, no doubt a reflection of her "strong-willed" character. Lady Shipley was so pleased to receive Marie-Anne again after that ancient "misunderstanding" and was sure they would all be the best of friends again.

Marie-Anne smiled and nodded and complimented the new upholstery in the drawing room. How very false the human animal could be, she reflected, when induced by circumstance. She had a fleeting thought of the women who had raised her, and who had been fond of saying that to fake a feeling was the lowest art – and the most valuable one.

The memory almost made her laugh aloud. Few things would be more mortifying to Lady Shipley than to know she was being silently compared to a group of elite prostitutes. Worse, that those women who had cared for Marie-Anne were infinitely more principled. In the midst of swallowing her laughter, Marie-Anne caught Mason's eye. She couldn't wait to share the thought with him, to tell him what *les dames entretenues* would have said about Lady Shipley. Then she remembered, even as he gave her a curious look that said he couldn't wait to ask her what was so amusing, that she must be careful not to show how very much she wanted to lick his neck.

"Mr. Mason tells us you enjoyed the art exhibition yesterday," said Dahlia eagerly when her father had made his excuses and retreated to the study. She looked very well today in her yellow dress. All the girls were lovely, with their glossy dark curls and soft brown eyes. They were like younger, fresher versions of their mother.

"Indeed, the art was wonderful. And it is so refreshing to spend an afternoon with someone who cares as little as I do for all the social bustle of London." This was something she and Mason had agreed upon: Dahlia adored moving among London society, and had not considered that marrying Mason might mean leaving it behind. "But Mr. Mason tells me there is great art to be found in New York, too, though he describes the city as very different from London. None of the social bustle, he tells me. Still I do not think it would be to my liking! But then you are more adventurous than I am, Dahlia."

Dahlia, who was not in the least adventurous, glanced towards Mason with a strained look on her face. Marie-Anne might feel guilty about this campaign to disenchant the girl if it were not so obviously a terrible match. After all, Mason came alive when he looked at art or spoke about it; Dahlia was bored to tears by the mere mention of it. He did not dance and she lived from ball to ball. He was confused and irritated by London society while she craved a daily infusion of it. It should not be too difficult to persuade Dahlia that she could do better for herself, especially if there was a way to remind her that a future duke was a romantic alternative.

But before Marie-Anne could think of a way to work that rejected suitor into the conversation, the poet arrived.

"At last! An end to the sublime anticipation of making your acquaintance, madame," he said as he bowed over her hand. "I see now why Phyllida has celebrated your elegance and beauty at every opportunity, and has warned me against losing my heart to your remarkable charm."

Marie-Anne found herself too stunned to reply. The lavish compliments were difficult enough to answer with any kind of grace, but worse by far were his outrageous good looks. It was preposterous. No man should be this handsome. It was the most impractical thing she had ever seen, and she greatly resented how it put a very melting feeling in her chest, and made her want to flutter her eyelashes and coo at him. It was only by exerting a heroic effort to remind herself that his name was Aloysius that she managed to gather her wits again.

"A heart that can be so easily lost is most unsatisfactory," she said lightly. "I should eat it for breakfast and be hungry again before noon. But of course you are only making your little poetry."

She smiled pleasantly to take the sting out of her dismissive tone. Not that being dismissive of poetry would do anything to turn Phyllida against this man. Marie-Anne contemplated the unbearably attractive fullness of his mouth while avoiding his velvety eyes, and wondered what could possibly cause any girl to abandon this Greek god. Short of inducing a pack of rabid dogs to eat his face, Marie-Anne rather believed they were destined for failure.

"His poetry is divine," offered Phyllida eagerly. "I'm sure he'll recite some for you, and you'll be as captivated as the rest of us. Just yesterday he wrote the most beautiful verse on the nightingale's song."

At this, Amy gave an unmistakable snort of laughter. As she quickly manufactured a cough to cover it, Marie-Anne gave a bright smile and asked if he had read Mr. Shelley's latest dramatic verse. It was the only thing she could think to say and she soon saw it was an unwise choice. Mr. St. James proceeded to talk endlessly and tried to impress with his knowledge, which caused Amy to grow very annoyed and Phyllida to look at him like he was some sort of paragon of manhood. Amy even went so far as to make an uncharacteristically waspish remark about how pretty words were as much a modern affectation as artfully windswept hair.

At this, Mason give a broad smile and a look of camaraderie to the other man.

"It seems there's only one sister in this family who appreciates artistic sensibilities, St. James. You've chosen well."

This made Phyllida gaze yet more lovingly at the poet, but also seemed to dispel some tension.

"I think it's very rude to talk about nothing but poetry when we finally have Madame de Vauteuil here." Lady Shipley's mispronunciation of her name grated on Marie-Anne nearly as much as the ostentatious accent she employed.

"Please, you must call me Marie-Anne," she insisted, to save herself from the verbal butchery. "We were almost family, after all. And you must remember I am not fond of formalities."

"Yes of course!" Lady Shipley looked delighted. "I wonder that you can bear the formalities at Summerdale House. The earl is well known for his propriety, they say he's very exacting. Is it true?"

There followed a thorough interrogation on all things to do with Lord and Lady Summerdale. It was tiresome, but Marie-Anne found herself almost admiring how Lady Shipley strenuously avoided the topic of Helen's past scandal. She could see the questions gleaming behind the woman's eyes, yet she voiced none of them. It was fairly likely she had memorized a list of other topics to discuss, so long did she monopolize the conversation with harmless minutiae.

Throughout the chatter, Marie-Anne stole frequent looks at Mason. He managed to appear desperately bored, which they had agreed was the best tactic to employ. He was really marvelous at it, the way he leaned back and gave barely audible sighs of impatience, without ever looking languid or effete in the pose. It was unforgivably vulgar of her, of course, to continuously examine the lovely bulge of muscle in his thigh – but really, what was her alternative? To stare at the impossibly pretty poet? She thought maybe she should, as the poet's beauty did not make her feel as though steam were rising from her skin.

"I cannot fault you for preferring to remain a guest at their beautiful home," Lady Shipley was saying, after a detailed inquiry into the décor at Summerdale House. "You are always welcome to change your mind and stay with us, the girls have longed to visit with you."

"And I am so happy to spend time with them," Marie-Anne smiled, and resigned herself to the fact that she would not be able to bring up Dahlia's rejected Lord Releford so long as her mother was present. Lady Shipley had no ability to hide her feelings, and her obvious eagerness for Marie-Anne to agree with her own preference of suitors would prove disastrous.

What she needed was to get the girls alone, away from their mother. She slid a quick look to Amy before turning to Dahlia and saying, "In fact I hope you have no great plans for tomorrow? Lady Summerdale's modiste will call, and I need you smart London ladies to advise me what is fashionable now."

As Lady Shipley had already mentioned a prior engagement, this kept her safely out of the way. Not that she didn't try to invite herself along, until Amy managed to whisper something at her that sounded very like: "She is here for us, mama, not to socialize with you!" Everyone politely pretended not to hear it, and Marie-Anne began to make her excuses and prepared to leave. She could feel Mason trying to catch her eye, but she couldn't spare him more than a helpless glance as she was quizzed by the girls about the modiste and when they should be there.

"Oh, are you leaving already?" Lady Shipley protested. "But I have hardly had the chance to ask you about the dowager countess, and I hear Lady Summerdale has the most envied staff. They say her cook is divine, and is it true the butler is a Hindustani? Oh, I should so like one!"

Marie-Anne blinked. "A divine cook?"

"Oh yes, that too, but I mean a Hindustani butler. It's the most fashionable thing, you know, and I do think it would go so well with this new red and gold scheme in the drawing room."

Marie-Anne blinked again. In just the proper shade, she supposed, and with a perfectly matched turban. She bit her tongue against saying it, for fear she would give the woman ideas. Loathsome people, Helen had always called them – not just the Shipleys, but all nobility, great and small. *A loathsomeness so varied and absolute that you can live among them for a lifetime and never reach the end of it,* she had once said.

"No, they would never think to match their butler

to the curtains," Marie-Anne finally replied. She could not quite keep the edge out of her voice, but did give a tight little smile. "They are always insisting on treating people with respect and humanity. And do you know, they think of their staff *and* Hindustanis as people." She clucked her tongue. "So eccentric!"

Mason choked lightly on his tea, sputtering a bit while the others sat frozen with polite smiles amid the tension. But it was not remotely surprising that Lady Shipley merely nodded in confident understanding, oblivious to Marie-Anne's disapproval and delighted to have this little insight. "The great families all have their little peculiarities. How charming," she beamed. "Just charming."

All the way home, Marie-Anne thought of a thousand other, more cutting things she might have said. But she also thought of how Helen had often said that people so perfectly convinced of their own superiority would never relinquish that conviction. Such an attitude must be doubly true of Lady Shipley, who was not only convinced of her own superiority but fanatically devoted to convincing others of it.

❧

After an early supper, she sat with Collins in the drawing room and, over a game of chess, related the details of her afternoon at the Shipley's. It was obvious why Helen had made fast friends with this butler. He really was an inveterate gossip with a heart of gold and an ability to remain very dignified as he related his tidbits. He had a great many of them, as servants talked among themselves with abandon, especially about disliked employers. Sir Gordon

Shipley was notorious for his severity and snobbery, and this was widely believed to be a reaction to how his own father had been rarely sober and always an embarrassment. He was almost more unbearable than Lady Shipley, who reminded every servant and shopkeeper that her husband was a baronet and privately lamented that this did not automatically open every door of Society to them.

"She does not understand how to be discreet in the way that they like," Marie-Anne told him as she considered moving a pawn. She was on the point of saying more on the subject – she so enjoyed discussing these people with others who, like her, lived among them without being one of them – but they were interrupted by a footman.

"Mr. Mason come to call, madame," he said, and Marie-Anne's belly performed a little flip of excitement. She was quite sure Collins noticed it, too, and so she concentrated on maintaining a bland expression while she said Mr. Mason could be shown in.

He gave his restrained little nod in greeting, the soft light chasing briefly across his glossy red hair as he moved. "Madame," he said as the butler left the room.

"Why do you do that?" she asked him.

"Do what?"

"You never give a bow like the other gentlemen. You bend your head, but only a little, and almost like you do not want to. Is bowing not the custom in America?"

"It depends where you go, and the situation. I don't think there is one American custom. Does it offend you?"

"Not at all," she reassured him. He looked terribly self-conscious. "It delights me to know there is a place where one is not always required to bow and scrape."

"Vive la revolution?" he asked in his darling American accent. She let her full smile spread out, and watched his own unfurl in response.

"Very good, now we know that Collins is not eavesdropping," she told him as she took a seat near the fire. "He would carry you off to the docks himself to banish you from the British soil, if he heard you say that. He is very disapproving of these revolutionary ideas. Hélène told me – Lady Summerdale, I mean. She said their cordial relationship was once very strained when she mentioned her admiration of your President Washington."

He did not sit, even when she gestured to a chair. He stood near the fireplace instead and asked, "Why would the wife of an earl admire Washington?"

"The daughter of an earl, too, and sister to one." Marie-Anne took slow and even breaths to calm the anger she immediately felt at the thought of those people. Helen had endured great cruelty from her aristocratic family and friends, because of what they called honor and decency. How savage these so-civilized people could be. "It is strange I never wondered why she was always so infatuated with the Americans. I thought it was only a fascination of the intellect, but today when Lady Shipley made that remark..."

"A butler to match the drapes, you mean?"

"Yes," she said, and wished she had a fan in her hand, so that she might snap it closed with a satisfactory slap into her palm. "Well. I see now, I think, why my friend would admire a government so determined to defy and destroy the aristocracy."

"Is she a secret radical?"

He seemed intrigued, eager to hear more, which made Marie-Anne laugh. "Not those two things together, no. She is very secret, and she is not very radical. But she has enough audacity to be a friend to me, thank goodness. Now tell me why you are here? I hope it is because Dahlia and Phyllida have both announced they have decided to die as spinsters and the only thing I must do now is to choose a dress to wear for Amy's wedding."

"Only a fraction as thrilling as that," he admitted, "but still thrilling. Dahlia is reconsidering. She was aiming to put your dressmaker to work tomorrow, to order a pile of dresses to dazzle all of New York society. She looked like I'd canceled Christmas when I told her there was no need for a fashionable wardrobe since I planned for us to live far outside the city."

"Oh, very well done! I must be sure to point out all the most practical fabrics and dreary designs tomorrow."

"But that's not even the best part. She interrupted my stirring discourse on the growth rate of hardwood forests in the Middle West to say she suddenly decided she wants a long engagement. Last week she was agitating to put an announcement in the paper, but tonight she said she prefers to keep it quiet until the season's long over."

Marie-Anne clapped her hands together in delight. "Wonderful! You see? I am sure more than ever she uses you to make Lord Releford jealous. If you marry and take her away too soon, it spoils her chance to win him back. And now she thinks you are not such a consolation, if she cannot get Releford." She stood and began to pace, thinking. "It would be good to push them together, you know? At a party of some kind. I would have one and invite him, but I do now know him."

"I thought he was friends with your Lord Summerdale."

"Yes, probably he is. Everyone is friends with Stephen, but he is not here, so it is no help to us." At his look of confusion, she explained. "To walk up to the son of a duke and say hello, this is a kind of unspeakable offense. Without an introduction, he might faint from the shock, which would be very unpleasant."

He chuckled, which pleased her immensely. "Ah. His ancestors would rise from their graves to chase us back into the nearest gutter where we belong, that sort of thing. What about the Huntingdons?"

"Oh yes! Joyce might know him. I will ask." She was on the verge of proposing that they have tea and cake to celebrate their progress, when she remembered the other half of her task. "This retrenchment is very good, but now for the problem of the poet." She scowled at him. "Why did you not tell me how impossible this will be?"

"Impossible? Why do you say that?"

"Oh *mon dieu*," she said, exasperated, and crossed herself before throwing her hands up. "You are worse than Amy, and what is your excuse, hm? It is without flaw, his beauty, and you have the eyes of an artist. Why did you not warn me of his face!"

"I never said I was an artist."

Marie-Anne would have none of this quibbling. "I

watched you with the paintings and I hear how you speak of them. The eyes and the voice of an artist, it is there in the things you notice. Also you said you draw with the pencil."

"That's not art. It's just scribbling." He was frowning back at her. She had made him very irritable. "I'd never call myself an artist, and there are plenty of flaws."

"In your scribbling?"

"In his face."

"Hah. Tell me one," she insisted.

He stopped short, clearly trying to think of any. "All right, his eyes have that perfect shape, and his chin – it's a good chin, and those are hard to come by in these circles, I'll concede that. Especially in profile. And there's the cheekbones, the less said about them the better, but the line of his jaw is... It's..."

"Designed to make a woman weak in the knees?"

"His nose!" he said, with a triumphant jab of his finger in the air. "His nose is boring. Insipid."

Marie-Anne crossed her arms and merely looked at him. He let out a sigh and sagged a little in defeat.

"All right, he's an Adonis," he admitted, in a voice that precisely matched her own helpless exasperation with the fact. "It's like Michelangelo sculpted that face. You're right, of course. Women can't resist it."

He looked so dejected, staring into the fire with his little scowl. She felt it tug at her heart a bit, and for a moment she wondered if his pose was calculated for exactly that effect. But there were those splotches of color on his neck creeping just above the collar, and now he was trying to compose his features hide his little burst of envy.

"Well." She gave a *tsk* and waved a hand in

dismissal. "Not *women*. It is girls who want perfection. A girl is enchanted by a perfectly smooth cheek, but a woman likes a little of the beard on it, to make it interesting." Her lips twitched. "Or freckles."

He looked up at her, his hazel eyes showing more green than brown in the firelight, and she felt very breathless. She suddenly could not remember what the poet looked like at all. Why on earth were they talking about some pretty boy with a ridiculous name, who was polished to a shine and spoke of boring things and had not once made her laugh? Mr. Mason made her laugh. He also made her mouth water, and she was having a terrible time hiding it from him.

"Miss Marie-Anne," he said in that slow and low voice that came out of him sometimes. It made her think of lazy, hot summer days. Sweat on the skin, laying back in the shade, feeling the heat seep right through and melt your bones. "I would very much like to kiss you," he announced. "Very much and very deep and very long."

She tried to imagine a proper and demure response to that. Unfortunately, her imagination was otherwise engaged at the moment.

"I would very much like to kiss you too," she replied, which was the wrong thing to say. One shouldn't simply blurt the truth, especially when they were alone in this room and he looked unbelievably tempting in the glow of the firelight, and now he was looking at her mouth and moving toward her, which was a complete disaster. A completely delicious disaster.

"But," she said, rather desperately.

He halted only inches from her raised hand. "But?"

"But of course we cannot do such a thing when you are engaged to be married."

After a very long and frozen moment, during which he continued to look fixedly at her mouth, he said, "Of course. And if I were not engaged?"

"Then I would kiss you, I think," she said simply. "Like you said. Very much and very... long." She did not say *very deep*, because already she knew she would have difficulty recovering from this conversation. "But you are engaged. And I am outrageous and even reckless sometimes, but I try not to be hurtful. Sometimes – it is rare, but there are times when honor is not just a foolish ideal."

He took a step back and said, "Right. And I'm not that much of a cad." He had the air of someone coming to his senses, and she suppressed a sigh of disappointment. "Or at least I'm trying not to be."

She raised her brows, relieved at his easy agreement, and summoned up a more lighthearted tone. "No, am I having a reforming effect? What a disappointment I have become!"

"I don't believe it's possible for you to disappoint, Marie-Anne."

She looked away briefly to avoid his admiring gaze. "Let us hope you are right, at least in the matter of convincing Dahlia to release you. It is a strong motivation, this kiss you promise me. That will be my reward, hm?"

It was equal parts delightful and alarming, how his smile could so easily go from pleasant humor to wildly suggestive. "A kiss," he said, with a long and lascivious look that touched every point of interest between her shoulders and her knees. "I think I can arrange for that to be a very satisfying reward."

Chapter Six

Freddy was saying something, but Mason's attention was entirely taken up with Lady Summerdale's breast. He considered exaggerating the line of it, or changing the angle of her hip so that it was more unmistakably sexual. It would take very little to turn it into a caricature, and just a little more than that to make it a grotesque mockery. He didn't like to do it, though. It didn't feel right to distort a body that was so perfectly formed by nature, and that he had managed to capture so exactly.

Instead, he altered the cartoonish figure next to her so that it leaned a little closer and leered more broadly. That was really all it ever took, anyway – show a man leering at it and the most innocent female figure was instantly interpreted as more sexual. It was the power of suggestion. Still, he added her hand, tickling the man under the chin in a gesture that was affectionate and flirting.

"There's an idea," said Freddy thoughtfully. He

was looking over Mason's shoulder, one of his more annoying habits. "Don't want to get too political, but play on Lady Summerdale's scandalous past like that and we balance the two stories."

"One story," corrected Mason, as he added a sash across the leering man's chest that read NORWAY. "Or one true story, at any rate. Her scandal was real, but this is entirely invented."

"Believable, though. What are they doing in Norway, anyway?" Freddie took a bite of whatever he was eating, probably dropping crumbs on the floor behind Mason's back. "Ought to holiday in Italy or Switzerland, like the rest of them."

Mason ignored him in favor of perfecting the expressions of satisfaction on the other figures who were waiting eagerly in a large bed behind Lady Summerdale's enticing form. There were three of them, labeled America, France, and Haiti. Maybe Haiti didn't belong – he wasn't sure how much the British public cared about that revolution. And he wasn't sure where to place her husband in the scene. What would an English lord do while his radical wife kept company with revolutionaries? And should he include something to remind readers that Norway had abolished their aristocracy last year?

"It would need to be more personal than this. Bring in the Irish," Freddy suggested. "That was the scandal, how she played the whore to an Irish peer. Maybe if they'd gotten their republic, she'd have wanted to be more than just his mistress. Either way, it's easy to make the case she has a taste for revolutionaries."

"Except for how she's married to the most upstanding member of the British nobility, who doesn't have a revolutionary bone in his body, and they are famously in love." Mason moved his pencil lightly over her eyebrow. Her body was easy to capture on the page, but her face was elusive.

"Well leave that out, but I tell you it needs more of the personal. Maybe add her French friend? That's more scandal *and* more revolutionaries."

"Freddy, that will not happen." Mason dropped his pencil and rubbed his eyes. It was late, and he had other things he'd rather be drawing now. "That French friend is going to get me out of this engagement. And she's going to manage it so I still have some kind of respectability with these people when it's done, which I'll remind you is necessary if you want to keep this game going."

He had no compunction about leaving Dahlia at the altar, if it came to that. She and all her acquaintance might consider it an irreparably damaging humiliation, but Mason didn't even come close to caring. If he dropped her, she'd still have her good name. She could even marry some decent man in the end, if she would ever lower herself to accept someone without a large fortune or an impressive title. Even more importantly, no matter what he did Dahlia would still have a roof over her head, clothes on her back, and food in her mouth. The idea of "ruin" among these people was blown considerably out of proportion.

The plan had always been to disappear and, like always, the people left behind would feel betrayed and bereft. The trick was to make sure they didn't feel that way until he was gone, and he needed a few more months until he had enough funds to take him very far away. Now that he was completely trusted among the Shipleys and all their circle – which now included Marie-Anne de Vauteuil and her invaluable high society friends – he and Freddy might get enough material to sell more papers than they'd imagined.

"Anyway, forget this," said Freddy. "It's suicide, going after Summerdale like that. Save it for when we're in need of desperate measures and ready to burn every bridge. We'll both hope it never gets that desperate. Besides, politics don't sell as well as the gossip. Did you finish the one with the marquess?"

Mason pulled the drawing of the marquess forward and handed it to Freddy. He slipped the Summerdale sketch into a folder behind a dozen other half-drawn and abandoned ideas. It really would ruin their whole scheme to publish anything like that. He'd only put his pencil to it because he wanted an excuse to draw Lady Summerdale, and when left to his own devices he always tended toward the political. Back in New York, the political work was the only kind that paid, and it was where all his experience came from. Freddy rightly insisted that others already did political satire in London, and the appetite for social satire was never satisfied. So that was where they had focused their attention.

"Oh, this is brilliant," said Freddy, beginning to laugh as he looked at the sketch of the marquess.

"You like it? I wasn't sure if I should make his wife look more sympathetic. You know – scoundrel husband, pitiful weeping wife."

"No, it's perfect. Let someone else play up the tragedy. This," he said with a gleeful jab at the drawing where the wife brandished a poker, "is comedy. No one has to choose sides to enjoy this version. *The Marquess cries Divorce at the wife who dared to witness his infidelity* – that's what we'll call the print."

Mason refrained from rolling his eyes. Nothing like re-stating exactly what was depicted, in case there was any doubt about a picture of a man in bed with a woman and shouting DIVORCE at his angry wife. But Freddy was in charge of words, so he left it alone.

"If we can get the mistress's name by next week, you can do another drawing on it then. If not, we'll have to think of something else. The divorce won't happen, so this story will be played out soon enough. It's not too soon to do another on Aloysius St. James, if you're ready to put that Shipley girl in the line of fire?"

Mason shrugged. "If we have nothing else, but it's awfully boring. She just sighs over him like all the others, while he writes bad poetry and looks pretty. Nothing new there."

"It's a new conquest, anyway, and we wouldn't want the public to miss out."

It might put Amy's future with her priggish vicar into jeopardy, but Mason didn't consider that worth his time or concern. Amy was sensible and he liked her well enough, but he didn't feel remotely responsible for her antiseptic romance. That was Marie-Anne's concern.

Except, damn it all, Marie-Anne was only helping him out of his own engagement for Amy's sake.

"God, it's like dominoes. We have to knock 'em down in the right order." He put aside the thought and reached for a fresh sheet of paper. "Let's not put her name on it. At least not until my engagement is safely ended."

"That can work. Build a bit of mystery, who's the new girl – that sort of thing. One day, Mason, you and I will write our memoirs and explain to the world how we created a libertine out of someone as dull as St. James. I'll lay odds he gets his wretched poems published on the strength of a reputation we invented, and he doesn't even know it. All the work, none of the credit, though the money's better than credit–"

"Freddy, are you going to leave anytime tonight? Or did you forget the tantrum you threw over having to pay for two rooms? If you don't actually use yours, I promise my own tantrum will be even louder."

When Freddy left, Mason retrieved the larger folder from where he'd kept it hidden away atop the wardrobe. He flipped past the sketches of Dahlia's hands, her father's artfully tied cravat, her mother burning her mouth on the soup at dinner last week. He'd used half a page sketching the flowers that were in Summerdale House, and now he used the other half to draw Lady Summerdale's waist. There was the beading on her gown from the night at the ball, and the curve of her forearm which he had to imagine because she'd worn long gloves.

He worked on it until it seemed alive to him, like he could touch the crook of her elbow and feel a pulse. Then he moved on to a new page, intending to try his hand at drawing a kangaroo but finding that his pencil had other ideas. It was Marie-Anne's smile that made it to the page. He drew her mouth again and again – her full smile and her little mischievous grin, her polite smile and her smirk, her moue of distaste and her lips pursed in disapproval. There was a natural upward curve to her lips, as though she were perpetually amused.

It was easy to think she *was* perpetually amused,

but he had seen her face when Sir Gordon and Lady Shipley pretended they had never treated her horribly. For that matter, he had seen she was not amused when she declared him a cad and rebuked him for flirting with her at the ball.

She truly cared about the Shipley girls, and was serious about keeping them safe from hurt. What's more, he was fairly certain it was not obligation to a dead lover that motivated her. It was just her nature to look out for them, no matter how exasperating they were. She cared, and as long as she thought he cared too, she would want him around.

How long ago had he learned to notice and use that sort of thing? Probably before he'd even learned to walk. *Like what they like or hate what they hate, and they think you're on their side without you even trying.* That's how his cousin had always put it. *Don't lay it on too thick, though.*

Mason looked at the page full of her smile. He didn't care what happened to the Shipley girls, but he wanted to kiss Marie-Anne de Vauteuil. He wanted it so much that even if he were to get free of this engagement tomorrow, he'd still help Marie-Anne with her plans. He'd do it because he wanted her to like him. Not to achieve some end – not to help him with Dahlia or get him closer to high society, and not even just because he rarely went an hour without thinking of kissing every inch of her. He just wanted her to like him as much as he liked her. And if he could get her to look at him half as soppily as she looked at that stupid poet, he thought he could die happy.

❦

"Won't you please consider coming to the opera?" Dahlia pleaded with him the next day. "I know you've said you don't like it, but Mrs. Heckerling has offered us her box and it's really so very important to be seen there."

"We're being seen *here*," he said to her with a sweeping gesture at the park. "And we'll be seen tonight at that card party, and on Saturday at the dinner you say is so important. I don't mind the park, Dahlia, and I like playing cards and eating dinner, but I'll be damned if I spend hours at something I don't like only so people can look at me."

"You are very disagreeable today, Mason." She said it fretfully, which was why he always found it hard to be unkind to her. Unless it was her parents or sisters, Dahlia was so anxious for approval that just faintly criticizing her felt like kicking a puppy. "Marie-Anne said I should ask you even though I was sure you'd say no. I think she worries you will not make a good husband for me."

"Did she say so?"

"Oh no, she would never say it." She paused to wave at a passing carriage, but did not ask him to stop so that she could greet whoever it was. "I remember her saying years ago that the world could always do with more love in it, and so one should never say anything to discourage a romance. Isn't that the noblest sentiment?"

Mason carefully considered how he wanted to respond to this before settling on, "If you value sentiment over truth, I suppose."

Her cheeks were growing pink, but he couldn't tell if that was a trick of the late afternoon light or real feeling. She was very subdued as she said, "She would never be untruthful. It is very ungracious of you to suggest it. I don't care what her past is or what my parents have said about her. Richard thought very highly of her and loved her passionately, and he could never love a liar."

She seemed so wounded that he almost pulled the carriage to a halt so that he could soothe her. But he remembered in time that he was supposed to be nurturing a rift between them. "Then it's a good thing I never said she was a liar," he said coolly. "You're the one who thinks she doesn't like me."

"Oh no, that's not what I meant! I think she likes you very much!" she protested, looking disheartened. "We seem to misunderstand each other rather often, don't we? I suppose with time we'll grow more accustomed to one another. Though I won't expect you to grow accustomed to the opera, at least not this week."

He guided the carriage out of the park and towards her home. There was no denying that an evening at the opera could easily provide fodder for next week's paper. This was the whole reason he'd ever bothered to flirt with Dahlia in the first place – to attend these sorts of things with someone who continuously and enthusiastically pointed out who mattered and who didn't, and why. He'd never thought it could backfire so spectacularly. Now everything seemed to be a choice between keeping his money-making scheme afloat and disentangling himself from her plans to marry him.

But if Dahlia was so desperate to be seen on the arm of her wealthy new beau at the opera tomorrow night, it was probably because Lord Releford would be there. And there was no reason not to take advantage and kill two birds with one stone.

"Why not ask St. James to join you? He loves opera."

He'd also make any man jealous, with that hair and that chin and the way even Marie-Anne fluttered when she looked directly at him. It only helped that St. James had been linked to an actress a few months ago, a possibly harmless acquaintance that Mason and Freddy had turned into a torrid affair with a few strokes of the pen. Now they could speculate in print if the would-be poet's new conquest was another actress, or one of the Shipley sisters, or some other notable citizen in the over-perfumed crowd.

"Oh yes, that's an excellent idea!" said Dahlia breathlessly, clearly seeing the superiority of the plan.

That settled the matter, thankfully, and Mason was so relieved to have an evening free of socializing that he didn't even mind when Dahlia's father, upon learning Mason would not be attending the opera, said, "Of course, it's only natural that you can't appreciate the more elevated entertainments to be found in London. But I think you'll find that if you apply yourself with diligence to studying the pursuits of those with more refined tastes, your own sensibilities will improve."

This was delivered in his natural voice: pompous, condescending, and at a normal speed and volume. Since Sir Gordon usually employed a slightly slow and loud voice when magnanimously explaining anything to the uncultured colonial in his drawing room, Mason thought their relationship must be improving. Which would not do at all. To counter it, he looked blankly at Sir Gordon for a while and eventually asked him where a man was supposed to spit in this city, as there was never a spittoon when you needed one.

He really couldn't wait to tell Marie-Anne about the look of horror this produced. Unfortunately, he saw her sparingly over the next few days and always in the presence of the Shipleys. At last she came to dinner one evening, her opportunity to meet Amy's almost-vicar.

"I am so glad to finally meet you, Mr. Harner!" she said when they were introduced, her enthusiasm firmly in place as she held out her hands to him and gave a radiant smile that made Mason's heart lurch. "It is a very special man, I think, who can capture our sweet Amy."

But Mr. Harner was deeply uncomfortable with this warm familiarity and, as he avoided her outstretched hands, Marie-Anne's enthusiasm began to die out. Her smile dimmed down to a pleasant expression that grew increasingly strained throughout the evening as she tried, and failed, to find anything interesting about Mr. Harner. The man was so dull his mere presence tarnished the silver.

"Does he take pleasure in anything at all?" She whispered it to Mason as he sat next to her after dinner at the card table.

"Reading to us from his favorite book of sermons." He answered her in an undertone as he reached for the cards. "But Sir Gordon threatened never to invite him to another dinner if he pulled out that damned book again. That made Amy threaten to kick St. James in the shins if he read any more of his poetry for the evening entertainment, which led to a squabble between her and Phyllida that made me very happy I never had sisters."

"So we must amuse ourselves with cards, I see," she said, and looked at him shuffling the deck. "You are very good at that! Do you gamble so much?"

He'd let his hands move without thinking, handling the cards as deftly as an expert. He stopped. "I was a bored child who played with cards, that's all. Dahlia," he said as she approached them. "We were just talking about entertainment. Will you play for us?"

"If you like," she agreed, "but Amy is so much better, and I was hoping Marie-Anne would show us her lace-making."

"Oh yes!" Phyllida came rushing across the room. "Won't you please, Marie-Anne? You can't imagine how often we've talked of it over the years."

Marie-Anne seemed amazed they remembered it at all, and protested she didn't have the materials necessary. When Sir Gordon began to frown and mumble something about his daughters engaging in a trade best left to common shop girls, Mason overrode him by asking how she had come to learn it.

"It was the business of my family for many generations," Marie-Anne explained. "It is why I learned English, you know, because my father's uncle came to England to open a business here. I was to come when I was old enough and help to teach the patterns."

"But then there was the war and Napoleon," said Phyllida eagerly, as though it was an old favorite story. "And no one wanted to buy lace from a Frenchman in England, isn't it too bad? But then Richard found you in Paris because you spoke English–"

"And loved cakes!" interjected Dahlia.

"Yes, and you talked about pastries and England

and he fell in love with you the very afternoon you met. He told us so. When did you fall in love with him, Marie-Anne?"

Marie-Anne arched her eyebrows at this impertinent question, and then gave a burst of throaty laughter. "The instant he said he would buy me any pastry I wanted, of course, and as much as I could eat of it!"

Phyllida's face fell at this, either because she knew it was an evasion or because she believed it was true and found it wholly unromantic.

"Well now I have to know – which pastry did you choose and how much did you eat?" asked Mason.

She cut a glance toward the settee where virtuous Mr. Harner sat in earnest conversation with the elder Shipleys. A wonderfully mischievous look came over her, and she raised her voice just enough so that it would carry.

"I have never seen them in England, but they are very popular in France. We call them *pets de putain.*"

There was a chorus of impressively varied gasps in the room. Dahlia's was one of simple surprise, Phyllida's of amusement, Lady Shipley's of anxiety, and Mr. Harner's of offense. Amy made a little choking noise and clasped a hand over her mouth, a clear attempt to stifle her laughter.

Marie-Anne simply smiled placidly and said, "I ate more than a dozen."

Her words lay there in the room, just waiting for him to pick them up. So he called upon his almost non-existent French vocabulary, furrowed his brow, and asked, "Something to do with a whore, is that right?"

"*Mais oui!*" She nodded approvingly, amid a fresh round of horrified gasps from the settee. "The farts of a whore." The girls were helplessly giggling now. "A whore's fart, that is the better way to say it in English. They are delicious. I don't know why they are called that, but..." She gave a very French kind of shrug.

"Well, because you don't know if a real whore's fart *is* delicious," mused Mason. "In my experience–"

"Dahlia!" Lady Shipley barked. "I think we would all like to hear some music, if you please. Immediately." She gave Mason a look of outrage before turning a quelling eye on Phyllida, who had collapsed into a chair with laughter. Dahlia, amused but eager to smooth things over, hurried over to the pianoforte where a purple-faced Mr. Harner helped her to choose a piece to play.

Phyllida recovered herself and began to talk to Marie-Anne about the dresses they had ordered from the modiste, questioning her about all sorts of wardrobe essentials that Mason had barely heard of. It was obvious Marie-Anne loved the topic, though, so he just sat back and listened to them while Dahlia began to play. Amy sat a little apart with, surprisingly, St. James – they sometimes managed to get along when they avoided the topic of poetry.

It was sweet, really. A cozy drawing room filled with a little family, ridiculous parents and silly but loving sisters, with music playing and a disapproving vicar and talk of ribbons and bonnets. Maybe he should just marry Dahlia. It was such a safe and simple life, dressing in fine clothes and eating good food every day and thinking of little more than which social event you'd like to attend next. There were all kinds of idiotic rules, but that was the case everywhere. He could learn them, and make himself happy here.

Then he remembered that there was the little problem of him not actually being a wealthy businessman. And how he was using every person in this room in a way that would appall them. And how, even if he wasn't involved in this business with Freddy, these people would never invite someone like him to be in this room, much less to be a part of their family. He was getting in so deep he almost forgot it, sometimes. *The illusions's for the gulls, not you*, his cousin had always reminded him. Somewhere, that cousin was still creating illusions for whatever poor bastards crossed his path. Cure-alls and card games and schemes he swore would make a poor man rich with no effort – Mason doubted the repertoire had changed much.

"Do you think panniers will ever come back into fashion?" Phyllida was asking Marie-Anne during a pause in the music. "Mama always says she misses them."

"Oh I would love it," Marie-Anne sighed at the thought. "But we should speak of something that poor Mr. Mason might have an interest in. I do not think he is fascinated by the fashions."

"I might be," he said, "if you tell me what panniers are."

She lowered her voice to ask Phyllida, "Do we think it is even more vulgar than the pastries, to tell a gentleman what is under a lady's dress?" Phyllida bit down on another giggle, which Marie-Anne seemed to take as an answer. "Very well, Mr. Mason, we will be shocking. They are a garment that is tied around the hips so the skirt spreads out, very wide. I remember when I was very little, I could hide under my mother's skirt and it felt like hiding under the dining table. I could not wait to grow up and wear the dresses, and the hats – so elaborate! But the style changed."

She began to describe a dress in detail, with many sweeping and ineffectual gestures, until she finally went to the writing desk and procured pen, ink, and paper. She set them in front of Mason and said, "You will do some of your scribbling for me, please, so Phyllida understands what I describe."

He tried to protest, but she was so insistent he gave in. Once he had sketched the outline of what she described, he couldn't help himself adding more and more detail until it matched her words exactly. When she described a wig and absurdly large hat, he added those too, and then, without thinking, he added a face with just a few strokes.

"But that's remarkable, Mr. Mason!" gasped Phyllida. "Marie-Anne, it's you, do you see? It's only a few lines, but it's her very likeness! However do you do it so easily? Will you draw me now?"

"I can try." He concentrated on looking completely unperturbed. He should never have picked up the pen, or admitted to trying his hand at drawing. Nothing of what he'd sketched tonight was in the style he used for the papers, but it was a mistake to show he could make a likeness so quickly and so true to its subject.

He took up the pen and drew how he imagined Phyllida might look in ten years, with more sophistication and polish. They were her features, but he put the focus on the angle of her cheekbones and gave her a serious expression she never wore in real life. If in the future he drew her for the papers, he'd emphasize the roundness of her face, make her more wide-eyed and full of spirit. It wouldn't look anything like this.

"I'm really not an artist," he apologized to Phyllida as she frowned in mild disappointment at the little sketch. "Faces are hard. I'll draw you a bonnet, or a bowl of fruit. Simple shapes are my specialty."

He did draw a bowl of fruit that night, back in his room alone. It was an attempt to stop himself drawing Marie-Anne's eyes, the playful gleam in them as she prepared to provoke Lady Shipley, or her disappointed look when Amy's fiancé failed to be amused at anything. He'd already drawn her mouth a hundred times, and the curve of her neck. She might even inspire him to try painting at last, so that he could spend hours reproducing the way candlelight reflected on her honey-colored hair.

But for now, he made himself draw as perfect a plum as he could imagine. When it was proving too easy, he added a bite out of it and worked long into the night to show the juices glistening and dripping down the velvety flesh. Texture work, he told himself – something that was difficult to get right with only a graphite pencil to create dimension and light, the illusion of moisture on the page.

When it was done, he looked at how the juices trickled in a sinuous line across the tender skin of the fruit. He couldn't even pretend to himself that it wasn't the most lascivious thing he'd ever drawn in his life. For God's sake, he couldn't draw a still life of fruit without making it about how desperately he wanted to taste her.

"Well, at least I can always start a side business in pornographic art," he said to the glistening plum before filing the page away.

Chapter Seven

A few days later he was giving excuses to Dahlia and her mother for his failure to make an appearance at some party the night before, when Marie-Anne arrived unexpectedly at their door. She asked if the other Shipley sisters were at home and when told that Phyllida was absent but Amy was in her room, Marie-Anne shouted up the stairs.

"Amy, *ma petite*, come down! I have something you will want to hear!"

While Sir Gordon grumbled his disapproval of this "hoydenish" behavior, Lady Shipley fluttered about saying she should ring for tea. Marie-Anne waved her off.

"No tea, I can only stop for a moment. Dahlia, you look very lovely in that green, you should wear it all the time. Here comes Amy," she said, flushed and smiling, when the eldest Shipley sister finally came in. "Do not look so worried, Amy, it is good news, at least I hope you will think so." She took Amy's hand

and reached out for Dahlia's, who grasped it re
"I am just come from Lady Huntingdon who gi
the same complaint you both gave me, do you
remember, when we were with the dressmaker? That
London has become boring. When the Season is no
longer fresh, it is stale, she says, and soon the city will
be so hot. So her answer is to go to her estate in
Surrey and invite you to come too!"

All the Shipleys gasped. Marie-Anne was
practically dancing with delight, so Mason just
watched her. She was so good at being happy. She
caught his eye, and said, "You too, Mr. Mason, and
Phyllida."

"And you too, I hope?" asked Amy.

"Yes, of course," laughed Marie-Anne. "The house
is very big and she will invite many others."

"But I thought–" Dahlia's elated look was
suddenly overcast by uncertainty. She shot a worried
look at Mason then at Marie-Anne, as though she was
afraid to believe this invitation was genuine. "Lady
Huntingdon has not invited us to anything at all this
season. Amy or me, I mean. I was introduced to her,
but…" She didn't say that Lady Huntingdon had
turned chilly the instant she had heard the name
Shipley.

"She knows you are very dear to me, all of you,"
Marie-Anne assured her. "She will also invite Mr. St.
James and she said I must tell you, Amy, that your
Mr. Harner may come too. But only if you want him
to come! It is for you to say."

"Who else is invited?" asked Mason. He managed
to sound annoyed at the prospect of a social gathering
that Dahlia was clearly salivating to be a part of.

"Yes indeed, and when shall we be going?" asked

reat excitement. "We will need to
: and there's my yellow silk gown,
g repaired but I must bring it."

said Sir Gordon, no less excited.

on, I'll send word to the milliner

completed as soon as—"

"No, no, there is no need to trouble yourselves," said Marie-Anne brightly, raising her voice so that it cut across their chatter. "It is only your daughters who have been invited to stay."

Her gaze didn't falter as she watched the excitement slide from their faces. It was spectacular, how she wasn't the least bit uncomfortable. Sir Gordon looked like he was slowly suffocating while Lady Shipley had a half-frantic expression, like she was desperately trying to understand. All the while, Marie-Anne – sweet-faced, perfectly composed, the faintest hint of anticipation in her eyes – politely waited for whatever they might say.

"But...but surely..." Lady Shipley looked like she'd had an idea that explained everything. With an air of great relief, she said, "Oh, but perhaps you don't understand, my dear, that Lady Huntingdon will of course be happy to invite us for your sake. Just as she invited Mr. Mason and Mr. Harner. I'm certain you need only ask her to extend us the invitation."

"Yes of course, I am very certain of that too," Marie-Anne agreed. "But I do not want to ask her."

"But why don't you want to ask her?"

"Because I do not want you to come."

"Why ever not?" asked a bewildered Lady Shipley.

"Because I do not like you," Marie-Anne replied pleasantly. The ensuing silence was so profound that Mason began counting the ticks of the suddenly audible mantel clock. On the seventh of these, she offered further explanation. "And it will be very genteel company, so I am sure you understand."

Mason thought he might actually injure himself in his attempt not to burst into laughter. Sir Gordon was turning purple and his mouth flapping open and shut like a lake trout. Lady Shipley clutched at her bosom and seemed to be trying to decide between a tirade and a swoon. Amy and Dahlia became fascinated with their own feet, which to judge by their expressions were hilarious and appalling and perhaps a little terrifying. Amid it all stood Marie-Anne, radiating perfect contentment.

"I'm told if you apply yourself with diligence to studying your betters, there's some hope for improvement," Mason offered to Sir Gordon, who seemed not to hear it, being too outraged with Marie-Anne to notice anything else. Mason looked to her. "Maybe we should ring for tea? They're always telling me how it soothes their nerves."

But Sir Gordon, after giving a kind of gurgling noise, had at last found his voice. "Impertinent little hussy!"

"Papa!" admonished Dahlia, while Amy gasped and put an arm out in front of Marie-Anne in a touchingly protective gesture. For her part, Marie-Anne only looked highly amused as Sir Gordon continued his blustering.

"...Nothing but a filthy harlot from the gutters of Paris," he was saying, as Lady Shipley nodded along. "Nothing to commend you save that our son was foolish enough to be seduced by a common strumpet–"

"Papa!" Dahlia's angry shout cut him off

decisively. She stepped forward with her chin raised, a supremely disgusted look aimed at her father. "You forget yourself."

Everyone, including Mason, was taken aback by how positively commanding she was. Her father began stammering, her mother faintly fluttering as Dahlia turned briskly to Mason and said, "Mr. Mason, I would be most obliged if you will escort Madame de Vauteuil home. I'll not allow her to be exposed to such insult for an instant longer."

"Dahlia dearest–" began a sheepish Lady Shipley.

"I beg you to keep silent or I will expire of shame right here in the drawing room, Mama."

And in stifling silence, Mason gathered his hat and gloves as Amy whispered that she would call on Marie-Anne tomorrow, and they hastily made their way into the street.

He considered offering to find a hackney, but he wanted to walk all the long way with her. Marie-Anne looked a little stunned. She uttered something in French that he couldn't hope to understand but took to be an expression of impressed amazement.

"Well! I have never dreamed that Dahlia is so..." She lifted her hand in an elegant motion, letting the gesture stand in for words. Turning up the street, she set off with him at a leisurely pace. "She was magnificent! I cannot understand why she ever thought she wanted someone like you."

Mason gave it a few seconds, but she just carried on walking with that confounded look on her face and no sign that she'd meant to give offense. "It's a mystery," he agreed, and prayed his flush of mild mortification would not creep too far above his collar.

"Did you see how she looked down her nose at

them? She would make a wonderful duchess one day. Even her boasting will not be called vulgar, it would be expected of a duchess! I think she may be perfectly suited for it. It is impossible she could resign herself to be the wife of an American businessman."

"It's my fondest wish that she won't be. I suppose the trip to Surrey will feature this son of a duke in the flesh?"

She burst into a smile. "Yes! I have put Joyce – I mean Lady Huntingdon – to work. She loves to... oh, how would you say, to play the Cupid. She invited Releford and she tells me he was not interested until she told him Dahlia would be invited also."

"And who else?" He hoped it didn't come out too eager, but he was more than a little curious. With a hostess like Lady Huntingdon and a guest like Releford, it could prove to be almost as fertile a hunting ground as the opera. Freddy would be in raptures at the possibilities.

"Releford will bring a friend, I think, and of course some of the Huntingdon family. There will also be women for Mr. St. James, to tempt him away from Phyllida." Here she looked up at him with that happy mischief in her eyes, clearly bursting with her news. "Maybe a singer, for certain another debutante, and–" She gave a dramatic pause. "A poetess!"

He looked down at her, so pleased with herself. If it wouldn't cause all kinds of indecent chatter, he'd pick her up right here in the middle of the street and twirl her around in her triumph. Instead, he just smiled back at her.

"You sure know how to make everything fun, don't you?" he marveled. Then he gave in and laughed, loud and long, and she joined him. When it died down, he asked, "Where in the hell did you find a poetess?"

"In hell is a good guess, if she as bad at poetry as he is." She affected a soppy look and put a hand to her heart as she recited. "'Like the breath of the morning dew, like the quivering strings of a golden lyre, kissed by –' Who were the strings kissed by?"

"Aphrodite, probably," supplied Mason. He'd managed to tune out that particular recitation of St. James' latest endeavor. "It's always Aphrodite."

She giggled at that as they turned a corner into a less populated street. "He is required to mention Aphrodite in every poem because he is a libertine, I'm sure. *Libertine* is much more flattering than hussy or – what did they call me? A harlot. No one ever says 'filthy libertine' or 'common libertine.' A man is permitted to be a harlot, and even proud of it, with a word like libertine."

She sounded thoughtful and completely indifferent, as though the words and how they were used were merely linguistic curiosities. He might have felt a more urgent need to defend her as Sir Gordon had blustered on, if she had shown anything other than this detached amusement. Of course, defending her would also require Mason to have any idea how a real gentleman would handle the situation. Pistols at dawn, probably, and a lot of fancy words, and other rituals he didn't know the first thing about.

"It doesn't bother you?" he asked. "What he said about you, I mean."

"No. Most of it is true, you know. My parents died and I could not go to my uncle in England, so I went to Paris where I was very poor. Sometimes I stole things to sell in the streets so we could eat. And with men I was…" She shrugged. "Well, I was not very concerned with their kind of virtue, and they will say this makes me a harlot and hussy and trollop and many other words I have learned since I came here. To them, these names they call me are the only truth. They do not care about my love for Richard, or his love for me. They do not care that I wanted only to be a good wife to him for the rest of my life."

They also hadn't cared that she was going to be mother to their grandchild, until it was lost. But he didn't say that, because he didn't want the wistfulness that came into her face when she talked about Richard to turn into real sadness. He also didn't want to hear about this great love of her life, or his childish jealousy might eat him alive.

No, what he wanted to know was how she was so impervious to their condescension. They looked at her and saw a common slut, disreputable and dirty, and they would never let her forget what she came from. Yet their opinion of her didn't seem to touch her, and he envied her for it.

Almost as though she could hear his thoughts, she said, "But there is a bigger reason it does not hurt me to be called these names. It is because, to me, these are not insults. It is not a sin to be poor or filthy or hungry. Even to call me a whore, I do not feel the insult. What is so bad about whores, after all? I have known many. They go about their business and no one is hurt by them. It is more than I can say for these 'respectable' people."

Going about your business without hurting anyone – that was as good a definition of respectable as he'd ever heard. She believed herself more respectable than them, and felt no shame because she had nothing to be ashamed of. He envied her for that, too.

"I believe you might make a good duchess yourself," he informed her.

She shouted with laughter. "It is possible I would! But I would be so miserable, I could never hope for it. I only want my little life in my little cottage in my little village." After a few moments of contemplation, she gasped in sudden realization. "Oh, but the dresses! I could wear such beautiful things. Maybe it is worth a little misery, hm? It is possible you are right, I would make a wonderful duchess."

"Well, Releford's father is the current duke, and he's widowed and ancient. You'd be a well-dressed widow within a few years, I bet. Get your dresses and get out." He gave her the smile he'd learned she liked best, and watched the curve of her mouth steepen and the dimple appear. "You help me out of my engagement, and I'll help you scheme to catch him."

"Hah. And I will reward you when I am duchess with a very handsome waistcoat."

"Make it a hat, in the worst possible color for my hair so Sir Gordon's eyes water whenever he sees me. Pink or violet?"

He delighted in her laughter all the way home, as she imagined the trouble she could cause as a duchess and he wondered how on earth she had ever convinced herself to want nothing more than a little village and a little life.

❧

"Describe their reaction in detail, if you please, Marie-Anne. I shall go to my grave wishing I had been there to witness it."

Though the entire Huntingdon estate was at their disposal and the guests newly arrived, Joyce had chosen to make herself at home in the room she had given Marie-Anne. Lady Huntingdon sat on a stool with her feet propped up on the bed as she watched the maids unpacking dresses. After thoroughly admiring each one, she told the servants to go and threatened them with dismissal if they lingered outside the door to eavesdrop. Marie-Anne was quite sure she meant it, too. The Huntingdon servants were entirely too cavalier about privacy, which concerned Joyce very little except in select circumstances. By giving this warning, she had clearly signaled to them that other guests might be fair game, but Marie-Anne was absolutely not.

Marie-Anne did not care in the least if the little scene with the Shipleys became gossip spread by servants, but she was happy enough to let Joyce to decide which whispers mattered and which did not.

"They were bubbling like champagne, they were so excited," Marie-Anne said, sitting herself down at the dressing table. "They were planning already, the wardrobe they would pack to bring here. And when I said they are not invited?" She made a grab in the air with her hand. "It was like taking toys from happy children. In an instant, poof – all the joy left them. Now I understand the happiness of ogres. It was very satisfying."

"The happiness of ogres," Joyce chuckled. "But they are the monsters, dearest, and they deserve so much worse. 'Because I do not like you!' Oh, it must have felt wonderful to say it outright. And to think I almost believed you'd forgiven them for the girls' sakes."

"Forgive them?" Marie-Anne gave an indelicate snort. "I am not a saint, I have said it many times. They did not allow me to attend my Richard's funeral. They put men at the doors of the church to stop me. There is much I can forgive, but never that."

"I should think not. Nor will I, for that matter." Joyce looked thoughtful. "What a shame you'll please them to no end in making their daughter a duchess. But if you will insist on it, do let's balance things by marrying their youngest girl to someone they'll positively loathe."

"Oh, this is a very good idea! Let's think. Do you have any young and attractive gamekeepers or gardeners? It is possible a very good body will tempt Phyllida away from the beautiful St. James."

Marie-Anne, who was completely serious, was startled when Joyce let out a bark of laughter.

"You may very well be right, my dear, but I can't think of any man here who fits that description better than Mr. Mason. And I can see you would not wish her or any other young lady to marry *him*."

Marie-Anne opened her mouth to disagree with this assessment of Mason's physique but, upon remembering how his thighs looked in his close-cut trousers, she shut it again. She then drew breath and prepared to object that Mr. Mason was a perfectly acceptable candidate for marriage but, forced to admit to herself that indeed she did *not* wish Phyllida to marry him, she closed her mouth once again. She had only just decided to change the subject to something less fraught when Joyce positively cackled.

"I shall sit you before the fire where you will serve as a fine bellows, if you keep flapping like that, Marie-

Anne. Though it's warm enough I daresay we'll not need to light any fires. Now," she said, regaining her composure as she stood, "I've assigned Lucy as your maid. She's experienced in dressing ladies, so you'll have help getting into those lovely new gowns. You may wonder that I've put you in this room, as the view is so unremarkable and the other guests are a bit farther down the hall. But I know you like the quiet and will take full advantage of it. Oh, and I must show you this."

With a notably innocent expression, she walked to the corner furthest from the door, not far from the bed, and put a hand to the wall. "The two wings of the house meet here, you see, and a great many rooms there are in each. The manor is far too large and very old, with so many of the little oddities one expects in old houses. Like this."

She pulled at the wood molding and a panel came open. Behind it was another wall, which looked to be made of a plain, unpainted wood. It was very strange.

Marie-Anne blinked. "There is a door in the wall?"

"Yes, rather unexpected, isn't it. Well, you see – before the renovations, it used to be that the only stairs were at either end of the house, so the servants would use this to pass more quickly between the two halves of the house. You have only to lift this latch here on the opposite door and it opens into the next room. There are joined rooms like this on the floors above and below, too. The doors haven't been used for decades. Well, not by the servants anyway. Most don't even know these panels are here."

Marie-Anne raised her eyebrows in question, but was only met with that determinedly innocent look. "I think you must want me to guess why you have given me a room with a secret door."

"I think you'll have little trouble guessing it yourself, my dear." She patted Marie-Anne on the shoulder as she passed by her, preparing to exit. "And you need not fear you'll be disturbed unless you wish it. I haven't told Mr. Mason it's there at all."

"Mr. Mason?" Marie-Anne asked, alarmed to find her voice rising into a higher register. "What has Mr. Mason to do with this?"

"Oh, did I not say? It's his room, on the other side of the panel."

Her friend gave a wicked smile and turned to leave. Marie-Anne rushed to stop her.

"Joyce!" Marie-Anne put a staying hand to the door, then found she did not know what to say. She hadn't said a word to her friend about her attraction to Mason, but obviously it was apparent. "*Quelle absurdité*," she finally managed. Then she sputtered. "A hole in the wall, I have never heard… And what do you mean to suggest…"

"My goodness, I never thought to see the day." Joyce looked at her in wonder. "Why, Marie-Anne de Vauteuil is positively scandalized! And you blush! I did not think you capable of it. Do you think Helen will believe me when I tell her? No, I daresay she never will. Oh, how I wish she was here, Norway can't possibly have anything as marvelous or improbable as—"

She was cut off by Marie-Anne's sudden burst of laughter, which continued for quite some time. Nothing had seemed quite so funny in a very long time.

"Oh," she gasped at Joyce. "Oh, I have been among respectable people for so long I am infected with the horrible propriety." She kept laughing until her sides ached. If Aurélie could see her now. If anyone she'd known in Paris – or, as Joyce said, if Helen could hear her protest the propriety of it – oh, how they'd laugh.

After some time she regained her breath and leaned her back against the wall. "But really! It is preposterous, a secret passage for a lover! Who was ever so scandalous to put it here?"

"Some Huntingdon long dead, I'm sure. After all, what good is a country house unless one can have a house party? And what good is a house party without rampant impropriety?" Joyce smiled as she surveyed the room. "To hear my grandmama tell it after a few glasses of sherry, romping about from one bed to another was the whole point – and still is in many circles – so they designed things to make it easier. Take advantage, Marie-Anne. Charlotte and I always did."

Charlotte. There was a name she had not heard for some time.

"You used to have this room?"

"No, but there is a hidden niche in the east salon that serves very well, and also the priest hole behind the north staircase. Then there is the folly beyond the hedge maze where we used to meet, the maze itself of course, and the abandoned hermit's cottage... I shall take you on a tour of all the best places for secret assignations." She patted Marie-Anne's arm. "We rarely go to any of them anymore, and only out of nostalgia."

"Oh really?" Marie-Anne was thrilled to be distracted by this unexpected news. "You and Charlotte are together again?"

Joyce nodded. "Very much so. Quite possibly forever. So do please remember to be less careless in your words to her, she'll arrive in a few days."

"Of course." Marie-Anne had, upon meeting Joyce's lover years ago, laughed at what she thought was an invented and intentionally bad French accent, only to learn Charlotte was from Martinique and speaking in quite her normal voice. The poor girl had looked as if she wanted to die on the spot, and Marie-Anne still occasionally woke in the night with mortification over it. But how wonderful, that the lovers were still together.

She smiled at her friend. "I am so happy you have her, *mon amie.*"

"As am I. And I am so eager to be happy for *you* that I have conveniently placed a handsome man behind a door next to your bed." Joyce opened the main door on the empty corridor and stepped out. "I spare no efforts in seeing my guests are well cared for, you see?"

"You are a very good hostess, Lady Huntingdon," Marie-Anne assured her. "I'm sure I will be very comfortable."

"Well if you aren't, my dear, it will be no one's fault but your own."

Chapter Eight

The manner in which so many women were drawn to a duke – that is, as a matter of principle, as though the idea of *not* being attracted to a duke was simply unthinkable and unnatural – had used to be a source of persistent bafflement for Marie-Anne. The allure seemed only marginally attributable to money and property, as so many men who were not dukes were fabulously wealthy. It could not be simply a matter of nobility, as the far more abundant titles – earls and viscounts and so forth – did not cause such extreme reaction, and even princes did not elicit the same quality and quantity of female sighs. Very few dukes were good-looking, though all seemed to believe themselves devastatingly handsome. And, having some experience of the average duke's character and personality, she knew for a fact that the appeal had nothing at all to do with hidden charms or fascinating depths.

No, she had long ago dismissed the phenomenon

as the inexplicable attraction of flies to shit. God had designed the world thus and as a mere mortal, she could not hope to understand the grand mystery of it.

She could, however, discreetly stick her dinner fork into the Duke of Ravenclyffe's hand where it had come to rest on her thigh beneath the table.

"Are you quite all right, Your Grace?" Phyllida inquired from across the table, as Ravenclyffe appeared to choke on the fish.

He nodded, coughing in earnest and reaching for his water glass. When Phyllida seemed anxious at his continued distress, Marie-Anne cheerfully pounded her fist against his back with as much force as she could muster – which was quite a lot, she found – until he finally spluttered to a stop and announced rather peevishly that he was perfectly well.

"Then of course I shall stop," said Marie-Anne. "It is so unpleasant when one is given attention that is not wanted."

Miss Ainslie, the singer who sat on Ravenclyffe's other side and who had earlier warned Marie-Anne about the duke's wandering hands, suppressed a titter. Marie-Anne instinctively avoided looking up at Mason. She could feel him watching the little scene, and knew if she met his eye that she would not be able to conceal her mild embarrassment at being treated so poorly.

A change of topic was called for. Marie-Anne cast about for something, knowing only that she should avoid the subject of horses as they were a particular passion of Ravenclyffe's, and she would not like him to think she was interested in anything about him. He had enough women inexplicably fawning over him.

"Phyllida, what were you saying about your walk

today?" she asked. "You found something when you played the explorer, I think."

"Oh, yes! It was not a thing, Marie-Anne, it was a person. A hermit!"

Phyllida's dark curls bounced as she talked excitedly, her eyes shining as she described the patch of tame wilderness she had wandered into. She was turning into the beauty of the family, Marie-Anne thought, and it had more to do with her vivacity than her features. Young, lively, overly romantic, and eagerly following meandering paths among the trees: it was a recipe for disaster. Marie-Anne made a mental note to give her a warning about Ravenclyffe, though Phyllida seemed blessedly immune to the allure of dukes. More importantly and unlike Marie-Anne, she had no sordid past and no reputation for loose morals, which meant she was likely to be safe from his advances. Such were the principles of noble men.

"It is very strange," Marie-Anne said. "Lady Huntingdon mentioned the hermit cottage to me, but I am sure she said it was abandoned. Hermits are very out of fashion now."

"Poor Mr. Mason, you are confounded at this talk of hermits, I see!" trilled the poetess, who was seated next to him. "I don't believe they were ever the fashion in America." Then she leaned in to tell him all about it, a private little conversation among the general chatter.

Her name was Miss Wolcott, but Marie-Anne only used her name if she was forced by circumstance. She thought of her always as The Poetess, and always with exasperation, for she had grown to very much dislike the woman. Full of her own inflated sense of importance, The Poetess had a ridiculously affected manner which was more irritating than amusing. Worse than that, instead of attracting Mr. St. James – which had been the entire purpose in inviting her, though she couldn't know it – The Poetess had immediately repulsed him. Apparently they could never be in accord because he had expressed contempt for a poet she admired. Now the two cordially ignored one another while Phyllida continued to fawn over St. James and The Poetess set her sights on Mason.

The whole situation made Marie-Anne want to throw things.

"The cottage is not abandoned, and he is a very good hermit," Phyllida was insisting.

Marie-Anne tore her eyes away from where The Poetess had put her face very close to Mason's, and was speaking in a low and breathy voice. She rather wished for a good reason to stab the duke with her fork again.

"What makes him a very good hermit? The point of a hermit is to hide from other people, and if you found him then he cannot be very good at it."

"It was quite an effort to find him! But I meant his wisdom, of course. That is the purpose of a solitary life, to gain wisdom."

"A very noble pursuit," said Marie-Anne, determined not to laugh at her.

"It is!" Phyllida agreed, and began to extoll the perceived virtues of this man who seemed to have done very little but sit in silence in the middle of the woods. From the corner of her eye, Marie-Anne saw Mason smiling at something The Poetess was whispering. Then he laughed, which once again made her want to throw things. How could he be genuinely amused by someone so absurd?

Thus far the house party had not been nearly as enjoyable as Marie-Anne had anticipated. Five days, they had been here. Five days of talking and laughing with Mason at every opportunity, that was true. But these five days were also filled with regular waves of resentment at the stupid Poetess, and five nights of trying to forget the convenient opening in her bedroom wall as she lay awake thinking of kissing him – and then thinking of quite a bit more than that while she pleasured herself, *faute de mieux*, with her fingers between her legs. And now she sat stewing in jealousy, feigning interest in an ornamental hermit, and stabbing randy dukes with the cutlery. It was perhaps time to consider that The Poetess was not the most absurd woman at the table.

Marie-Anne cast a forlorn look at her plate, wishing for some bread to appear. Sadly, it did not.

"My grandfather hired a man to be a hermit," Lord Releford was saying. He was seated with Phyllida to one side and Dahlia to the other, and seemed very content with this arrangement. "I believe he went through several men, in fact. They found it too difficult to adhere to his strict rules about bathing. After a few months any man would want a wash, but Grandfather said if a hermit didn't look ramshackle then he wasn't worth paying."

As Phyllida assured him her hermit was very clean and perfectly well-groomed, Marie-Anne rallied. She might be failing in separating Phyllida from her libertine poet, but things were going according to plan with the other Shipley sister. Releford was not only a true gentleman, he was utterly taken with Dahlia. Though he was in line to be a duke himself, he seemed less objectionable than most. He could even be forgiven for inflicting the lecherous Duke of Ravenclyffe on them, if he managed to woo Dahlia well enough that she would break off her engagement.

The signs were very encouraging. Telling herself it was entirely for the sake of Dahlia's romance, Marie-Anne decided to take her aside after dinner to press her on the matter at last. It was past time for them to talk frankly about this engagement. When it came to it, though, it was Dahlia who took Marie-Anne's arm and asked her if she wouldn't like to stroll out to the terrace to enjoy the warm night air.

At a sufficient distance from the open doors of the drawing room, where the others were, Marie-Anne spoke freely.

"Now we are where they cannot hear us so I will tell you I do not like this Ravenclyffe. He is the kind of man a woman should be careful of, I think."

"How do you mean?" A crease of concern had appeared on Dahlia's brow. "Has Ravenclyffe offered you some offense?"

Marie-Anne patted her arm. "Nothing I cannot manage, little cabbage. A woman of scandal is very experienced in these things. I only mention it to say I am surprised he is a friend of Releford, because they do not seem very alike. Mr. Mason has told me that you know Lord Releford very well?" Even in the dim light, she could see Dahlia was blushing as she nodded. "And I have seen myself how he looks at you."

"Mr. Mason?"

"No, Dahlia, I meant Lord Releford. In fact, I have never seen Mr. Mason look at you as Releford does."

"How does Lord Releford look at me?' she asked, with barely disguised hope.

Marie-Anne gave a snort. "As I look at a cake when someone is too slow in serving me a piece of it." Dahlia gave a choked sound. Marie-Anne stopped their meandering stroll and faced her. "I hope we are friends enough that I may speak plainly?" At her tiny nod, Marie-Anne went on. "Well, it is simple. I think your affections are not for Mr. Mason. I think they are for this Lord Releford. I am not wrong?"

Poor Dahlia looked like a child afraid of getting into trouble. She bit her lip and gave a sheepish nod. "It's very bad of me, I know, but I like him so very much and…oh, whatever shall I do?"

She suddenly looked close to tears, so Marie-Anne quickly led her to a stone bench in a shadowy corner of the terrace. "What to do? Exactly what you want to do, of course. You will let Releford eat your cake. After he marries you, of course," she amended hastily, which successfully banished Dahlia's tearful expression and replaced it with a strangled laugh.

"But Mason—"

"Mason deserves better than to be the second choice. You must be honest when I ask you this, Dahlia – do you believe you will ever want Mason in the same way you want Releford?"

"I thought…I did think it was possible, truly I did. I do like Mason, and it was very exciting at first. But then it began to feel like the gravest mistake, because we are so very awkward together. And then – well, to own the truth, Marie-Anne, I see how he is with you. So very easy and relaxed, both of you, and always laughing together. Oh, he is amiable enough with me, but already you are better friends than he and I will ever be. When I see it, I am reminded of how Releford and I used to be."

"Yes, Mr. Mason and I have a natural sympathy as foreigners." Marie-Anne carefully kept her tone unworried. "But I think it was more than just friendly for you and Lord Releford, no?"

"It was. But then he was very rude about mother and father, and while I cannot fault his sentiments, he was unforgivably harsh. Then he said Phyllida was acting disgracefully and even if it was true – well," she sniffed. "We had a row and he dared me to find any man more tolerant than he of my family. So I did."

"Ah. And now you regret it." She watched Dahlia give a miserable nod, and did not resist the urge to put a consoling arm around the girl. "Well you may take comfort in knowing he also regrets it. I am sure of it. One word from you and he is at your feet. Do it before he becomes so desperate he writes poems to your lost love. We cannot withstand more terrible poetry."

That earned her a wobbly laugh. "I should have to release Mason from our engagement first. I confess I do not think it will break his heart, but I dread the thought."

"It is good you did not make the engagement public, so his pride is as safe as his heart. He will not be cruel to you, so why do you dread?"

"Because... what if I release Mason, and then Releford won't have me?" She was obviously mortified at the possibility. "I can't bear the thought."

"Of what, being alone? I promise you there are many worse things. For example, you could hold on to a man you do not want only for fear the other man won't have you," she chided, and then patted her arm reassuringly when she saw the girl was a little abashed.

"You're right," Dahlia said with a sudden resolve. She sat up and squared her shoulders. "I'll speak to Mason right away. Tomorrow. I will take tonight to consider my words and then..." Her courage seemed to flag a little. "It's very daunting."

"*Courage, petit chou.* One awkward moment, and you are free."

She looked up to see others moving to join them on the terrace. Mr. St. James was exhorting Charlotte to be more lyrical in her description of her native Martinique, and Joyce was worrying over her husband's insistence on walking without aid of his cane. "Only promise me you will not run away with Releford in a fit of passion and leave me here with all of these people. I will be tempted to hide with Phyllie's hermit."

❧

Marie-Anne was not used to feeling even a little ashamed of herself, which is why it took her so long to identify the uncomfortable twinge. Once she realized that she was unduly excited about the end of Dahlia's engagement, and that this excitement came almost entirely from the knowledge that she could soon feel free to kiss Mason, she began to experience a self-conscious touch of guilt.

It always tastes better with a little guilt for spice, is what Aurélie used to say. But dear Aurélie had been the kept woman of a married man, so she *would* say that. Virtue, Marie-Anne had learned at a young age, was a very relative thing.

All day she had watched Dahlia work up her courage to speak to Mason. If the girl could overcome her indecisiveness and do it, she would surely feel only a deep and abiding relief. And Marie-Anne had no doubt it was the best thing for Dahlia, in every way. Just because Marie-Anne benefitted from it too, that was no reason to feel ashamed.

Or so she told herself as she sat near her open bedroom window that evening, hoping for a breeze as she used a wet cloth to wipe the perspiration from every crease of her body. The maid had helped her to undress but even free from gown and stockings, she felt warm and slightly sticky until she'd rinsed herself off. It had been a very warm day, and very long, and it was only at the end of the night when everyone was preparing to retire that she had finally heard Dahlia ask Mason if she could have a word. Marie-Anne had beat a hasty retreat to give them privacy.

She would have to wait until morning to know if the engagement was ended.

She didn't want to wait.

There was a glass of wine on her dressing table that had seemed like an excellent idea when she realized she might have trouble getting to sleep because of the suspense. She sipped at it now, but it did little to distract her. The panel of wall that she had fixated on nightly was suddenly irresistible. She pressed her ear to it, hoping to hear something. Then she opened it and listened at the seam of the opposite door, the one that was the only barrier to his room. She heard nothing. What on earth would she even hope to hear?

A giggle escaped her, which only repeated itself more loudly when she considered that Mason might hear his wall laughing.

She put a hand to the latch. What was the use in being considered outrageous if one rarely did anything truly outrageous?

"Well, Joyce," she murmured to herself as she tied her dressing gown over her shift and drank down the rest of the wine, "Let us make your grandmama proud."

She lifted the latch. The panel pushed open easily enough but when it issued a loud creaking noise, she stopped. She looked through the crack into what appeared to be a very large room. Of him, she saw only an elbow resting on a desk. There was a lamp next to him, and she watched him stand, take up the lamp, and come toward the door.

He was close enough to touch, but he didn't look inside or open the panel further. She felt a sudden surge of affection for him. He was very endearing, standing in his shirtsleeves and looking so befuddled in the lamplight.

"Are you home to callers, *monsieur*?" she asked, and of course he jumped at the sound of her voice. "Bravo," she cheered, as he barely managed to keep from dropping the lamp in his amazement. She pushed the door open more fully and stepped into his room. "A house fire would be very inconvenient."

She refrained from laughing – though only barely – as he stared at her and then examined the panel. It was very amusing, his incredulous face going back and forth, back and forth. She smiled and nodded to reassure him he was not imagining her sudden appearance. How refreshing it was, that he too clearly thought this was preposterous.

"That's your room?" he asked, looking through

the panel.

"Yes. Our hostess tells me it is normal for a country house that is old like this. One grows bored in the country, so they build these little diversions."

He looked at a loss for words. "What kind of..." He shook his head. "But what if..." He gave the open panel a slight push, winced at the loud creak, and finally gave a resigned kind of shrug. Then he began to laugh. It was deep and resonant and utterly sincere, and it was quickly becoming her favorite sound. "Oh god," he finally said, "these people are ridiculous. How the hell did I end up here?"

"All my fault!" she cheerily reminded him. "But what is this?" She took a step to reach the desk where he'd been sitting, and picked up the paper that had caught her eye. "This is Ravenclyffe. How perfectly you have drawn him."

All Mason's laughter had stopped the instant she picked up the drawing. He rushed to the desk and swept up the other papers before she even had a chance to glance at them. She would have felt deprived if she were not so delighted with the sketch before her.

"It's not even close to perfect," he said, charmingly flustered.

She waved a dismissive hand. "The features are not exact and it is very simple, but still it is exactly him. His face, the – what is it? The leering, that is the word. But he does not leer here, and still you show that he has a filthy mind. Debauched, you know? Well yes, you must know, you have drawn him that way."

"Yes." He was tucking the other papers into a large folder. "He asked if I wanted to see his chestnuts, if you can believe it. What did he say to you?"

"It was not words with me. But what do horses have to do with this?"

He frowned at her, confused. "I don't know, what *do* horses have to do with it?"

"You said he invited you to see his chestnuts."

His look of bafflement persisted a few moments before a look of dawning comprehension took over his face. "Oh!" he cried softly, stretching the syllable out a very long time as though the solution to a mystery had suddenly revealed itself. "Horses. Chestnuts are *horses*. That makes so much more sense. Because of the color, I suppose."

"Of course. What did you think they were?"

But as soon as it was out of her mouth, she realized what he must have thought. She could not stop the shout of laughter that escaped her. She clapped a hand over her mouth, but could not hope to contain it. He was saying he didn't know the first thing about horses, which only made her nearly howl with laughter, so she stifled the sound as best she could. Then her imagination served up an image of what he must have looked like in the moment – round, shocked eyes, and that purple flush creeping up his face while Ravenclyffe probably wondered what on earth was wrong. Her sides began to ache.

"Oh *mon dieu*," she gasped out as she made her way to chair before the empty hearth, where she collapsed completely. "How did you…why did you think–" She interrupted herself with another snort of laughter.

"Well what else would you think when a man says he'd love to show you his chestnuts?" Which was a reasonable enough question, but it only made her laugh harder. "Especially when he leaned in and whispered it, like it was an illicit proposition. He was downright furtive about it."

"What did—" she panted for breath, clutching her sides. "What did you answer to him?"

"I don't remember." His laughter was not quite as uncontrolled as hers. He sat himself in the chair across from her. "I'm sure I said I was flattered—" She let out a sharp *Ha!* "...But that it wasn't a proposition that appealed to me."

"You have a formidable strength, to resist the invitation. To view the chestnuts of a duke! Mere mortals can only dream of such wonders."

He was laughing rather helplessly now too, though she suspected it was because she was making such a spectacle of herself. Marie-Anne wiped the tears of mirth from her eyes and fought to regain some control. "I would give anything to have been there to see it," she sighed at last, once she had her breath back.

She settled back in the chair and began to feel the warmth in her belly and the mistiness in her head that said she'd had more wine than she realized. Between that and the laughter, she was very content.

"I complained to myself that this visit was not as amusing as I thought it would be. But I go through a secret door in my wall and I am given this story. It restores my faith."

She felt him looking at her and knew she was sprawled too carelessly in the chair, and in only her dressing gown. But what did it matter? She felt warm and wonderful, and she loved the feel of his eyes on her.

"You make me want to paint," he said softly, and

she looked at him, looking at her. "I've never learned it. I haven't even tried. But you make me want to put color everywhere."

His eyes moved across her face and she knew the colors he saw: the amber hair falling against her flushed cheeks, the blue of her eyes, the pink of her lips, the deep burgundy of the dressing gown. It was strange to think of him, with his vivid red hair and his golden freckles and dusky green eyes, sketching with his pencil in just grays and blacks. It seemed to her that everything he touched would have to take on color. She was sure every part of her that he touched would come alive.

"Dahlia said she would talk to you," she blurted, impetuous words that changed the nature of his look.

She felt the excitement in him, and it was exactly like her own. There was the tiny flare of his nostril, the flick of his glance to her mouth, the heat that rushed through her when he looked in her eyes. He knew now, why she had come to his room.

"She did talk to me," he said. A slow smile spread across his face, because he was so wonderfully wicked. "I thought I'd have to wait until tomorrow to thank you."

"It went well? I mean – she was not upset, I hope."

She wished she hadn't asked it. It made her think of little Dahlia, nervous and determined, trying to do the proper thing. Marie-Anne did not want to think of proper things at all.

He shook his head. "She shook my hand, wished me well, and called me a friend. I believe she was greatly relieved."

"I thought she would be." She took a very deep

breath and gave voice to her doubts. "But she was so ambivalent when she spoke to me. I worry she is not committed to her decision."

He immediately heard the equivocation in her words. "Now just a minute," he said, eyed narrowed. "I was promised a kiss."

Her unruly mouth let a burble of laughter escape. "And you are such a cad you will insist on it!"

"Being engaged is what made me a cad. If I'm released from my engagement, I'm not a cad anymore."

"Hah. Once a scoundrel always a scoundrel." To her surprise, he looked a little abashed at that. She softened, banishing the laughter that might hurt him. "Truly, she was uncertain when I spoke to her. When she tells me the engagement is broken, and when she tells her sisters, that will make it absolutely certain."

He looked a little like the Shipleys had, when she'd said they were not invited to the house party. Well, so much for the happiness of ogres – she was not happy at all. Here she was in perfect déshabille, with a ravenous hunger for the man alone in this room with her.

Oh, virtue really was very relative, she reasoned. And she had never liked it much anyway.

"But perfect conviction is very overrated, I have always said this," she told him, and he looked up at her. "A kiss, then. Just *one*." She smiled her own slow, wicked smile. "For now."

She would have leaned forward to give it to him, but the look he gave her rather melted her into the chair. As before, his eyes took her in slowly, every bit of her from top to toes. It was thrilling, and she felt a rush of warmth between her legs while every inch of her skin began to tingle in anticipation.

He slid from the chair to his knees before her. "Well if I only get one, then I'd like to make it count," he said in a delicious voice, and then put his hands on her knees.

She brought her hand up to her mouth to cover the soft gasp of surprise which was almost a scandalized laugh. They were suspended like that for a moment, with her wide-eyed and smiling in disbelief while he raised his brows in a devilish dare. Then he nudged her knees gently, a questioning exertion.

He murmured, "Very much and very deep and very long, I think I said?" And she was only human. She let her knees fall apart.

She felt like a giddy girl, shy and excited and inexperienced – which was nonsense, she told herself as the dressing gown parted and his hands pushed the lacy hem of the shift up her bare legs. But she had been a girl, almost, the last time she had enjoyed this particular delight. Richard had never been very inclined to it, and it seemed to be out of the question for…what was his name? She was rather forgetting things, as Mason put his face between her thighs. The village shoemaker that had been her lover, he had not done this and his name did not matter at all because Mason was breathing her in hungrily. A deep breath, a rush of air at the top of her thigh that told her he loved the scent of her arousal, that he was taking her deep into his lungs because he was as lost in lust as she was.

But he took his time. The way his tongue moved leisurely over her, a slow and luxurious journey as it moved closer and closer to the center of her, was not only meant to tease. It was for him too. He loved this, she could tell. He wanted to taste every last inch of her. She leaned back in her chair and opened her legs wider, the pleasure and the wine chasing through her veins as his tongue reached deep inside her, eager to take in every last drop.

He made a sound, a groan that sent vibrations through her and made her gasp. His tongue finally moved upward in a slow, broad stroke across the place she wanted it most. Oh God, he knew what he was doing. She pressed a fist to her mouth to keep in the shout of pleasure she wanted to let loose. Instead she made little whimpering noises, teeth pressed against her hand as she panted and his mouth continued the most delicious torture.

He brought one hand away from where it smoothed over her thigh and added it to the pleasure. A finger inside her – two, or more, she couldn't think past what an idiot she had been to say only one kiss – and his mouth over the most sensitive part of her. She grew frantic with desire. Even as she thought she never wanted it to end, she could not wait to reach that end. He groaned again and sucked gently at her while she gasped her approval.

She looked down to take in the sight of his head between her legs, red hair gleaming in the lamplight. His fingers pressed inside her just so, his lips and tongue never relenting, and her free hand reached down to twine her fingers in his hair. Wonderful, thick hair that she gripped to hold him there as she rocked her hips forward, trying desperately to get more of herself into his mouth. His tongue played with her in earnest, his fingers urged her on until she finally reached the peak and shattered – a slow shattering that seemed to go on and on and on, that took all her breath and temporarily made her forget how even to breathe. And all the while, he tasted her, his tongue never missing even the littlest bit of her as she moaned and jerked beneath him.

"Oh," she finally sighed, when she got her breath back and realized he was not stopping. He kept his mouth on her, his fingers moving gently and his tongue knowing exactly how and where to move on her, until she felt the excitement building again. One kiss, she had told him. Very much very long, he had said, and so she could not fault him.

She really could not fault him at all.

She might have said so, but she was urgently occupied with stifling her cries of pleasure again, sudden and strong. She had forgotten pleasure could be so intense, so drawn out. So very, very good.

When it was over she was completely limp, and not a little bit stunned. She looked down at him as he pulled his hand away and placed a last kiss on her thigh. He rested his head there and looked up at her with a satisfied, dreamy little smile.

She let her fingertips linger in his hair, running circles through it as she slowly came back to a sense of herself. "Well," she mumbled, with a contented little sigh. "I cannot wait to learn what our second kiss will be like."

Chapter Nine

Marie-Anne considered it one of her greatest acts of self-control when, the next morning, she did not dismiss the maid, make her excuses, and fling herself through the wall again. It was certainly all she wanted to do, and virtually the only thing she thought of.

The only thing that prevented her from doing it was a lingering worry over – of all the predictable and tiresome things – what the servants might say. They would notice patterns and then gossip among themselves, and there was no pretending that they would not be looking for improper behavior from the semi-notorious Frenchwoman in their midst. It occurred to her that she had never before been required to exercise discretion in matters of the heart. She had been open about all her lovers, all her life. Well, except for Jeremy, because the village would have been scandalized. But Jeremy was different. She had liked him, but not –

She sat up abruptly in her bed. Yes this was different, but she did not want to think too much about it. She threw off the covers and headed for the wash basin. It was another warm day. Once she was dressed, she could find Dahlia and assure herself that Mason had been irrevocably released from any obligation.

"Well, so what if I am a little infatuated?" she murmured to herself. She had not been infatuated for many years. And what was a little infatuation, when even the most practical woman would be hopelessly besotted with a man who could use his mouth like that? "*Very* infatuated," she amended.

She took her time at the basin as she washed, resolutely keeping her back to the secret panel while thinking how much she really did want to kiss his mouth, in addition to many other parts of him. If she were a more respectable person, she would throw herself into the task of ending Phyllida's fascination with her libertine poet. But she much preferred to neglect that and throw herself instead into reviewing her options for another evening's ravishing entertainment, because she was brazen and shameless and respectability was wildly overrated.

When she finally made her way downstairs, there were only a few guests remaining at breakfast and Dahlia was not one of them. Nor was Releford, or the other Shipley girls. She settled herself next to Miss Ainslie at the table and politely smiled as the singer regaled her for at least the fourth time with tales of her grand success on the stage in Vienna. Marie-Anne was nearly finished with her toast and wondering if she was still required to look impressed, when Amy came in the room.

"Marie-Anne, there you are!" Amy beamed at her. "I wonder if you will walk with me in the garden, when you have finished your breakfast?"

"I am finishing now, you see?" She gulped down the last of her tea rather inelegantly and stood. "Let us go before the sun grows too hot."

Mason entered the dining room as they left it, which her body greeted with a sudden but brief sense of vertigo. She joined Amy in wishing him a good morning as they passed, and looked up at him only in the very last second. His face was perfectly composed and cordial, but his glance burned right through her.

Oh, she rather loved that burn. It made her desperately hungry for so much more of him.

A sudden and very deep pang pulled at her as she walked toward the garden. Norway was a horrid place, not least because it was so very far away. She desperately wanted to talk to Helen. It was a part of infatuation, of course, this intense need to whisper with a dear friend. Her heart seemed to be moving very quickly and she would very much like Helen to help her decide if it was reckless. She could talk to Joyce, of course, but Joyce was far too blithe with regard to romantic entanglements, and anyway they were not close in the same way as she was with Helen.

Nor could she enjoy confiding in Amy, who was very caring and trustworthy, but entirely too practical. It was doubtful she ever swooned in her life, dear girl, and though Marie-Anne had only met her fiancé the one time, she was certain he was not the kind to induce breathlessness. She was suddenly very sad for Amy on this account. Swooning was wonderful, after all. Every woman should swoon from time to time. Possibly she could convince Amy that it was vital to the circulation of the blood, and that the staid and boring Mr. Harner was therefore a danger to her future health. That might appeal to her practical soul.

But, one sister at a time.

"Where is Dahlia?" Marie-Anne asked as they stepped onto the garden path. "I want to speak with her."

"She's gone riding with Releford," Amy said happily. She was flushed with excitement. "That's why I wished to speak with you in private. Dahlia has broken her engagement with Mr. Mason! She spoke to him last night. Now we can hope she will come to an understanding with Releford and it's all your doing, Marie-Anne, I'm sure it is!"

Marie-Anne did not contain her broad smile as they clasped hands in excitement. Amy might not swoon, but she was capable of great happiness and her glee was contagious. "You have seen how he looks at her?" Marie-Anne asked her. "It is not so difficult to end something when there is a happy alternative, we only needed to push her toward it."

"Yes, and I can't imagine she'll tell everyone she meets how very superior Releford is, as she did with Mr. Mason. She won't need to, of course." The relief in Amy's voice was overwhelming. "And Releford is very respectable, not at all like so many of the men she flirted with. There can be nothing but praise from Mr. Harner's uncle."

Marie-Anne looked at her curiously. "It made you so distressed, that this uncle did not approve?" Which seemed a less combative way of saying that Amy seemed happier to be free of disapproval than she was to see her sister well-matched and in love.

"His disapproval distresses Mr. Harner so," she

answered. "Mr. Harner is himself always very forgiving and kind, but of course I do not wish my relations to be the cause of any strain in his relationship with his uncle." Before Marie-Anne could tartly reply that he did not seem to care equally about causing strain on *her* relationships, Amy said, "Mr. Mason did not seem upset at all, did he? Just now, he looked perfectly content."

"Yes," agreed Marie-Anne. "His heart was not engaged."

Amy leaned over to take in the scent of the beautifully flourishing roses, and then adopted a very careful tone. "If you tell me he confided as much to you, I would not be shocked. In fact, Dahlia told me that her own heart was not at all engaged. She likes Mr. Mason – we all do, except for mother and father of course – but she has never loved him."

"That was very obvious to me," said Marie-Anne, "or I never would have interfered. But I am relieved she does not regret her decision."

"Not in the least. She confessed to me that in observing his manner with you, she felt some envy. Not because she resented your ease with one another, but because she felt certain she could never feel such ease with Mr. Mason."

Marie-Anne cleared her throat lightly and tried not to feel nervous over where this conversation seemed headed. "Yes, she said to me that it made her long for Releford. So we must be glad for them, and hope he is even now declaring himself to her."

"Dahlia is younger than me," Amy went on as though Marie-Anne had not spoken. "Her memories are not the same, nor as vivid as my own. While your rapport with Mr. Mason reminded her of her own with Releford, it reminds me of nothing so much as you and Richard."

"Amy, *ma petite*–"

"Marie-Anne, you must never think that you are bound to remain loyal to Richard's memory for our sakes," she continued doggedly. "Or that your past indiscretion with him is something for which you must pay penance for the rest your life."

"I have never thought those things," Marie-Anne protested faintly. She really never had, and found it very presumptuous to assume she felt guilt over these things and must be preemptively forgiven! But Amy, like her sisters, apparently liked to think of Marie-Anne as eternally grieving and forever repenting.

Amy seemed hardly to hear her protest. "I would not speak so but for the fear that you might feel constrained to be only friends with Mr. Mason when I think it possible you could one day be very much more."

Well. That was unexpected. "Oh."

"I know I need not ask you to forgive my impertinence, as you are always encouraging it. You will tease me for being so practical, but – well, I worry about your situation, and Mr. Mason is very good and very wealthy and he seems to like you very much. Dahlia would not be hurt in the least if he were to marry you. That is all I wanted to say."

Marie-Anne struggled between amusement and affection. In the end, she only smiled indulgently and slipped her arm in Amy's companionably as they walked. "I count a baroness and a countess as two of my dearest friends, and if we are lucky there will soon be a duchess who thinks herself in my debt. I promise you, *ma petite*, you do not need to fear I will starve a beggar in the streets."

Amy laughed a little. "I confess I had not thought of that. Little Dahlia, a duchess. Mother really will be unbearable, and father too. It's a very good thing I like my sister so much or I could not be happy at the prospect."

They amused themselves by speculating how insufferable Lady Shipley would be as they strolled back to the house, stopping to admire the roses that grew in even more profusion just outside the drawing room. It was there where they heard voices drifting from the open window.

"But that's Mr. Harner!" Amy straightened up, startled. "He was not to come until next week."

She began to move toward the terrace so that she could enter the house, with Marie-Anne close behind her. But Mr. Harner came outside, and Mr. St. James with him. Both were very agitated, and Mr. Harner seemed to only grow more upset when his eyes fell on Marie-Anne. Nevertheless, he gave a stiff bow in greeting.

"Miss Shipley," he choked out. He was brandishing what looked like a thin sheaf of papers in his hand. "Something must be done. I will not have you suffer for the indiscretions of your sisters or this...this..." He gestured at St. James, clearly too disgusted to think of a word for whatever Mr. St. James was.

"But whatever is it?" asked Amy, wide-eyed.

Mr. Harner thrust the papers into her hands. It was, Marie-Anne saw, a pamphlet – one of the weekly papers that circulated, documenting the latest news and gossip. This one was illustrated, which meant it must be very popular indeed. It had been curled tightly in Mr. Harner's hand, and Amy flattened it as best she could.

On the page was a drawing of a man who was very obviously Mr. St. James – or at least, Marie-Anne thought, exactly as St. James would like to appear: perfectly wind-swept hair and an air of wild romanticism. He was pictured at the opera, a very lively scene in which he was surrounded by women who were all shown from behind except for the exceptionally lovely actress on the stage. But rather than looking at the stage, he was gazing at the woman next to him. Beneath the picture was written *St. James plans his Next Conquest.*

Amy had turned a very deep red. "It is not so very different from what they have written about you before, is it, Mr. St. James? And Phyllida is not pictured."

"Indeed, it might be any woman with a lovely coiffure and gown, with her back turned like that," said St. James. Marie-Anne had always thought he was proud of his reputation as libertine, but now he seemed angry at Mr. Harner for bringing it up. "I see no need to distress Miss Shipley, and to rush all the way here from London to do it."

Mr. Harner ignored him and jabbed at the pamphlet. "In the text, Miss Shipley, you must read the text."

"At the opera...His affair with the celebrated actress..." Amy read, blushing even more. She continued to scan the lines for the offending information. "Oh! Here – Mr. St. James has lately been a frequent guest in the home of Sir Gordon Shipley, one of whose daughters the notorious libertine conspicuously favored while attending the opera!"

"You must see now that these are inventions." Mr. St. James was speaking not to Harner, but to Amy. He seemed quite concerned that she believe him. "Phyllida did not attend the opera that night. I accompanied Dahlia at her invitation."

While Harner protested that this was even worse, as it implied St. James was dallying with both sisters, Marie-Anne couldn't help but to think it was all very silly. So what if Phyllida's infatuation with St. James was known in the papers? She hardly hid it, and it was already known among all her acquaintance. And so what if he *was* a libertine – he seemed decent enough to Marie-Anne, who had seen many a libertine in her day. She had come to believe that, like his hair, it was an affectation. After all, she'd had no occasion to brandish eating utensils at *him* in an attempt to defend her thighs.

But here was Harner, insisting that if his uncle caught wind of it, it might ruin his prospects. The rumor would cause no damage at all if Dahlia were to announce an engagement to Releford. No one would talk of anything else, and having a duchess as a relation would solve any number of social ills.

"I have said my piece and will take my leave now," Mr. St. James was saying, his color high. "I would not like to cause Miss Shipley further distress."

He bowed quickly to both ladies – pointedly ignoring Mr. Harner – and went back into the house. Marie-Anne put a hand on Amy's arm and nodded toward the hedge maze where Dahlia now walked with Releford. They were arm in arm, smiling as only a pair of lovebirds would smile. Dahlia waved at them from afar, and rested her head on Releford's shoulder as they strolled off into the garden.

"There, you see!" said Marie-Anne with satisfaction. "It seems already there is a happy resolution, do you agree?"

Amy laughed with relief, and even jumped up and down a bit in her rejoicing.

"Oh how wonderful!" She squeezed Marie-Anne's hands enthusiastically. "How very *wonderful*." She turned her shining face to her fiancé and said, "Mr. Harner, my sister Dahlia has only recently abandoned her attachment to Mr. Mason. And now I have good reason to believe – *we* have reason to believe that she will marry Lord Releford. Is it not most excellent news?"

She was breathless with excitement, but his expression turned stiff and he looked toward the open doors to the house, as though anxious to think anyone had observed her great emotion.

"Yes. Excellent. Of course you are very happy for your sister." He employed the same tone one might use with an overexcited child. "It is natural you would forget yourself in such a moment."

Amy's bright smile immediately melted away. She tipped her head down as though to hide her face, and blinked rapidly. "Pardon me," she choked out. "I seem to have become quite foolish. Do forgive my outburst."

"Oh no, not at all," said Mr. Harner earnestly, and Marie-Anne remembered now what Mason had said – that Harner was always pleasant yet somehow always criticizing. "Few ladies comport themselves with the elegant restraint that is your usual manner, Miss Shipley, when you are feeling less careless. I offer my congratulations on the happy news."

Amy had gone very still. She resembled a china doll – very pretty and fragile and lifeless – and Marie-Anne saw with absolute clarity that this was exactly how Harner wanted her to be.

"Me, I know nothing of this elegant restraint." Marie-Anne said as pleasantly as she could manage. She wondered if she looked elegant now, as she restrained herself from scratching at his eyes. "It pleases you so very much, this restraint?"

He looked irritated that she had spoken to him. "It is not a matter of what pleases me, madame, but–"

"Wonderful!" She fixed a smile of supreme satisfaction on her face. "We will not care what pleases you, as you say. We will care instead what pleases Amy. For myself, I would be ashamed to steal a smile from her. But I am not so civilized. I am famous for it, in fact!"

Her playful tone confused him into silence, but Amy saw her hostility. "Marie-Anne, *je t'en prie*," she whispered, sliding into French with a quick look of apology to her fiancé. "Do not make a scene. I'm sure when you are more acquainted with him, you will like him better."

Marie-Anne spoke her reply in rapid French, seeing that Harner found it difficult to understand. "I'm sorry, *ma petite*, but it reminds me too much of how your parents treated me when I first came to England. As if I should be ashamed to be happy. Your brother told them he loved my smiles and my sorrows and every other thing that came from my heart, do you remember?"

"I remember," said Amy in a hushed voice. "But I am not like you, Marie-Anne. I do prefer to be more reserved in my manner."

"Hmf. When you prefer it, that is what you are. When you prefer something else, you should be that something else." She bit her tongue from saying that she thought Amy had chosen a husband who was too like her disapproving father. There was an unmistakable impatience emanating from Mr. Harner now, so she switched back to English and said stiffly, "It is rude to speak in French if you do not understand, *monsieur*. Please forgive us."

"Not at all, not at all," he soothed in the most gratingly condescending manner. "It has been a most eventful morning. I myself was so overset by this detestable pamphlet that I have quite forgotten to give my regards to our kind hostess. I wonder if you will do me the very great honor of presenting me?"

And so Marie-Anne spent the next few hours clenching her jaws shut in an effort to be perfectly inoffensive. Joyce was politely bored by Mr. Harner, and made her escape quickly. But her husband the Baron was far more in sympathy with the would-be vicar, so Marie-Anne sat next to Amy and quietly endured their talk about favorite theologians, the efficacy of hartshorn jelly as treatment for gout, and memorable card games in which they had participated. Only for Amy's sake did she force herself to keep every improper impulse in check. She thought of it as a kind of experiment, an attempt to understand the appeal of this vaunted "restrained elegance."

She entertained herself by imagining Mason without his clothes. She would be able to lick his neck very soon, that was a cheering thought. She planned to spend a great deal of time feeling the muscles in his thighs – if she did not suffocate from this stifling conversation first. The only time she seemed able to breathe were the few moments when she glimpsed Phyllida through the window, practically dancing as she came up the path from the woods. She was with some Huntingdon cousin whom she quickly abandoned when her gorgeous libertine poet appeared. Phyllida walked with him toward the garden, arm in arm and chatting merrily. It's what Dahlia and Releford were probably doing as well, somewhere. Marie-Anne would love to find Mason and do the same. Yet here she was with the demure Shipley sister and her dull fiancé, nodding politely as the subject of proper field drainage was thoroughly explored.

A footman finally interrupted them to announce a light buffet had been set out for afternoon refreshment on the terrace. Marie-Anne jumped up with unseemly haste, desperate for a more lively conversation partner over the meal. But it was Charlotte who claimed the seat next to her. The girl was excruciatingly polite and Marie-Anne was so afraid of saying a wrong word to her again – the two of them trying so hard to prove they liked each other - that it was a new round of biting her tongue.

By the time it was over she was more than ready to be wildly improper. Maybe she'd take off her stockings and swim in the fountain. Or strike up a conversation with The Poetess about the poetry of Sappho, to see if she could make Mr. Harner blush. Or just hide in the priest-hole with a bottle of sherry.

She'd taken no more than a few bites of her food, but when she looked up to see Mason appear, she put her plate aside. Here was a far better option. Here was recklessness come strolling in, disguised as a gentleman in a very fine suit.

"I believe I will go to rest in my room a little while," she announced. She caught his eye. "I am so very hot."

Joyce admirably hid her smirk an instant after it appeared, and quickly engaged her husband in a conversation about the weather.

Once in her room, Marie-Anne kicked off her slippers and released the few buttons she could reach on the back of her dress. Fortunately, the maid came quickly and soon the dress and petticoat were removed. She heard the girl sigh, "So pretty," as she loosened the corset string, just as she had sighed this morning when she'd laced it up. The corset was new, and already a favorite item in her wardrobe. It was silk, pale blue and embroidered in pink and white, and though Marie-Anne had seen far more shocking undergarments in her day, there was something undeniably erotic about it. She couldn't wait for him to see it.

But she did have to wait. She supposed she really should feel a little embarrassed to be listening at the panel, waiting anxiously for a sound that told her he was in his room alone. When it came – the thudding sound of his main door closing – her stomach gave a girlish little flip. Oh really, was there anything better than this? She had almost forgotten what it was like to feel breathless and giddy and positively famished.

Once she heard his footsteps near, she lifted the latch. The panel swung open easily to reveal him standing there, waiting for her with his jacket off and loosening his cravat. His hands stopped as he stared fixedly at her corset. She let him look, though she was terribly impatient for him to bare his neck, and drew in a slow, deep breath so he could fully appreciate the view.

"Did I say this door in my wall was ridiculous?" he asked absently. "I take it back. God bless the genius who thought of it."

"It does not creak today," She stepped into his room and pushed the panel silently closed behind her.

"I found some oil and aimed it at the hinges," he explained, still staring.

"This is how you spent your morning?" She began to unbutton his waistcoat, because he was entirely too slow. "Hunting for oil?"

"And talking with that jackass Ravenclyffe." He helped with the last few buttons and pulled off the waistcoat. "And tasting you at the back of my throat."

She reached up to pull off his cravat. "I spent it in learning that Dahlia has announced she is not engaged to you, and being very proper and very bored, and wanting to do this."

She licked his neck, and it was exactly as delicious as she'd expected. He sucked in his breath as her tongue moved over his skin, which was even more delicious. Everything about him felt wonderful. He was solid and so very warm, and his hands ran delicately over her corset as though he would memorize the embroidered details with his fingers. Best of all was how he put his weight against her, all his sublime strength and heat surrounding her and filling her senses as he pressed her gently to the wall.

"If you say only one kiss, I'll…" He trailed off as her hands smoothed down his back and over his buttocks. He had lovely muscles all over him. "Jesus, I might actually cry."

She pulled her mouth away from his neck long

enough to ask him, "Where do you get these splendid muscles?" She tugged his shirt up so she could feel his belly. It was not the body of a typical gentleman. "Do you cut the trees yourself?"

"Trees?" He put a hand in her hair, piled loosely on her head. She could feel his pulse, rapid and heavy at his throat, and reveled in the sound of his breathlessness. "Oh, trees. Something like that. So more than just one kiss?"

"More," she said. She leaned her head back against the wall, dizzy with the smell of him. His mouth had all her attention. She felt mesmerized by it. "Many more. As many as possible."

He looked up from where his fingertips moved softly across the swell of her breast. Her stomach gave that little flip again, to see his eyes so full of desire for her. "I've never seen you so serious."

That made her smile. "I am very serious about my pleasure," she told him, and then kissed him. He responded with great enthusiasm.

It went on for ages. It was like being a girl again, like those days when kissing for hours was expected, when there was nothing *but* kissing. Well, kissing and roaming hands, and pleasure spreading out slowly through every inch of her body. Like last night, he was not too impatient for more. He was content to taste her, to explore every corner of her mouth and lips as though he had sworn to memorize her with his tongue. It was utterly marvelous. She had time to wonder where on earth had learned to use his mouth like this, and more time to consider that she didn't really want to know and didn't really care anyway so long as he kept it up.

But finally, after a very, very long time of kissing,

the aching throb between her legs grew unbearable and she was the one who grew too impatient. She curled her hips up, pressing against the hard length of him. He responded with a groan and an answering pressure. He was wonderful, how he did no more than that, how he waited for her desire to direct him. His mouth moved to her throat now, down to her breasts, sucking at her as she panted and searched for the buttons on his trousers.

He was hot and hard, and he gasped in the most delectable way when she wrapped her hand around him. She put her lips to his ear and panted, "Lift my chemise."

He obeyed with alacrity, and she did not need to say anything more after that. He took control, pulling her leg up over his hip, pushing hard and fast into her. He stayed there, filling her for a long and breathless moment while she tightened her leg around his hip, silently begging for more. Then he kissed her as he slowly drew back, teasing her with his withdrawal until she gripped his shoulders in desperation and he thrust into her again to the hilt.

It stole her breath. He did it again and again, a little faster and withdrawing less each time, so controlled while she was wild with excitement. His mouth was over hers, a plundering heat that smothered the whimpering, wailing sounds she made. He drove her higher and higher until she finally reached the peak of it, and it seemed endless. Waves and waves of pleasure, with him buried deep inside her, his own shudder of release barely registering as she pressed mindlessly against him.

When she had some sense of herself again, she was vaguely amazed they were still upright and the sun still shone. She was dazed, and it seemed to take a very long time to get her breath back. It was entirely possible she would never remember how to do anything but lean against him like this, skin to skin, awash in satisfaction.

"*Merci*," she mumbled without thinking.

His chest heaved against hers, just as out of breath, like they had run a marathon. "Likewise."

She put her mouth to his again, lazy and limp but still wanting his kisses. She thought she could probably kiss him for days without stopping, which was an alarming little fact as it meant – it had always meant, with her – that her heart was deeply entangled. Still, she did not deny herself. It felt too good, all of it.

"What's that?" He had stilled, whispering against her lips. Then she heard it – a soft tapping from her room and a voice calling softly. Someone was at the door of her room.

Reluctantly, she pushed him away. "I must answer it. I'll come back tonight." Then she frantically pulled the panel open and latched it behind her. She made sure the panel on her side was closed securely before throwing on her dressing gown and running to the door.

She did not open it but called through it, only to hear Joyce on the other side.

"I am so very sorry to disturb you, my dear, but he says it cannot wait. Did I wake you?"

"No. Who says what?" she asked, trying to pin a large and unruly piece of hair back where it belonged.

"It's a messenger from Summerdale House. He says he is under very urgent instruction from Helen and that he must speak to you without delay."

She jerked the door open so fast her arm hurt. Joyce stood there with the maid beside her. "Is Hélène unwell?"

"No, my dear, she is perfectly fine, I made him swear it to me. But he has said she left him some vital instruction and it's a matter of urgency, and he will speak only with you. I thought it worth disturbing you and I do so hope I am right. Here's Lucy, she will help you dress and you can come to the library without delay."

∽∾

"But it must be a mistake."

She sat in the small library and tried to believe this was not some bizarre dream. There was still that liquid feeling at the base of her spine, and her mouth was still pleasantly sore from so much kissing. Before allowing the maid into her room, she had taken a moment to wash quickly between her legs, and now she was extremely aware of the lingering dampness as this square-faced man told her that Mason had no prosperous business.

"I could of course be mistaken in my interpretation of the facts I have discovered, madame. It is also possible I am missing some information."

He was so modest in this statement that she knew he did not believe himself to be wrong. He had no doubt at all. As secretary to Lord Summerdale, he would never say such things if he had any doubts. She very much wanted to deny it completely, call him a meddling old fool, and escape this room. But she knew she was already more than a little foolish about Mason, and that she had always been too quick to disbelieve unhappy news about a new lover. She would make herself listen to these accusations.

"I do not understand it," she said. "He lives as a wealthy man. The finest clothes and... You say yourself the hotel in London where he stays is very exclusive."

"We must conclude that he has ready access to funds, but I can assure you that no bank in London has heard of a Mr. Spencer Mason of New York. It is possible to make further inquiries among tradespeople and at the hotel but unless you feel the matter is pressing, it is perhaps more advisable to await the return of Lord Summerdale before taking such action."

Bribes. He meant bribes, to shopkeepers and servants. Handfuls of coins and whispers and speculation. In Paris when she was a girl, men had come around weekly, offering her a *sou* if she would tell them who came to Aurélie's room, or if Delphine had been drinking, or where Luísa sent letters. Always discreet, always so civilized, these well-dressed men with their purses full of coins.

"If the matter is not pressing, then why are you here?" she asked him, irritated.

"I hope I have not misjudged, madame. Lord Summerdale instructed me to discover whatever possible of Mr. Mason's situation, and indicated that it is a matter of grave concern to Lady Summerdale because of your acquaintance with Mr. Mason. Once I had discovered that at least three gentleman are seeking to invest a substantial sum in Mr. Mason's timber business, I felt it my duty to learn more about the business. As I have said, it is unknown among several persons who should by all rights have heard of such a large and prosperous enterprise."

He paused, but she could think of nothing to say. She only twisted her fingers together in her lap and told herself she was lucky to have such friends looking out for her. She did not feel lucky, though.

"I cannot yet judge if it is entirely a lie. The prominence and prosperity of the business may only have been, ah, exaggerated," the secretary was saying. His name was Mr. Meeks, which seemed appropriate to his very deferential manner. "But I felt it prudent, knowing that Lady Summerdale felt very strongly, to apprise you of my findings immediately. Before three months ago no one had ever heard of him, yet now he has all of London believing him to be a man of consequence and has convinced several gentlemen to invest in a business that appears not to exist. I cannot call it anything but suspicious."

It was hard to believe she'd been so limp with delight only moments ago. The picture this secretary painted was thoroughly disheartening. It did not seem possible that Mason was a charlatan. She had seen that he was very practiced at lying, but he was not so practiced that she was fooled.

Unless she *had* been fooled, and just hadn't realized it.

She remembered his face at the ball when they had first met, and how mortified he had been, the way the purple crept up his neck. That was not fake. The way he had looked at those paintings at the exhibition, too – that was not a lie. And he had treated Dahlia very honorably, really.

"He does not seem to me like a monster," she said. "Has he done anything so unforgivable?"

"No indeed, madame. Those men who wish to

invest have not yet given over any money, and he does not live on credit, nor leave a string of debts in his wake. As I say, it is only very suspicious."

"Well then." She sat up straighter as she came to the conclusion that she must confront Mason with this, just as she had done when she discovered he was engaged. Maybe the surprise of it would cause some more truth to spill out of him. It was far more palatable than the supposedly civilized method of spying and bribing for information.

"I will put my guard up. Thank you for coming, Mr. Meeks. You did not misjudge. I will send word to you if I learn anything more."

"As shall I, madame."

Chapter Ten

While Mason waited for her that night, he recreated bits of her on paper. To leave evidence of this little indulgence was unthinkable, so he only let the shape of her appear for a moment before disguising her as something else. The line of her throat when she threw her head back in passion became a river that ran down a narrow hill, and the sweep of her collarbone was transformed into a vine. Her knee he turned into the face of a little fox, and the tender flesh of her inner thigh became its soft tail curled around its body. He drew her mouth, open and panting, swollen with kisses, a lock of hair curling at her chin – but then made himself stop before adding more details and depth. He could get every tiny crevice on the surface of her lips just right, he was sure of it.

He turned it into a flower instead. He was busy transforming the curl of hair against the line of her jaw into a leaf around a stem, and giving up hope that she would visit him tonight as promised, when he heard her at the panel.

She knocked lightly, which was so unexpected that he wondered if it could possibly be someone else. He turned the drawings face down on the desk before carefully approaching the panel. There was no way to open it, and it locked from her side – an arrangement he'd call unfair if secret doors had anything to do with fairness or logic. Just as he was debating whether to whisper something at the wall or knock in return, she pushed it open.

There was no eagerness in her, no enthusiastic embrace as there had been hours ago. She just stood and looked at him thoughtfully. All through the evening he'd felt her watching him, careful to never meet his eye as she huddled with Dahlia in a corner of the drawing room after dinner. He had told himself she was exercising discretion to keep the other guests from suspecting a romance between them, which would inevitably lead to talk about her past.

But now she finally met his eye. It was more than just discretion. He couldn't guess what, but he knew enough to be wary of whatever was going on behind the perfect blue of those eyes. He gave her his warmest smile.

"Just passing by, or will you stop in for a while?"

He gestured wide to invite her into the room, and she stepped in. She left the panel wide open, and he glimpsed her darkened room beyond before turning back to watch her. Her dressing gown was tied securely and she wore stockings and shoes – signs that she was here to do no more than talk. He tried not to be so disappointed. Of his favorite things to do with Marie-Anne, talking was a close second to making love with her. But it was still second.

She crossed to the desk where she looked at the face-down stack of drawings without turning them over. It was almost like she was looking for something, the way she slowly took in all the details of the room. A little prickle of suspicion ran up his neck. She was up to something, no doubt about it.

"A bundle of mischief," he mused aloud. He leaned against the mantel and watched her turn to him, her brows raised in question. "It's the first thing I thought when I saw you at that ball, in your fashionable gown with your respectable friends, trying to look like you're not full of surprises. But you are."

"Me, I am full of surprises?"

He nodded. "You've got one right now. Go on and let it loose, I'm braced and ready."

For a moment – just the barest hint of a moment – he thought she might step forward and kiss him, or pull off her dressing gown. But the devilish spark that had appeared was gone in a blink. She watched him very closely, which was every bit as alarming as it was thrilling.

"It is a surprise for me too," she said, "To find that I still like you very much even after I learn you are worse than a cad. You are...what? An impostor, maybe? A fake. A fraud."

He felt his face instinctively arrange itself into an expression of polite confusion. "I'm a fraud?"

It was pure reflex, his mouth buying time while his brain began sifting through the dozen plausible stories that were always ready and waiting to be deployed. But which to use would depend on what she said next, how much she knew.

"Yes, a faux businessman. Or I think maybe there

is a business, but it is not how you describe. You are a liar, Mr. Mason."

He held his perplexed look but as he should have predicted, she did not react in the tried and true ways. Even adding a hint of injury to his expression did not cause her to show doubt, and women so reliably apologized when faced with a man's bruised ego. The usual rules did not seem to apply to Marie-Anne de Vauteuil.

"Go on," he urged her. "I'm interested to hear more."

She considered him a long while as he did his best to hold her gaze and look innocent. It was something of a stalemate until finally there was a flicker of uncertainty in her eyes. It was followed by tell-tale signs of doubt: the quick glance away, her tongue darting out to wet her lips, her hands clasped briefly together. What a relief. He could work with doubt.

"I think about you too much," she said quietly. "From the first time we met, you know? Always I am hoping to make you laugh. I am too happy when you look at me, and too sad when you do not. You walk in the room and I forget a little how to breathe. Already you make me a little foolish, Mason. Please do not lie and make me a fool."

It was like a punch to the gut. The truth. It was the perfect card to play, except for the fact that she wasn't playing.

He could still lie. There were a hundred different illusions to spin. But she made him forget how to breathe a little, too.

He dropped his eyes to the floor. "How did you find out?"

"Does it matter?"

"I don't suppose it does." He found it hard to look at her, though he really didn't want to look anywhere else. If it was the last he'd see of her, he'd rather take in as much as he could. He wondered if he should slip out now in the dead of night, or wait until dawn to make his way back to London. "Have you told our hosts yet?"

"I have told no one." When he did not hide his surprise, she shrugged. "I have thought about it all this evening, and still I cannot make myself care that you have no timber business in America, or any money in the banks of London."

It must have been through Summerdale, somehow, if she knew about his banking habits. But that was far from the most interesting bit of information here. He crossed his arms and frowned a little and, incredibly, fought against telling her she was crazy.

"Full of surprises," he muttered. "Now why don't you care?"

"Why should I care that you lie to all of London society?" She lifted her shoulder in another shrug. "Bah, society. I care for them as little as they have cared for me. They spat on me. Even now, I know they only tolerate me because I have an important friend who tells them they must respect me. But they will return to spitting on me again, if they are given the chance."

She spoke of it the same way she had spoken of the insults the Shipleys had hurled at her – casual and detached, like she was discussing the weather on an unexceptional day. He had the most absurd urge to take her hand and run with her away from this place, laughing into the night. Maybe they could go to her little village. Sensible, decent people were probably thick on the ground there.

"If you don't care, then why in the hell are you all the way over there? And with so many clothes on?"

She gave him an exasperated look. "You will please stop insulting me with this pretending. You know very well why I do not throw myself into your arms when I learn you are a lie. It is a very elaborate deception. I hope it is not meant to harm – but this is only a hope. So you must tell me why you do it." She frowned and stroked her fingertips across his dinner jacket, which was draped carefully on the chair. "And where you get the money for such fine clothes."

He only considered misleading her for the tiniest moment, and only because it would be so easy to call it another misunderstanding. She would be perfectly willing to believe that, like his engagement, he had bumbled into the situation. But it was an easy impulse to reject. He liked her too much. Even more, he loved this feeling of them being on the same side.

He took a deep breath and nodded at the papers on the desk. "Turn them over."

She did. Her expression lightened when she saw the first page, covered in disparate drawings of foxes and flowers and vines that were really pieces of her in disguise. She liked it. A warmth spread through his chest as she smiled in pleasure at it. Then she frowned again. "Keep looking," he prompted. "The others."

The next was a page filled with trial sketches, a face at many different angles and in a few different styles. She blinked at it in surprise and sat down at the desk, where she put it aside to look at the next sketch – the same face, in its final and polished version.

"It is Ravenclyffe. But how…" She looked confused and not a little impressed. "You have drawn him so differently, but still it is him every time. *C'est une magie*, I would never know all are from the same hand."

He grinned at that. "No need to flirt, darling. I'm already a little foolish about you, too."

She bit her lip prettily as she blinked at the drawing in her hand. He wanted to kiss her senseless again, all the more because he knew she wanted the same. Here they were, admittedly crazy about each other and doing nothing about it. Decency was a strange thing.

"Keep going." He nodded again at the drawings she held. "The next page."

It was the most comical of the sketches. It showed Ravenclyffe being laced into a corset by three servants, one with a foot braced against the duke's rear end and the other two with the corset strings over their shoulders as they strained in the opposite direction, as though they were hauling a barge. She let out a faint snort of laughter and went to the next page, which showed Ravenclyffe comparing his ridiculously elaborate snuff box to Lord Huntingdon's.

"This one – the style is familiar." She moved her finger in a circle around his face. "You sell these to the papers?"

"We *are* the papers. My partner writes the stories and I provide the illustrations. The printer tells me there's more and more interest in buying the prints separately, but most of the money comes from the weekly pamphlets we produce." He plowed ahead with it. Better to get it all out before she reacted, while she still just sat there looking. "Freddy – my partner, he's not exactly accepted in the circles where the best scandals happen. So I invented someone they'd let close. It sells better, when you're the first to know the latest news."

She dropped the pages suddenly, as though they burned her, and looked up at him with the beginnings of anger. "You mean gossip. You lie so you can be close enough to hear the rumors, and then you print them."

"It's usually completely true," he assured her. "Or as close to the truth as we can get. And it's nearly always about these superior society types."

"Who?" she demanded, all trace of good humor gone. "Who else besides Ravenclyffe and Mr. St. James? It is you who drew him at the opera to spread gossip about Phyllida. I saw the pamphlet only today. It was this same style, I recognize it." She was definitely angry now. "Who else have you made into a mockery?"

He held up his hands in a calming gesture. "None of your friends. This week we'll print that Dahlia is rumored to be engaged to Releford, but that's not mocking anyone. Hell, it'll probably even do some good for her sisters. And St. James – he was nobody until we called him a libertine, I promise it's profited him as much as us–"

She slapped a hand onto the desk. "Do not tell me it is charity!" She stood, color high and eyes bright. "There is money in the mockery. You think I do not know? I have lived this! And I have seen far worse than the little jokes they made about me so long ago, *much* worse. To pay for your very fine hotel and your gentleman's clothes you must have ruined many people, I think."

"Ruin?" he scoffed, incredulous. "What does it ruin, Marie-Anne? Some lady doesn't get invited to her favorite ball or some lord gets turned away from his club. That's ruination for these people, a little pointing and laughing. It's only their pride that gets hurt. They don't lose their homes or their wealth. They aren't thrown into the gutter to beg for their dinner, and you know it. You know how they make their fortunes off the backs of the people they spit on for entertainment, so please spare me an appeal to their sensitive souls. Ruin is what they do to other people."

Her jaw clamped shut as she took a few rapid breaths, considering. He passed the time in wondering when he had grown so vehement on the subject. It was true he didn't do this for charity. Or as a misguided stab at justice, for that matter. But he liked it for more than just the money.

Marie-Anne gave an abrupt nod, conceding a little.

"It is true what you say, most of the time. But not always. You think I have lived in my little village so long, counting my few coins, because gossip does not harm?"

"The gossip did that, did it? Not the Shipleys?" he asked. "From what I can tell, it's never the talk that does it. It's the people who don't stand by you when you get talked about, they're the ones that do the damage. "

Her lips pressed together. "Very well, but you must believe me that to put it in the papers makes it worse for some people. I have seen it wound very deeply. There are some who do not deserve it."

"Maybe not. But I won't lose any sleep over the

Duke of Ravenclyffe being laughed at by all of London."

She sat slowly down, calm again as she looked at the drawings on the desk. "This was your business in America too?" She gave a startled look, a thought occurring to her. "You are really from America, aren't you? Or is New York a lie, too – and this Kentucky."

He couldn't stop the smile that tugged at his lips. He loved how she said *Kentucky*. "That's not a lie. I grew up in Kentucky, and the Indiana Territory too. Then I ran to Philadelphia and Boston and New York." He didn't want to tell her everything. There was too much, and very little of it was the same kind of honest poverty that her own young life had been. Best stick to the relevant sins. "I worked on the docks, mostly, unloading cargo. Shifting barrels in warehouses and taverns, wherever I could get work."

"The muscle." Her eyes lingered on his shoulders and chest, shown in all their coarse glory in the loose shirt. "It is not from cutting trees."

"I've cut some trees in my time. But I never owned acres of land, or a timber business. In Boston, I started drawing caricatures. It was an honest way to get a little extra money, for a change. Then a man from a New York paper said I could make more there." He shrugged. "So that's what I did for a couple years. Used four different styles, and sold to every paper that would pay."

"This has made you a little wealthy?"

A rueful laugh escaped him. "It made me a little less poor for a while, that's all. It was just starting to take off when I had to leave. It was political work," he explained, hoping she wouldn't want a blow by blow account of New York politics and all the feathers he had ruffled there. "I made the wrong men angry. Freddy had seen my drawings, knew someone at the New York paper. He wrote to say he thought I'd do very well for myself in London. So here I am."

She examined him, sitting back in her chair a little. "And you do very well for yourself, as you say. Well enough to live as a gentleman."

"By the skin of our teeth." He looked down at his very fine boots. They cost more money than he'd ever spent on anything in his life. Every time he sneezed, he checked to be sure they weren't somehow scuffed or damaged beyond repair. "It takes a lot of investment, to turn me into a wealthy-looking man. We only started to turn a profit a few weeks ago."

She leaned forward, elbows on the desk, eyes closed, and rubbed the bridge of her nose. Later he would try to draw her in exactly this attitude. Portrait of a Disenchanted Woman, he'd call it. He wondered if it was disappointment at his lack of wealth, or at his lies.

"Why did you not simply marry Dahlia, if you have no scruples?" she asked him. "She would bring some money. Enough that you would not have to work on docks. Maybe the same as you would make from these papers."

He leaned his head back against the wall and gave another humorless laugh. "Well, I could say it's because I'm really not a cad, but that's being overly kind to myself. I'm just a different kind of scoundrel. I wanted money, not a wife. That's the game: get the money and get out, try not to get tangled up in the law. A marriage is about as entangled in the law as you can get."

She did not reply, and he tried to think of

something to say that would steer the conversation away from this line of questioning. Get the money and get out and on to the next thing, the next place, the next game. It was how things worked, the only way he knew how to keep going. But now he wondered for the first time where it would ever end, and if he wanted it to. She seemed likely to ask him exactly that, and he wasn't ready to answer.

All he knew for sure was that he didn't want to go yet. He hadn't had his fill of her – her smiles and her kisses and the taste of her and the way she said his name with her accent. The way she looked at him, like he was worth looking at. The thought that she might send him packing now that she knew about him was thoroughly depressing.

When he worked up the courage to look at her again, he found she had spread the pages across the desk to look at them. She lingered over the drawing that had been the curve of her throat and was now a river.

"It is so beautiful," she said. The words cut into him, painful pleasure. He'd never let anyone see these kinds of drawings, the ones he made in secret. Only the humorous sketches were meant to be seen.

He went to the desk and looked down at the page. "It was you." He traced a finger over the arc of water on the page, then lifted a hand to skim just barely over the line of her throat. She looked at him with wide eyes and trembled faintly. He took his hand away, loving how the heat of her was still there on his skin, as warm as if he'd held sunlight. "I turned it into this."

She looked down at the drawing again. "So much talent," she said very softly. The pride swelled in him, to see the admiration in her. "Yet you use only the crudest part of this talent, to bring out the worst in the people who see it."

She said it like she said so many things, as only a simple observation with no scorn attached.

"I use it to feed myself."

He gathered up the pages and stacked them neatly together. He should do at least one more of Ravenclyffe, but he hadn't thought of another scene to draw yet and he doubted he'd be able to concentrate at all now. The small traveling case with the false bottom where he stored his drawings was only a few steps away, and she watched as he put the pages into the large leather folder and dropped it in.

"Will you tell them, Marie-Anne?" He didn't turn to her to ask it. He suddenly felt very tired. "I can leave tonight, if so. I'd prefer to avoid a scene."

"Wait," she said sharply as he began to pull the concealing partition into place over the pile of paper. She nodded at the few pamphlets scattered next to the folder. "Who else have you written about?"

"I don't write, I told you. That's Freddy's job." He picked up the handful of pamphlets and held them out to her. "I don't have all of them, but this should give you an idea." She took the pamphlets and stared down at them as though reluctant to look past the top page. "I hardly ever understand why something's scandalous. Freddy just tells me which stories are worth an illustration. He's written a little something on just about everyone who matters, but more than half the time it's old news. When it's not old news, it really is harmless."

The topmost pamphlet in her hands showed the drawing of the Marquess. She traced a fingertip over the figure of the wife brandishing the poker. She made as though to speak, but then stopped and gave the barest trace of a smile.

"Almost I was saying that this one is not harmless." She spoke without looking up at him. "But that is wrong. There is talk that the marquess will not allow his wife to see her children because she is too emotional – but everyone knows she never sees her children anyway. She hates the children. It is all an act, their drama." Now she looked up at him. "At the worst, he will take away her allowance and she will not have twenty new gowns every year. Then she will complain to her friends about a husband she has never cared for. And life will go on."

He nodded at the drawing. "That's the one that let us turn a real profit. People love the drama, but turning it comical is what made the story popular."

"It is also that it is a marquess. No one would laugh so hard if you draw the merchant and his wife. But if there was money in drawing the humble man, you would not hesitate?"

"I might hesitate. But I'd probably still do it. Just like you stole things in the streets of Paris, so you could eat. I'm guessing you stole more from common merchants than you did noblemen."

Marie-Anne didn't contradict him. She looked down at her hands, which curled the stack of pamphlets into a thick roll. This conversation was the longest he had seen her without a smile or a laugh, so it was a relief to see something of her usual humor creep into her face again.

"This wife of the marquess you drew – one time she came into a jeweler's shop where I was choosing a gift for Richard. She said I was evidence their standards had fallen, and the jeweler asked me to leave." Marie-Anne smiled a little, as though it were a fond memory, then gave an impish look. "Maybe I do not care so much if London laughs at her."

He was still too doubtful to let himself return the smile.

"So you won't tell everyone about me?"

"I don't know." She was thoughtful again, rustling the pamphlets in her hands. "There is very much for me to consider. Where would you go?"

He shrugged. If he was revealed, he could hardly show his face among respectable society anymore. It would be back to living in the kind of place people like him belonged. Rather than saying he'd find a garret among the criminals and whores while finding a quick way to cheat honest men of their money, he just said, "There's a lot for me to consider too. I thought I'd have a few more months before anyone figured it out."

"Well then, we will both consider. It has not been a restful day. In fact, it is very much the opposite." A smile tugged at her lips again, a little teasing without the suggestion they indulge in further energetic endeavors. "Time and sleep will let you think, that is what a friend of mine used to say. Goodnight, Mr. Mason."

She was through the panel before he could do more than echo her goodnight. He wanted to ask her to drop the Mister and just call him Mason, as she'd been doing for weeks. But asking it would have been as dispiriting as the sound of her dropping the latch into place.

Chapter Eleven

In spite of the improved weather, Mason sat in the salon with the unbearable Duke of Ravenclyffe, hoping to catch a glimpse of Marie-Anne. She did not appear, which meant he had to pretend to pay attention to the duke's theories on the study of phrenology, specifically how skull size proved the superiority of the European people. Mason understood he was supposed to be grateful for Ravenclyffe's reassurance that most Americans were included in "these blessings of Providence" but rather than thanking the idiot duke, his response was silence and a skeptical look. This was the best way to make smug men doubt themselves enough that they inevitably sought his approval, without even realizing they were doing it.

It didn't take very long. Ravenclyffe had been hinting for days that he'd like to invest in the fictional timber business, but he obviously could not bear to seem eager about it. Now he abandoned his pride –

or at least a small part of it – and said outright that he wanted in. Or rather that he was "not averse to lending financial backing to a profitable enterprise."

A flash of color outside the window caught Mason's attention. "Can't say I'm looking for more investors," he said vaguely, and decided it was just a bird and not a thoroughly captivating Frenchwoman passing by.

"Naturally I have the utmost faith in John Company, but the prudent man bets on more than one horse. There are still far too many natives in India, they're sure to make more trouble. As I say, the anatomy makes it plain – the cranium alone is proof, but our most prominent naturalists…"

Mason tuned out the nonsense by imagining how satisfying it would be to fleece Ravenclyffe out of thousands of pounds and then just disappear. Even more satisfying would be to do it and then publish a series of drawings about it on his way out of town. They could call him The Duped Duke, deceived and swindled despite his large-capacity skull and a jaw so inconspicuous that it was barely distinguishable from his neck.

Somewhere at the back of his mind, Mason could hear his cousin scorning him for toying with an idea for drawings instead of reeling in the biggest fish that had ever nibbled on his line. That was cousin Jody's way – big risk, big reward. Or big disaster. He'd more often met with disaster, and Mason had learned from that. Still, it would be smart to lay the groundwork for a fleecing. Just as a kind of contingency plan, in case he had to abandon the scheme with Freddy. Always good to keep every option open.

He'd have to pursue it later, though, because

Marie-Anne appeared in the salon, looking fresh and pretty in a gown of periwinkle blue. Amy's priggish vicar was at her heels, though Amy herself was nowhere to be seen.

"Mr. Harner, you must believe me," Marie-Anne was saying. She was using the overly cheerful tone that meant she would dearly love to strangle someone. "This is a wilderness in name only. The trees are groomed as well as Mr. St. James' hair, though they are not nearly so thick."

"Nevertheless, Miss Shipley would be so distressed if you should lose your way–"

"Amy would be very amused if I could be lost so easily. I will tell her it has happened when I want her to laugh, I thank you for this excellent idea. Ah, but here is Mr. Mason!" She beamed at him in what seemed a very pointed manner. "I have prepared a hamper, you see? Just as you suggested."

"Right," he answered readily enough. He'd suggested no such thing, nor exchanged a single word with her since she'd left his room last night, but he was happy enough to follow her lead. "And you have your bonnet, so we're well prepared to face the elements. No need to worry, Harner."

"There, you see?" She handed the small hamper to Mason as she put the bonnet on her head. "Phyllida wants her hermit to meet Mr. Mason, and I want to meet the hermit. We go together, and more than three visitors will overwhelm this lonely man in the woods. I must insist you stay."

Feeling sure that Harner would have protested further were he not so occupied in bowing and stammering at the duke, Mason decided the two insufferable men deserved each other. Especially since the duke was eyeing Marie-Anne's figure like she was a prize piece of horseflesh for sale.

"Ravenclyffe was just telling me all about India. Weren't you saying you might travel there some day?"

Though Mason had addressed this to Harner, the duke spoke to Marie-Anne.

"Yes, we were discussing the work of your esteemed countryman, Monsieur Georges Cuvier. The most fascinating theories, madame, I should be delighted to acquaint you with his work if you are unfamiliar."

"Georges Cuvier?" she asked distractedly as she adjusted the ribbon under her chin. "Yes, I have seen many times when he stood in the rue du Vieux-Chemin talking to a goose for hours. The goose did not find him so very fascinating."

"Oh no, my dear lady, I mean Georges Cuvier the famous naturalist. Wrote the *Règne Animal*, you know."

"Yes, Baron Cuvier, this is him, I am sure of it. It is very well known his mind is weak. Sometimes he forgets to put on trousers, and he has tried many times to eat his cravat with butter and cream. The poor man, he is to be pitied."

"Mr. Harner will say a prayer for him, won't you, Harner?" Mason asked. "And then you can talk to Ravenclyffe about India."

"Yes indeed, we hear the most remarkable reports from the missionaries who have traveled there," began Harner, full of eagerness, and Marie-Anne and Mason wasted no time in making their escape while the two men were distracted in conversation.

He carried the hamper and followed her outside, past the garden and toward the hedge maze. It seemed they really were headed for the copse of trees referred to as "the wilderness" which was really just a few neatly contained acres of woodland. Mason had laughed when he heard it the first time, thinking it was a joke. Everything was so tame here, and they seemed to use words to add grandeur and excitement to the most mundane things.

"Did you really know that Cuvier person?" he asked Marie-Anne as they walked.

"Of course not." She smiled until her dimple showed itself. "But the terrible duke has spoken of him to Charlotte, because her mother is creole. He is very rude. It is bad manners to cut off his tongue, but I thought it is possible he will hesitate to repeat the teachings of a lunatic."

"You, my dear, are a very quick thinker."

"Just like you." Her smile faded. There was a little coolness to her, the polite distance she used often with people she did not like. He had never felt it from her, not from the moment they had met. He supposed he deserved it, even if it did feel like he might freeze to death. He'd probably always deserved it.

"Are we really going to see Phyllida's hermit?" he asked.

"Yes, and she tells me he wants to know about American trees. I hope you have sufficient lies ready?"

"Always."

The way her mouth pursed made him wonder if he should not be so blunt, but the last thing he wanted to do was mince words with her. He strode ahead a few steps and put himself in front of her, causing her to stop. She looked up at him expectantly.

"I'm sorry, Marie-Anne. I should've said that last night."

"You lied to me," she said, with more sadness than accusation.

"It wasn't personal. I lied to everyone."

"Yes, but I thought..." Her gaze fluttered prettily down to his mouth, and then to the ground. "I thought we were friends."

"We were. We *are*, or else I would've kept on lying." She was destroying him with that sullen little frown. "Look, I have no pride at all. I'd get down on the ground and beg forgiveness right now, but we're in full view of the house and lord only knows how these people would use the spectacle against you. But say it, and I'll do it."

"What? You talk nonsense—"

"What do I have to do, Marie-Anne? I'm sorry. I hate that you feel deceived. I swear I won't lie to you anymore."

The frown was gone and she gazed at him, thoughtful. Maybe she saw that he was remembering how her skin was like velvet, and how she had opened to him so readily and panted so desperately. He could smell her even now – all imagination and memory, of course – the taste of her still filling his mouth and making him salivate right here in this very public, very civilized place.

Maybe she saw all that. But he hoped she also saw that he meant it when he swore he wouldn't lie to her. The idea that he'd hurt her feelings made him want to lay down and die.

"Well," she said finally. "My vanity is very satisfied. You care for my feelings before you ask my decision about you. I thought it would be the first thing you asked."

He didn't say that he'd refrained from asking because he was afraid of her answer. He just smiled with relief that her resentment seemed to be gone. "I reckon if you were planning to tell everyone I'm a fraud, you'd have done it already."

She sniffed. "Maybe I will tell them tomorrow."

There she was – a little teasing, a little taunting, a little laughter just below the surface. They were friends again – entirely on her terms, which he did not in the least object to, just as long as things were easy between them.

His smile was irrepressible.

"Why tell them when you can have it to hold over me? You can amuse yourself for days, making me dance to your tune."

She clucked her tongue and rolled her eyes. "Why would I want this? You are a terrible dancer." She made a gesture to shoo him out of her path, and they continued their walk toward the trees. "The pamphlets, they are entertaining. They are not vicious, it is true. Well, some are a little vicious, I must confess this, but so far it is never my friends who are treated badly in your papers."

"We try not to be hateful," he agreed. "Freddy's testing a theory that comedy sells just as well as tragedy."

"I want to meet this Freddy."

That surprised him enough that he stopped his exploration of the hamper. It was full of bread and fruit and cheese.

"Why do you want to meet Freddy?"

"He is in charge of the words, no? And to choose what is the story, to say which picture you will draw.

You told me this."

"It's more of a conversation between us, about the drawings. But why do you want to meet him?"

"It is to satisfy my curiosity about him, to see if he is a terrible scoundrel." The spark of mischief had reappeared in her eyes. "And maybe there are other stories I would like you to tell."

"Oh *ho*, what's this?" He stopped walking and waited for her to do the same. He was hard pressed to hide his admiration as she blinked in mock innocence at him. "Why, Miss Marie-Anne, I believe you're looking to misbehave."

She flicked the briefest glance over his chest and down to his thighs, and playfully raised her brows at him. "Always!" Then she laughed and moved on, as he tried to ignore the renewed lust she had conjured with a single look.

He caught up to her. They were in among the trees now and, as promised, the path was perfectly maintained and all the nature very orderly. Her brief burst of flirtatiousness was gone, which was a shame. It was a perfect place for a hidden kiss or two or twelve. He wanted to ask her if she'd come to his room tonight, but she was all business.

"In France there was a philosopher who said the poor should eat the rich," she said, smiling a little to herself as though it were a private joke. "I had a very dear friend, Aurélie. She said the poor are more clever than philosophers, because they know it is better to milk a cow than to slaughter it for a single feast."

"And which cow are you particularly looking to milk?" He pushed away the troubling thought that she sounded a little too much like his crooked cousin right now.

"It is you and your Freddy who do the milking. You will do it until you must stop, or until you want to. I understand this." She gave a fatalistic shrug. "As you say, you must feed yourself. But I do not see why you cannot accomplish something more than filling your pockets, when there is a chance."

She described one of the drawings he had shown her last night, the one where Ravenclyffe compared his prized snuffbox with another man's. She voiced her appreciation of how he had positioned the men so that the snuffboxes were obvious proxy for their cocks, two gentleman comparing their precious, over-embellished little toys. But it was the little background scene that had caught her imagination. He'd drawn a lady shielding a young girl from the scene, and admonishing her to stay far from the men.

"I like that you make him ridiculous," she said. "But I like it more if you also give him this reputation, in every drawing, so that he is known to be ridiculous *and* degenerate."

"You want to go after Ravenclyffe?" He had no idea how Freddy would feel about that. "I know we made a libertine out of almost nothing in St. James' case, but I'm not sure how easy it'll be to do the same to a duke."

"It is not out of nothing," she objected. "And I would not want to make him seem so romantic as a libertine."

"More of a cad, then?"

She gave an indignant huff that had no small amount of disgust in it. "This word is too kind, cad. It is the genteel way to say a man is not honorable, but he is more than dishonorable. The pig. And I do not ask you to invent, it is all truth."

He considered this. "So your point is to give a general impression that mothers should keep their daughters out of his reach, something like that?"

"Oh yes, I would very much like that. He is a duke, you know? You cannot destroy a duke, you can only hope all his acquaintance will laugh at him. Already you are drawing pictures to do this. I only suggest there is this other thing to ridicule."

Freddy was the final decision on what the story was, but Mason didn't say that. She could answer all the challenging questions about why it would or would not work when she met Freddy.

"I'll draw it," he said. "I'll put together a few more drawings and take them to Freddy when I meet him tomorrow. Will you come to my room tonight to look at the sketches?"

She laughed. "Ah, the ancient invitation! You say this to all the women?"

"Only the ones who are serious about their pleasure," he assured her, and had the very great satisfaction of watching her blush.

༄

"I think it is perfectly understandable he would remind you of a farmer," explained Phyllida as she spooned jam onto her bread. "He lives in nature, and so is possessed of the wisdom one can only acquire when one is liberated from the bonds of civilization. A life devoted to the contemplation of the soul among the creatures of the forest is not so different to a life spent in service to the soil."

Mason decided that if Marie-Anne could keep herself from laughing at this statement, which was one of the most ludicrous things he'd ever heard, then he could do it, too. Never mind that this wise hermit had said barely more than two sentences before accepting the offered sandwich, tugging respectfully at his cap, and leaving. Never mind that the sole reason for the existence of an ornamental hermit was to entertain within the dreaded "bonds of civilization." And never mind that seventeen-year-old Phyllida Shipley was about as familiar with wisdom as she was with the definition of a forest: she was determined to be fascinated.

Now the three of them sat before the picturesque little cottage – which would be more rightly described as an artfully designed hut – and shared the contents of the hamper while Mason stared dreamily at Marie-Anne's mouth and Phyllida compared the rigors of being a hermit to farming.

"I think your typical farmer spends more time contemplating his crops than his soul," Mason offered. Phyllida scowled, so he added as seriously as he could manage: "And he's the poorer for it, I'm sure."

"Indeed he is not, Mr. Mason!" Phyllida was brimming full of hope that she could make him understand. "An ideal life is one spent out of the corrupting influence of society. Our souls are born in a state of perfection, do you see, and wander far from it through the influence of civilization. Education interferes with our natural state. Do you see, then, how a simple farmer is necessarily closer to the divine than the learned man?"

He considered telling her that learned men tended to be wealthy men, and that most farmers would gladly sell their alleged proximity to the divine for a fraction of that wealth. It would fall on deaf ears, though. She was patently uninterested in common sense, and it was more expedient to agree with her.

"I do see it now," he said in a tone of dawning enlightenment. "You're much better at explaining these ideas than the poems St. James composes. He gets himself tangled up in the mechanics. What was he trying to rhyme the other day? 'A countenance noble' with 'morality immobile'?"

"I preferred 'savage beauty' and 'ravaged esprit'," said Marie-Anne, who thankfully did not look at him or both would have burst out laughing. "Such persistence in creativity! It is to be admired."

Phyllida grew unusually quiet as she unwrapped cheese and sliced more bread. Normally, she would take this opportunity to praise St. James' poetic sensibilities. She finally mumbled something about how he had been working on that poem for months and still wasn't finished. "I fear he may be in want of inspiration."

"You are inspiration enough for ten poets, Phyllie," Marie-Anne insisted loyally. "If he needs more than you, then he is a very poor poet."

"I wouldn't say that's the only thing that makes him a poor poet," Mason muttered. But he did it quietly, so that only Marie-Anne heard him.

Immediately after dinner that evening, he excused himself so he could prepare the new drawings alone in his room. He briefly sketched out three ideas, and then began calculating how long he could reasonably wait for Marie-Anne to come through the door and help him decide which one held the most promise. It would only take a minute, and then maybe she'd kiss him. Maybe she'd pull his trousers open again in that deliciously impatient way.

Or maybe he'd spend all night fantasizing in an empty room. She might not come at all. Over dinner, he had made mention of his intention to go to the village tomorrow. A few of the other guests invited themselves to come along, including Marie-Anne, and he could only assume she had some plan to get free of the party so that they could meet up with Freddy. She was clever enough, he had no doubt. But a part of him still hoped she would want to discuss it with him tonight.

Just when he had decided to give up, and pulled his favorite of the sketches toward him so that he could add more detail, her soft tap came at the panel. She wore a friendly smile of greeting as she entered, and also all of her clothes. He exerted a mighty effort to hold back his sigh of disappointment.

"You have been drawing?"

She came forward and he slid the pages across to her. She smelled wonderful. He had brought another chair to the desk in the hope that she would stay long enough to sit, and now she drifted down to it as she looked at the sketches.

"I liked that one best," he told her. She held the drawing of Ravenclyffe seated in the salon, surrounded by empty chairs as he leered at Miss Ainslie who stood at the piano, singing. A cluster of young ladies peered fearfully at him from afar while two housemaids in the corner discussed his lewdness. Marie-Anne smiled a little as she examined it. Then, as he watched, she gave a delicate shudder of disgust.

"It is very vivid, how you make him drool at the singer." Her finger hovered over the group of young ladies at the side of the drawing. "But this will not do.

You have drawn Phyllida, and here is the youngest Huntingdon niece, it is obvious. And these chairs here – everyone will see it is this estate, and this party of guests. It is too exact."

He was so distracted by the idea that the Huntingdon estate was identifiable by its chairs that it took a moment for him to register the rest of her concerns.

"I can change their faces if you like."

"And the room," she insisted. "And the singer too. You cannot draw a scene from this house, do you not see?"

"I can't say that I do. Is it a secret that Ravenclyffe is here?"

She was scowling at him again like it was perfectly obvious and he was a thickheaded dolt. He felt a horrified flush beginning to creep up his neck, as it always did when he suspected he was making an ass of himself. But her exasperation was fading a little now, and his mortification ebbed with it.

"Lady Huntingdon is my dear friend," she explained patiently. "Very dear, and very loyal when others abandoned me. She has invited you here because of the lies you told, and now you gather stories from her guests like...like fruit on the ground, hm? To be welcomed into a private home, it is a privilege. To share it with strangers, to make the private public – this is a betrayal of her trust and her hospitality."

Well, that was damned inconvenient. He could say that the Huntingdon servants were so famously indiscreet that it hardly mattered – the doings of this household were hardly a secret. But right now all he wanted was to wipe the serious look from her face.

"Let's change the scene, then." He pulled up a fresh sheet of paper. "And the ladies' faces. You can describe new dresses for them, too."

This didn't lighten her mood as he'd hoped. She put the drawing down and squeezed her hands together. He'd never seen her less than perfectly self-assured, and her uncertainty alarmed him enough that he put the pencil down and reached across to put a hand on hers. This amused her a little.

"I worry you so much, do I?" She quirked a brow at him and pulled her hand away. "It is not so grave. I am wondering if I should tell Lady Huntingdon about you. It is very bad of me, to decide for her that you are harmless."

"That seems pretty grave to me," he said carefully. "How about if I just promise you that I won't draw a single thing you don't approve of? I won't use anything I learn here unless you say I can."

"Ha," she scoffed. "You do as you please without asking approval, as I do." Her obvious skepticism made perfect sense, but he was still a little insulted by it. There was no chance for him to defend himself, though, because now she was tapping the empty page, eager. "But it is for me to think, and it is for you to make a new drawing now. Come, I want to watch you!"

So he picked up the pencil and worked. The same idea but different in the particulars, with her making suggestions all the while. She was a little exasperating, hanging over his shoulder and dictating the most trivial elements when he wasn't ready to add that level of detail yet. He finally pulled away and put a hand over the paper to shield it from her commentary.

"For God's sake, Marie-Anne, just give me

another half hour and I'll be ready to bother with the pattern on their stockings. Until then, sit. Over there. I'll tell you when I need your help."

She blinked at him out of startled blue eyes. "*Eh bien!* Truly you are an artist." Then she swiftly returned to her chair, pointedly looking away from him with a smile playing at the corner of her lips.

He couldn't tell if she was mocking him or not, and he really didn't care. Among these people in their fine clothes and enormous homes, he doubted himself with every breath, holding on through sheer luck and guts in the face of his colossal ignorance. But this page before him was something he knew with absolute certainty. He knew how to hold the pencil and let his hand move without thinking too much, how to form the shape of the empty spaces and how to recognize when it was good. It was the only thing he was certain of, and he didn't need her hanging over him and making him nervous about it.

She looked through the folder full of drawings he had left on the corner of the desk, and he worked. Some part of him could sense her watching him intently from time to time. She was hell on his concentration, so he exerted a mighty effort to block her out. He was determined to do this and do it well, like it would prove something vital if he could draw it as she wanted.

Most of the sketch was done, just a few more details to add, when she spoke softly from her chair.

"It is beautiful, Mason."

She was looking at one of the drawings from the folder, rapt, and he hesitated to see which it was. Her face was mesmerizing. He wanted to draw her like this, too – full of soft wonder, her eyes shining. She looked up at him and he felt a kind of vague panic beginning to build in his chest to see she was entirely serious, even a little bit reverent.

"It's just a drawing," he said sharply, as though he had not carefully chosen this selection of his work, hoping she might look at them and have exactly this reaction. He leaned over to see which one she held.

It was the drawing of Lady Summerdale – or really, just a piece of her torso. Shoulder to hip, it showed the beaded bodice, the delicately puffed sleeve of her ball gown, and the length of one bare arm next to her curving waist. As he watched, Marie-Anne's hand floated over the paper as if she wanted to touch, but was afraid of damaging it in some way.

"It is Hélène," she said, and gave a little sniff. "Oh, you make me miss my friend. Almost I can believe she is here, it is so real. Well, it is not quite right how you placed the seam, and she wore gloves with this gown – but this is not important."

He cleared his throat of the thousand things caught in it. "How did you know it was her?"

She gave him a scornful look. "She is my friend! Who else has this body, so perfect like a goddess? No one. Even if you wrap it in a horse blanket, I would know it. This." She touched a finger lightly to the inside of the elbow on the page. "She is so alive, I almost expect it to be warm to the touch. It is exquisite."

It was painful – actually, physically painful, the hot tangle of joy and fear that suffocated him. Part of him wanted to rip the drawing out of her hands like a jealous child, and part of him wanted to point out every flaw in it, tell her how wrong she was. An even bigger part of him wanted to laugh and turn it into a joke that made it small and unimportant, something that didn't matter.

Instead, what finally emerged from the mess of feelings strangling him was a faint, "You mean it?"

"Of course. It is enormous, your talent. I..." She shifted through the pages. "And this one of the old man. And here, the cat. This one, it is Dahlia's curls, no? How do you make the light shine when it is only pencil on paper? You are extraordinary."

She pulled them out one by one and detailed everything she loved, admiring so many of the little things that he had worked at for hours, things he never thought anyone but himself would notice. When she reached the drawing of the lascivious plum, she pressed her lips together and passed over it without comment. It was only then that he remembered there was anything he enjoyed doing with her more than this. And he didn't even miss that so much, if this was to be the consolation.

Chapter Twelve

Marie-Anne was forced to admit to herself that, despite how terrible it was to make money by lying to people and publicly humiliating them, she was far more in sympathy with Mason than she was with any of the Huntingdon guests. As she watched one of Joyce's many nieces struggle and fail to hide a look of disgust at a villager who had dared a cordial greeting, she reflected that most of the people mocked in Mason's pamphlets deserved far worse.

It was ungenerous to judge them so harshly. After all, they could not help how they were raised. She vividly remembered Helen's stories of how hard it had been when she, the daughter of an earl, had first come to Bartle, determined to live as simply as any villager. When she had described cleaning out her own chamber pot for the first time in her life, it had made Marie-Anne laugh until tears rolled down her cheeks – not least because she couldn't imagine growing fully into adulthood without ever once having to clean up after oneself.

As she and Mason walked with the handful of other guests through the village, two of the ladies – the tiresome singer and The Poetess – seemed to be engaged in some kind of battle. They were boasting about their various travels, and who was better acquainted with a certain Hungarian musician, and all manner of experiences that would apparently prove one of them more worldly and sophisticated than the other. Presumably they were hoping to impress the villagers, being unaware that the villagers were far more excited at the prospect of two fine ladies fighting in the street than which of them could name more canals in Venice.

Moving on to deciding who had the more discerning palate, the ladies eased into a debate over whether the preserves served this morning had been quince or fig. Marie-Anne was standing a little away from the rest of the party with Mason, who was watching the arguing ladies closely.

"Will you put this scene in your papers?" she asked him, careful to keep her voice low.

"Not unless it comes to blows." Despite his grin, he seemed perfectly serious. "I wouldn't put it past Miss Wolcott, either, she might say she's a simple poetess but I'd lay odds she's tough as a hedge apple."

"Apples do not grow in hedges."

"No," he said, distracted as he watched the ladies snap at each other. "And the preserves weren't fig *or* quince. Should we tell them it was elderberry, or wait to see what happens? It really would make a great print, and both of them would love the publicity."

"You mean it, don't you? Already you are planning how to draw it, I can see."

He pulled his attention away from the scene to look at her. "What? No, I was joking. I promised you I wouldn't use anything from these people unless you said I could."

His anxious frown gave her an unexpected sense of satisfaction. Good. He *should* be concerned. There was a kernel of resentment in her still, even though she had spent the last two days assuring herself that he was not malicious or spiteful. She couldn't quite understand the lingering anger until this moment when, suddenly, she realized it was not his lying that had so offended her. It was that he had used her in the hopes of getting close to her friends. Charmed her and used her and planned to run away the instant he was discovered.

That was only part of her appeal to him, of course, and a small part. She could see very plainly that he liked her for herself, and it was more than probable that they would have become lovers no matter what her social connections were. It was very real, their attraction, and so she did not fault him for acting on it. She could not help but be angry, though, with the part of him that had hoped to use her.

A better person would tell him this. But she did not want to be better. She much preferred to nurse this little resentment for a bit, because she was petty. And also he was very handsome when he wore a look of concern.

She smiled at him, and his frown deepened. "You look wonderfully worried."

"You like that, do you?" he asked.

"Oh yes, it is very becoming. This expression draws the eye to the freckles on your forehead. I forget they are there sometimes, but the frown reminds me."

It would have been interesting to hear his reply, but alas – the squabbling ladies were making such a nuisance of themselves that a local goose had taken exception to the noise. It ran at them, flapping its wings and hissing. One of the villagers shouted and ran after it while the ladies screamed. As the goose was chased away, priggish Mr. Harner stepped forward. He seemed inclined to comfort the frightened ladies, but his charitable instinct was thwarted when he evidently remembered that the singer did not conform to his idea of respectability and The Poetess was entirely too vulgar for his sensibilities. Thus he reeled towards and recoiled away from each lady in turn, trying express solicitude while hiding his distaste, and Marie-Anne began to regret implying that Mason should not draw this scene. Perhaps it was not worthy of the gossip papers, but she would dearly love to have it memorialized.

"Oh Marie-Anne, do stop laughing or I shall succumb as well," implored Amy in a constricted voice. She was valiantly stifling her own laughter.

"Never. It is bad for the health." But even as she said it, the humor was draining from her. Mason had picked up a fallen reticule and handed it to The Poetess, who now clung to him as though she could not stand without his support. "It puts pressure on the internal organs if you do not release it," she said vaguely, as she watched The Poetess take Mason's arm.

"That cannot be true, surely you are joking?"

"It is time to go to the vicarage, *non*?" She raised her voice and called to Mr. Harner. "You do not want to miss your appointment, you are expected at the vicarage!"

Gratifyingly, The Poetess let go Mason's arm and the little party snapped to attention. They gathered together so that they could pay their visit. This was how they would be occupied while Mason met with a business associate whom he had explained was very private but was also – and quite conveniently – a dear, unnamed friend of Marie-Anne's. So they were free to go to the village pub while the rest of the party was otherwise occupied.

Marie-Anne took one last look at Amy, who was listening attentively to Mr. Harner. He was probably telling the poor girl that she should not be amused at such spectacles and to please refrain from visibly enjoying herself while at the vicarage. What a disagreeable man.

"Now you're the one who looks worried," observed Mason as they walked away.

Her frown instantly dissolved. "And does the expression look very good on me too?"

"Everything looks good on you. You look even better with everything off."

Oh, this was how it was going to be, was it?

"This is a brazen falsehood," she replied, desperately hoping her cheeks were not as pink as they felt. "You have never seen me with everything off."

"You're right, madame, and I apologize. What will it take to get you to remedy that?"

She cleared her throat and tried to think of something clever to say. It was exhilarating, to talk with a man like this. She had been feeling a little homesick for her own village today, especially when they passed the bake house and the smell of fresh bread reached out to her like the warm embrace of a friend. But it was very safe and predictable there. Nothing was safe or predictable about Mason. Not even a little chat as they strolled on a summer day.

"It is very attractive for a man to be so sure of himself," she informed him. "Except for when it is not attractive."

"Right, and it's up to us to blunder around learning which is which." He turned to her as they came to the pub, maneuvering so that she had her back to the wall of it. "I wonder if you'll give me a hint, though."

"A hint?"

"Yes. See, I'm very sure that you want to kiss me again. But I'm not sure why you don't."

She really was no good at hiding it, so she didn't bother to try. He put his hand to the wall just above her shoulder, leaning in. Her gaze dropped to his mouth and lingered there while she thought of all the wonderful things he had done with it. She was certain he was thinking of kissing her here, in public, even though he knew he shouldn't. Not that she could blame him for being sorely tempted – it was perilously easy to forget the world around them when they stood close like this. She was breathless. Her skin was hot all over. She wanted to reach for his buttons and invite him to lift her skirt.

"Perhaps it is a test." Her voice came out husky and seductive, without even trying.

"A test?"

"Mm, yes." She let her eyes drift down briefly to the fall of his trousers and saw his flesh stirring against his thigh, evidence of his excitement. Involuntarily, she wet her lips and let out a sigh, which only caused his body to react more – to say nothing of what her own body was doing.

"What exactly am I being tested on?"

It was hard to remember, when all she really wanted was for him to touch her. Anywhere. But they were in the street, and he was a very poor judge of what he should and should not do. Which was the whole problem. "I wonder if it is possible for you to resist something that tempts you, when it is there for the taking."

She watched him as he filtered through the part that pleased him – that she was there for the taking – and gradually grasp the less appealing point of what she'd said. As she waited for him to gather his wits, she attempted to cool her blood by counting the freckles along his hairline. It did little good. Nonetheless, she had reached twenty-two golden flecks and six dark ones, all scattered beneath red hair made brilliant by the afternoon sun, when he dropped his hand, stepped back the tiniest bit, and spoke.

"Full of surprises," he muttered. "Now why would you–"

"Mason, why the devil are you out – oh."

A young man, very short in stature and smartly dressed, had appeared. He smiled at Marie-Anne in what she was sure he believed was a very charming way. It *was* very charming, really, if one did not compare it to Mason's smile.

He struck Mason lightly on the arm, never taking his eyes off of Marie-Anne.

"You're meant to introduce us, Mason. Don't tarry, now, get on with it."

"Freddy, this is Marie-Anne de Vauteuil. Madame, this is Freddy, a scoundrel with no surname I know of."

"I'd think twice before accusing a man of being a scoundrel without name, Mason. Frederick Lowery, madame, there's a surname for you. A very great pleasure to meet you."

He was quite good at pretending to be perfectly content standing here chatting. But Marie-Anne had been trapped in too many awkward social situations herself, and easily recognized his impatience for her to be gone and leave them alone. She spoke so that he would not have to find a polite way to ask her to go away.

"Not such a great pleasure, I think, when you learn I know about your pamphlets." It was always great fun to say such things with good cheer. She was rewarded with an expression of frozen panic very like a rabbit that had been spotted by a hunter. "Yes, it is true, I know you are a scoundrel just as Mason has said. And still I speak to you! I am very shocking myself, you see. Shall we go inside?"

She did not wait, but turned and entered the pub. It was a very neat and welcoming establishment, and she felt another pang for Bartle. Now that Dahlia was set up with her respectable son of a duke, there really was little reason for Marie-Anne to remain here interfering in the affairs of the Shipley sisters. Any embarrassment Phyllida might bring by associating with a libertine poet – or, it seemed now, with a humble hermit – would be mitigated by Dahlia's forthcoming marriage. In all fairness, Marie-Anne had done what she had promised to do, or near enough to it.

And yet she could not feel that there was no need to worry for Amy's situation. It did make perfect sense for Amy to marry a quiet, reserved man of the church: she was not enamored of London or its society, and she had always said she had no ambitions beyond a modest life caring for a few children in her own small home. Mr. Harner could give her that, so long as his benefactor uncle allowed it, and Marie-Anne had no business objecting. It was only that she could not feel that dear Richard would be content with this match for his sister, if he could see it. And Marie-Anne could not be happy to return to Bartle if she could too easily imagine Amy's sadness.

No, she should stay through the summer at least. To be sure everything was settled with the Shipley girls. And to be sure of these two men. Rapscallions, was that the word? What a delightful word. She would practice saying it later, so she could spit it out easily the next time she was inspired. For now, though, she would like to know how little honor this Freddy had. She sat next to Mason, their backs to the wall, and Freddy seated himself across the table from them.

"I will call you Freddy," she announced. "As Mason calls you, but not with so much affection. And no, you may not call me by my name, you will say madame until I decide if I like you."

Oh, this was very enjoyable. He looked wary of her and a little chastened. No wonder so many members of the peerage went out of their way to look down their noses at others. It was extremely pleasant to feel morally superior.

"Don't look at me like that," Mason defended when Freddy turned an accusing glare on him. "She put half the pieces together herself and threatened to shout the house down unless I gave her the other half. And here we are."

"Right," said Freddy, not questioning this rather exaggerated account. He turned his very dark, very brown eyes to Marie-Anne and muttered out the side of his mouth to Mason. "Any special tricks to make her like me?"

A dark pink flush began to appear on Mason's neck just above his collar, which meant he had, like her, immediately thought of something lascivious. The dear man. With a fleeting regret that she wore laced boots instead of easily removed slippers, she wound her leg around his below the knee, rubbing her foot lightly up and down his shin.

She blinked at him as innocently as she knew how. "Go on. I am all anticipation to know what you will say."

He seemed to think for a very long time. She had learned that Mason flushed red when slightly embarrassed, and purple when horribly mortified. Since he did not go beyond a deep pink on his throat, she could be reasonably sure this was a pleasant and forgivable torment she inflicted. His neck must be monitored regularly for signs of mortification, of course, because she was not a monster. Alas, attending to that task was a reciprocal torment, considering how very much she wanted to lick his neck again. It tasted as divine as it looked, no matter the color.

"Cake," he said finally. "Ply her with cakes. She's inclined to like anybody who does."

"Is that so?" asked Freddy.

"This is nonsense," Marie-Anne assured him. "I am not so easily won."

"Any particular kind of cake?" Freddy seemed hopeful.

"Good cake." Mason looked very steadily into Marie-Anne's eyes, like it was some kind of dare. She supposed it was. "The kind that makes your mouth water just to think of it. Soft and sweet in your mouth. Give it to her the right way and she just melts, like butter in the sun."

Freddy seemed oblivious to the delicious shivers this put up and down Marie-Anne's spine. "I can ask if they have cakes here, but it won't be anything near as good as the Huntingdons have been serving you."

She hastily withdrew her foot from Mason's leg. It felt dangerous to be so close, and touching him did nothing but make her aware of the sudden pool of heat between her legs. Like butter in the sun indeed.

"I will not like you because of cake," she told Freddy. "I will only like the cake. Now, you will show me the newest pamphlet, please. There has been one printed since last week?"

"She objects to our methods, Freddy," Mason explained while the other man reached inside his jacket to remove the pamphlet. When Marie-Anne looked at the drawing that took up a whole page and covered her mouth to hold in her laughter, he smirked. "But she seems to like our material in spite of it."

Mason had drawn a simple scene depicting Dahlia's engagement. Releford was on one knee, clutching her hand as they looked adoringly at one another. Behind them was a gallery of portraits, generations of bewigged Relefords looking on in varying degrees of mortification and disgust – not at Dahlia, but at the Shipley parents. Her mother was pictured swooning comically while her father appeared to be dancing an undignified jig.

She began to skim through the writing in the pamphlet while Mason opened his folder to give his drawing of Ravenclyffe to Freddy. Most of the stories in the paper were about Dahlia's engagement, or related to it, from listing all the heartbroken suitors – including Mason – that she left in her wake, to speculation about which of the Releford jewels she might wear at the wedding. Other major items in the paper included more gossip about the marquess (odds this week were against divorce) and rumors of cannibalism among a party that had set out to explore a South American jungle.

Marie-Anne had just been savoring a small paragraph devoted to a duchess whom she particularly disliked when she could no longer ignore the men's discussion.

"Look here, Mason, either we make something up out of whole cloth or we don't use the drawing. Hang your scruples, there's no other way if you haven't made another sketch. And I don't like the idea of inventing tales about Ravenclyffe. He's a duke, you know."

"There's the singer, Miss Ainslie," offered Mason. "I'd be happy to wager he's propositioned her."

"Singers and actresses." Freddy dismissed this with a wave of his hand. "They exist to be propositioned by dukes. It's got to be someone respectable."

Just as Marie-Anne opened her mouth to announce that no amount of cake could make her like Freddy after that statement, Mason snapped his fingers.

"Miss Wolcott. She fancies herself a poetess, but she fits your definition of respectable. I think she does, anyhow. Ravenclyffe tried to get her alone in the hedge maze more than once, she told me. Once he caught her in the library and she had to fend him off with a volume of Homer, I think it was. Or I could be confused on the details, she tells a lot of stories."

"Wolcott?" Freddy was making notes. "The Wolcotts from Derbyshire, you mean? Brother fought and died in Portugal?"

Mason shrugged and looked to Marie-Anne as though she might answer it. She blinked at him, amazed, and waited – and blinked and waited some more, until she finally accepted that he truly did not understand.

"*Mon pauvre*, you have suffered an injury to your head, perhaps? Or no, I think there is a witch or a goblin who steals your memory, it is the only explanation."

"What?" He was perplexed.

"What! It is not even an hour since you swore you would not use any gossip from the Huntingdon guests."

"Yes, but it's *Miss Wolcott*," he said, as though that explained everything. "She tells her stories to anyone who'll stay in earshot for more than five seconds together. The servants, the other guests – I'd bet she's told half the village by now. Hell, she's probably turned it all into a series of godawful poems already."

This was all absolutely true and Marie-Anne wouldn't dream of disputing it. And though in the usual way of things she would be inclined to mock anyone who uttered the phrase "but it's the principle!" she was forced to concede that, in this case, it was indeed the principle. He had not even stopped to consider his promise before blurting to

Freddy.

She addressed herself to Freddy. "The kind of man Ravenclyffe is, there is no lack of stories like this. You must go and find them. Or only write little hints of what he is like, without naming any ladies. That will be enough."

"It won't be, I tell you," objected Freddy.

"You think there is anyone who will say it is wrong? No, everyone will recognize this man Mason has put on the paper. He will recognize himself."

Freddy scowled at her. "And if we don't do as you say, you'll have both of us run out of town, is that right?"

She gave him a brilliant smile. "Yes! I am so glad you understand. Now we can speak of more important things. I wish to know why Mason squanders his very great talent on these silly papers. Can you tell me why?" Freddy just looked at her, apparently overwhelmed. "Come, you must keep up!" she scolded.

He just looked at her for a long moment, then shifted to look at Mason and slowly shake his head at him in deep disappointment. "It's a good thing you make us so much money," he said to Mason, then to Marie-Anne: "It's hardly squandered, madame. Aside from our profits, every eye in London is on his work."

"This is not what I mean. He is a very great artist and you have him making these little pieces of no consequence—"

"There's no need for exaggeration, Marie-Anne," Mason interrupted. "I told you I'm not really an artist."

Of everything he'd ever done or said, she'd found

nothing as scandalous as this declaration. "Not an artist! *Mon dieu*, there is a time to be modest, but – no, it is not true. There is no time to be modest when one has such skill."

"No, there's no time to sit here talking," he countered. "We have to meet the rest of the party and walk back to the manor."

It was only because of the purple on his throat and the way his mouth hardened that she abandoned the topic. They parted ways with Freddy and made their way up the village street towards the vicarage in silence. He had seemed a little shy but perfectly comfortable when she had looked through his beautiful drawings last night. She should have asked him then, where he had learned and if he would ever try to paint and use color. Maybe that was why he was so concerned with earning money now, so that he could afford to study. She would ask him sometime, when they were alone and when he was not upset about it.

"I have to say, Marie-Anne, you seem like you have just as hard a time as I do, resisting when you're tempted. Do you ever keep a thought to yourself?"

"It is rare," she agreed, glad that his color had died down. "But I try to be careful of people. When *you* are tempted you see only what you want, and if it is available? Well then, you take it."

He stopped walking and looked at her. It did worry her, how he had seemed to reject the idea that what he was doing could really hurt someone. She suspected that he was not accustomed to considering the consequences, probably because he'd planned to run away before there were any.

"So you're testing me, is that it?" He raised his

brows and it made half of the freckles she'd counted on his forehead disappear into the furrows created. She had to try very hard not to look at him like a love-struck girl there in the street. "You want to see if I can resist when what I want is there for the taking."

She was visited by a brief vision of him taking her. Oh *merde merde merde*, this would be very difficult. Still, she shrugged as if it was a perfectly reasonable and simple course. "If you can resist me, then I think it will prove you can also resist this very tempting information that surrounds you."

"Resist you? Forever?"

She could not help giving a burst of laughter at the woeful note in his voice.

"I think not forever. But for a little while. To prove that you can, you understand?"

He narrowed his eyes at her. "Well it seems we are entering into a wager to see who can resist the longest."

Now it was she who raised her brows at him. "You think you are so tempting to me?"

"Madame," he said in that slow, sweet way that he had, "I know it for a fact."

And though she pretended otherwise, it was disconcerting to know how right he was. He was very assured of himself, and he had every right to be. At least it was a wager she wouldn't mind losing. Not in the short-term, anyway. And the short-term was all there seemed to be, with Mason.

Chapter Thirteen

Upon their return to the manor house they were greeted with what sounded to Mason like a very one-sided argument taking place in the drawing room. He would normally have gone immediately to investigate, because it seemed obvious he should. But he was learning that he was even more ignorant than he'd suspected about the proper course of action among this finer class of people. And Marie-Anne was forcing him to consider that his moral instincts might be as lacking as his etiquette.

He looked to her now, prepared to follow her lead. She had paused in the act of untying her bonnet.

"But that is Phyllida," she said with alarm.

Amy was already hurrying toward the drawing room. Marie-Anne followed swiftly behind, as did the other guests, and Mason wasted no time in joining the parade.

"I shall never forgive you, never!" Phyllida was shouting. Her cheeks were pink, a hand pressed to the base of her throat, her lips trembling. She had inherited her mother's fondness for high drama. "It is a betrayal of the very foundation of our friendship, sir. How can you think I would welcome it, how *can* you!" And she burst into tears.

The poet St. James stood at a very respectable distance from her in the drawing room, looking only a little pained. He was good at posing like this, stoic and noble and infuriatingly handsome. It was the same suffering-artist look he always put on after reading out a piece of his poetry to an unenthusiastic audience. Amy had rushed to embrace her weeping sister and it was only when she looked up at him, furious, that St. James began to look heartsick.

"What exactly did you do, St. James?" Mason asked, a little surprised at how aggressively it came out. He thought he'd become inured to Phyllida's dramatics, but a weeping girl was still a weeping girl.

"Faithless!" cried Phyllida now, dashing the tears from her face. "I would never have envisioned such treachery from you, never. All your promises to me were lies—"

"I never promised anything, I swear it." St. James addressed this to Amy, who still glared at him. "On my honor—"

"Honor! You speak of honor!" Phyllida had caught a second wind now. She drew herself up, all offended dignity, and slowly pointed an accusing finger at him in an impressively theatrical gesture. "You are a stranger to honor, you dreadful...you perfidious...you *cad*."

Now everyone was staring at St. James who, it must be said, did not have the look of a guilty man. He looked instead like he wanted throw up his hands and declare her a lunatic, but was too much a gentleman to do so. Mason sympathized deeply, and thought it best to get everything out in the open as quickly as possible.

"Well spit it out, St. James, so we can sort out if there needs to be a duel." This earned Mason several looks that clearly told him he had no right to say it. But since Marie-Anne didn't look appalled or tell him to shut his fool mouth, he didn't care. "Don't worry, I don't have a pistol. Just a burning desire to know what all the fuss is about."

St. James gave a curt nod. "I have informed Phyllida of my intention to pursue the study of law."

Mason waited, with everyone else, for him to continue. There was only silence, though, apart from Phyllida's choked gasp – as though she'd never heard anything so mortally wounding.

"And?" prompted Mason.

"And he is abandoning poetry!" cried Phyllida. When the response to this aggrieved declaration was a deafening silence, she looked beseechingly at the incredulous faces surrounding her. "But don't you understand? He forsakes the Muse! To become a *lawyer!*"

Marie-Anne turned abruptly away so that her face was hidden, but not before Mason saw her hand come up to cover her mouth. He thought he might have to do the same, if he wanted to avoid laughing in Phyllida's face. Amy was far more gracious and composed.

"Is that all, Phyllie dear?"

"All!" Phyllida gasped, appalled at her sister's sangfroid. "We cannot all be content with dull church mice, Amy. Some souls yearn for a wisdom and beauty that can never be found in a vicarage – or in tedious books of law. A lawyer! I can find nothing to admire in it, nothing at all."

"I think it very admirable that Mr. St. James should look to the future and choose a profession that might provide a comfortable living."

"But I was promised *poetry*," wailed Phyllida.

Amy clearly wished the audience would have the decency to disperse, but there was no chance of it as long as there was such quality entertainment to be had. She patted Phyllida's hand in a soothing gesture and avoided looking toward Marie-Anne's back, which was now shaking with suppressed laughter. Mason felt a renewed flood of gratitude that she had gotten him out of his entanglement with the ridiculous Shipley family.

"It's a terrible disappointment, of course," Amy said quietly to her sister. "And yet just as you must be true to your own nature, so must Mr. St. James be true to his. In time, I'm sure you will come to see that it is for the best. You have often said, Phyllida, that the superior soul must strive to be above such temporal concerns."

Mason almost applauded. This was the practiced art of the long-suffering older sister who knew exactly how to end a tantrum. Phyllida visibly gathered herself and nodded at her sister. "Temporal concerns. Just so. Yes, one must rise above," she said, sounding like a martyr serenely facing an arena of lions.

She let go of Amy's hands and turned once more to St. James.

"I could never be a lawyer's wife, Mr. St. James. I could not bear it. I suppose I must wish you luck."

"I regret that my decision has caused you distress,"

he said stiffly.

"And I regret that you have abandoned your dreams, and all my hopes with them," she sniffed, lips trembling. "Farewell, Aloysius."

And so saying, she made a slow exit, cloaked in an aura of great tragedy and with all eyes on her. It was the best show Mason had seen since he'd come to England.

కఞ

"My imagination is a terrible failure," Marie-Anne said that night when she had finished howling with laughter. She'd managed to compose herself very well after Phyllida's scene, but gave in to hilarity within seconds of stepping through the panel into Mason's room. "I thought it was only possible that he would lose interest in her. I did not consider she could possibly lose interest in *him*."

"It's the first evidence I've seen that there's any hope for her." Mason was sketching her laughing eyes, or trying to. It was hard when she kept wiping them and moving her face, but now she was calming down and settling at last in the chair.

"What can you mean, any hope for her? She scorns a man because he will abandon bad poetry and because he will work in the law. She is very full of nonsense."

"I don't agree. If she was full of nothing but nonsense then his ambitions wouldn't matter to her. That pretty face of his would've been enough to keep her hanging on."

She blinked, surprised. "But... oh no, I think you are right!" Dismay came over her face. "If it were me

I would stay with him. His profession would not matter to me, if I could look at him every day. This is very concerning, to find I am so frivolous. More than Phyllida, even!"

She genuinely seemed a little appalled at herself.

"At the risk of being too self-assured, Marie-Anne, I have to say that if you were anything like frivolous you'd be naked and on that bed with me right now." He started over on his drawing, concentrating on that instead of the thought of her naked on his bed.

The tiny crease at the corner of her eye was what most betrayed her. It only appeared when she was teasing. Because of it, he knew she was not serious before she even said a word.

"Perhaps if you looked like Mr. St. James, I would be inclined to be more frivolous."

He looked at her. Not to study the shape of her eye, but just to look straight at her and through her blatant attempt to play on his jealousy. He let his mind fill up with memories of her hot mouth on his throat, and how she had thrust her hips against him and moaned. She could see it, what he was thinking of.

"Perhaps if you were naked on the bed, we could be all kinds of frivolous together."

He should count it as some kind of victory that she could not hold his look, but he didn't feel remotely victorious. He just felt a little dizzy from all the blood rushing south. She was going soft right in front of his eyes, easing back in the chair, her hand smoothing slow and languid across the fabric of her gown against her knee. The outline of her legs was clear and made him think of the plump softness of her inner thigh. He could taste her still, all the flavors of her still vivid in his mouth even though it had been days. It had been forever.

It took a moment to realize she had said something. He had only heard her faint murmur and thought of her moans, because he was that far gone into his imagination. "What?"

"You are drawing," she said. Her voice was like her body, all soft and slow and suggestive. "You remember I am here to ask what you draw?"

He held up the page of poorly proportioned eyes, embarrassing scribbles that he'd be ashamed to show her except that she wanted proof.

"This will not sell gossip papers," she said.

He shook his head. "St. James being scorned by Phyllida Shipley and abandoning poetry – that would sell papers."

"But you draw me instead."

"I'm trying to. You've got me a little distracted." Maybe he should go back to drawing her mouth. He knew how to do that.

She lifted her shoulders just barely, an attempt at nonchalance. "It is you who talks about naked on the bed. You distract yourself. You see how I sit here innocently? I came to see art."

He would have challenged her on the word – she said "art" as though he had any right to the word – but he was far more interested in how her breasts now rose and fell in shallow breaths. It was not performance. He was sure she didn't even realize how plainly she showed she was aroused. The other things were purposeful, like her trying to make him a little jealous, and lingering in his room even after knowing he wasn't telling tales on her friends. She was reminding him that she was there for the taking, and that he was supposed to resist the temptation she offered.

It was as much a punishment as it was a test, and he didn't doubt he deserved it. The arbitrary nature of it was the worst part. How would he know when he'd proven himself? When she fell into his bed, he supposed. Or when she gave in to her obvious desire to kiss him. And it *was* obvious.

She wanted it every bit as much as he did. Which meant he had something to work with.

He had exactly no experience in seducing women – at least not romantically or sexually. The rules he'd set out for himself long ago prohibited significant cruelty, so he'd never played that game. He knew how to charm and persuade for other reasons, though. It was all the same principles: coax down the defenses, give them a glimpse of what could be, wait for them to fall for it.

Deciding it was worth a try, he said, "I'll draw something for you. Not like how I draw for the papers." It was the most open and artless he'd ever seen her, no defenses at all when she looked at his secret drawings. To realize it was a revelation, that anything he'd done could have evoked that in her. "Anything you want. You can watch."

She looked up at him, delighted. "You will not be annoyed with me to hang over your shoulder? Oh, but no – I will not dictate. Only watch." She got up and came around to his side of the desk, standing over him and the fresh sheet of paper he placed there. "I want you to choose," she said. "Something beautiful to you."

He looked up at her, long enough to make her breathing go quick again, then gave her a slow smile.

The pencils were lined up, graphite in varying degrees of sharp and rounded, and he reached for the first.

"Something beautiful," he agreed, and began to draw with the smell of her filling his senses.

He'd never considered letting anyone watch him draw this sort of thing before. The silly things and sketches for the papers were different. Those weren't meant to be life-like or lovely, and he was happy to show them to anyone who cared to see. But the things he loved to make were hidden away, his own secret, purposeless indulgence. They didn't make money. No one wanted them but him – and now her.

He moved his hand along the paper. It was all sinuous lines. Graceful curves and delicate folds appeared under his pencil as the heat of her body warmed his arm where she stood next to his chair. He felt a distant terror behind the thrill, the danger of giving this part of himself to her, of exposing himself to her judgement. It was only fitting that coaxing down her defenses would require him to take down his own, that seducing her meant tempting himself to the point of yearning.

"It is...a flower?" she asked, her voice husky and sweet. "I do not know it."

She had leaned down closer to the page, and he could feel her breath against his cheek. He turned his face to observe her and saw the wonder in her eyes, the obvious enchantment as she studied the page. She thought it was beautiful. She didn't have to say it, because her face showed it.

And it was beautiful. Anyone would say so, even if they never saw what he had put there. He rubbed a finger carefully over a line to smudge it a little, to create a more diffuse shadow in the declivity between the petals. He put his mouth to her ear and whispered, "It's you. I hid it in a flower. But it's you."

There was a little jolt of controlled surprise that ran through her as she saw it, and then the unexpected blush that was like a slow-blooming rose, the color spreading delicately over her cheekbones, up to her hairline, down to her neck. All the while a mix of emotions played across her features: a little scandalized, amused, bashful, and still reluctantly enchanted. Thank god it hadn't offended.

"Mason!" she admonished softly.

"You said something beautiful." He brushed his finger soft and slow on the page, up and down the inner curve where in real life, his tongue had pulled the sweetest sounds from her. Her flush deepened. This time it was not modesty, but lust.

The defenses down, the glimpse of what could be – and now he only had to wait for her to fall. Just let her be pulled in by the gravity of her own wanting. Her hand came up over the page, her finger atop his as he traced over the secret lines of her body. It was very possibly the greatest discipline he'd ever shown, that he didn't lean into her, turn his face and catch her mouth when he knew she wanted him to.

"Marie-Anne," he rasped.

"You think I cannot resist, hm?" Her eyes were closed, concentration in her face. She was trying quite desperately to keep control of herself, and it thrilled him.

"I can't think of any reason you should," he answered honestly.

Her eyes opened. The blue had gone smoky, unfocused. "To prove you can resist temptation. You remember?" A sleepy smile pulled at her mouth.

"You try to make me so hungry that I will make it easy and give in first."

"Well," he murmured, trying to think clearly. He put his face closer to the warmth of her neck and inhaled the scent of her hair, her skin. She gave a delicate shudder. "There's no need to make it so difficult for yourself. I'm right here, and the bed's right there."

"Mm, yes it's true," she sighed happily. "But you have miscalculated. To satisfy this, I do not need a bed. Or you."

She pulled away a little away from him to lean back against the wall. There was no more little embarrassment or shyness in her. She looked directly at him as she pulled her skirt up with one hand, and slipped the other hand between her legs.

He made a sound that was somewhere between amazement and protest, only because he could not believe it. He could hardly decide where to look – the serene smile on her face or her hand moving softly beneath her skirts. "Marie-Anne."

Her eyes drifted open to look at him, and she made a little humming sound. "Do I shock you?"

Somehow he was out of his chair and standing, arms braced on the wall on either side of her head, looking down at her as she pleasured herself. Her skirts hid her hand from him, but the obscenely contented look on her face was quite a view. So much for seduction. Just that deftly, she had turned the tables so that he was the one fighting his too-obvious lust. She was astounding.

As tests of endurance went, it was fiendishly designed. A good thing he had learned discipline, how to play the long game, to delay the immediate payoff in favor of the greater reward later on. That's what he told himself as she sighed and played with herself, as her heat rose up to touch his skin, as he held himself rigid and hot and hard, never closing the few inches of distance between their mouths.

"Is this part of your pleasure?" he whispered after a while. "To torment me?"

"Oh no. My pleasure does not require you. But it is, I confess, much…more–" Here she gasped sharply – "More extraordinary, when you are part of it."

"So you do this often? Without me, I mean." Now he was just torturing himself.

She gave a brief, broad smile. "Oh, I always think of you," she assured him. "I like especially to think of how it was to look down and see your head, your red hair between my legs."

"Jesus."

"Shh!" Her free hand came up as she made an urgent sound, dropping her skirts and pressing her fingers against his mouth. He kept his eyes on her, a relentless focus on her face so he could memorize the way she looked in this moment instead of imagining burying himself in her. He thought he might explode without her ever touching him, as she writhed and bucked against the wall, her fingers moving furiously, her hand now gripping his shoulder for support as she came.

When it was done, she sagged against the wall and looked up at him with that dreamy look that he'd seen on her in the aftermath of their lovemaking. He closed his eyes against the sight, afraid it would send him over the edge. He remained frozen on the edge of explosion, desperately trying to think of the least arousing things he could imagine in the hopes of keeping control.

"Satisfied?" he finally ground out.

"For the moment, yes." She brought up the hand that had been between her legs and traced the fingers across his mouth, sending a new flare of lust shooting through his groin. She knew how he loved it above all, the smell and taste of her. "But I have a very great appetite."

She patted his cheek fondly and slipped around him, wishing him goodnight over her shoulder as she closed the panel behind her.

ༀ

He didn't stop trying. As long as he didn't put anything he saw here in the papers, she would give in sooner or later; he hoped with a bit of effort on his part it would be sooner. The game was less torturous and more enjoyable when it was played fully clothed and at a distance. He gave her heated looks every chance he got, and watched her respond. She was terrible at hiding it. He joked with her and with others in her hearing – absurd and playful, double entendres when he could manage it – anything that might make her laugh, because laughter was the way to Marie-Anne. She couldn't resist it.

But it was flirting with Miss Wolcott, the somewhat unbearable poetess, that he suspected would yield the greatest returns. He made the mistake of complimenting a bit of her poetry, which meant he had to seem fascinated by every other bit of it she trotted out for his approval. Luckily, he was an uncultured American bumpkin, which meant he could just look suitably awed and mumble his appreciation of such fine words as *pulchritude* and how she managed to find a rhyme for *contumely*. Every time he did so, the awful poetess cooed and batted her lashes, while Marie-Anne very, very pointedly ignored him. It was a promising tactic.

One afternoon she waved at him from her place on the lawn, urging him to join her and the group of ladies who had set up their easels. They were painting in watercolor. Phyllida seemed to be trying to paint her hermit's cottage, but the other girls were using Marie-Anne in her straw bonnet as their model. It was no easy task, as she kept talking and gesturing from her place on the grass.

Mason waved back at her but did not go out to join them. He felt an unexpected pang of envy to see the paints and canvases, the ease with which the girls pursued their pastime. They taught art to ladies here. Just so that they'd have something to do, apparently. None of them seemed to think it was a miraculous gift, the kind of thing that a grubby little criminal boy from a backwater would have given anything for.

"Do you miss her?"

Mason startled at the sound of St. James' voice behind him, but hid it behind his well-worn expression of polite puzzlement. "Miss who?"

"Dahlia. You have hidden your wounds well, but…" St. James trailed off as he gazed at the ladies in the distance. He looked awful, or as awful as someone like him could look. His clothes were neat and his shave as close as ever, but there were hollows around his eyes as though he hadn't slept in days, and his hair had less than half its usual buoyancy. He looked longingly toward the place where Phyllida and the others dabbed at their canvases.

"I wouldn't say I was all that wounded," Mason assured him. He'd barely even thought of Dahlia since she'd obligingly taken herself back to London a few days ago, the better to plan her wedding. "Are you all right, St. James?"

This produced a heavy sigh from the erstwhile poet, who turned to Mason and said, "Yes. Of course. Quite all right."

He put on a brave face as he uttered this patent lie. Clenched jaw, painfully straight spine, mournful eyes – oh, God, the eyes. Damn it. Mason would have to draw him now, there was no avoiding it any longer. It had been easy to resist committing the perfect lines of that face to the page when all it did was spout fake sentiment in terrible verse, but there was no resisting real emotion.

"If you don't mind my asking," Mason said, gesturing to seat beside him on the terrace, "Is it the girl you'll miss more, or the poetry?"

St. James sat. "That's a very ungentlemanly question."

"That's because I'm not a gentleman. Come on, I won't tell a soul."

"If I say it's a wrench to lose the girl, my reputation as a libertine is rather ruined, isn't it?" He smiled. "But since you're sworn to secrecy, I'll tell you it's the poetry I'll really miss. Or the attempt at it, I should say." He glanced at Mason's carefully composed face and chuckled. "You need not be so polite in hiding your thoughts any longer. I know I have no talent for it."

Mason was at a loss for words for a moment until he finally blurted, "You do?"

"Yes." His smile was perfect too, and it occurred

to Mason that he hadn't seen it before. Never this happy and unselfconscious, anyway. "It was dreadful. Execrable. Really just abysmal."

"You seem awfully cheerful about it."

"I do, don't I? Well, I always knew I was bad. But I did think with practice, I would improve. I believe I *did* improve a little – but only a very little. And it's hard to keep on mangling something I love as much as poetry."

He continued to gaze at the cluster of girls painting their summer scene. Mason revised his opinion of the man to one of admiration. It took a special kind of courage to knowingly make an ass of oneself. Regularly, and publicly.

"But why would you do it if you didn't have to?" he asked, curious. "Couldn't you just study law from the start?"

"Well one has to try, doesn't one? Or I suppose not, but I naturally incline to these sorts of romantic ideas. Flights of fancy, my father says. I thought if I really threw myself into it, you know..." He watched, wistful, as Phyllida leaned over Amy's shoulder to say something that caused her to laugh. "If you want a thing so badly, if you love it like it's a part of yourself – the best part of yourself... Well, you must try. What else can matter?"

He wasn't sure anymore if St. James was talking about poetry or Phyllida, the way he was looking at her.

"That's the most poetic thing I've ever heard from you."

St. James gave a discouraged sigh. "Shame it doesn't rhyme, though."

Mason worked very hard not to laugh, and tucked it away to tell Marie-Anne later.

Chapter Fourteen

She had stopped coming into his room nightly, but at the end of a week she stepped through the panel and asked what he would give Freddy for their next paper. He showed her the sketches, which were based on London tidbits Freddy had written out in a letter to him.

"Nothing about the libertine St. James, or Phyllida," he told her, and she nodded in satisfaction. He entertained her with the story of how St. James had been knowingly torturing them all with his verse all this time, and managed to make it so amusing that she snorted with laughter. "We'll have to rely on Miss Wolcott for our poetry from now on," he said. "She's not nearly as bad at it as he was. I'll encourage her to write an ode to Ravenclyffe's snuffbox."

It worked a little too well. The laughter was gone from her face in a blink. It would probably be a step too far to tell her how adorable she was when she was jealous.

"Ravenclyffe will take his snuffbox and leave here soon," she said through tight lips that he very much wanted to kiss. "She will have to write the ode to the so handsome Mr. St. James instead."

He reminded her that the two poets hated each other, and tried not to smirk at this evidence of her jealousy. She scowled and said goodnight, and left his room.

The next day, Ravenclyffe left and Marie-Anne wore a red gown to dinner. She sat beside St. James and asked him all about his plans to study law, lamented that he too would be leaving for London soon, and licked at her spoon while giving a coy look to Mason. It didn't matter that he knew what she was doing, he was jealous nonetheless. She looked stunning in red.

Freddy sent word that rumor had reached London about the libertine St. James having dropped his latest girl, and speculation was rampant as to whom he'd seduce next. Mason made sketches that suggested the poet had renounced his ways and was considering a withdrawal from society and the life of an ascetic. In an effort to please Marie-Anne – and because, truthfully, it made for a better story – he added in an implication that St. James' change in character was the result of having observed the lecherous Ravenclyffe up close, and wishing desperately not to be anything like him.

"Yes, this I love very much!" she grinned when she saw the drawings.

They were walking along the far side of the hedge maze, and he wondered what he could do to persuade her to slip behind a thicket for an afternoon tryst. How many pamphlets must be printed before she believed he would not exploit her friends? And more practically, how long could he stay here if he couldn't exploit them? He was obliged to go where the usable stories were and that, very unfortunately, was far from Marie-Anne.

"You will meet with Freddy tomorrow to give him this?" she asked, and he nodded. "He will be annoyed that there is no more excitement from the Shipleys for him to put in the paper. But perhaps Dahlia's mother will make a fool of herself at their engagement ball."

"I believe you mean probably, not perhaps."

She laughed in agreement and passed the sketch back to him. He could not help himself – he caught her hand and held it, palm up, while he traced a thumb lightly over the veins of her wrist. Her pulse leaped.

"You study me so closely. Are you thinking of drawing me?" Her skin was growing hot under his touch, so quickly.

"I'm thinking of pulling that dress down and sucking your breasts." Her pulse leapt again, in time with her sharp intake of breath. "Since you asked."

The best part – or the worst, he really couldn't decide – was how obviously it excited her. He was learning that a blushing virgin couldn't hold a candle to a woman who knew exactly what she wanted and felt no shame for wanting it. But then, no woman he'd ever met could hold a candle to Marie-Anne, in any sense.

"There is nothing to stop you," she said, meeting his eyes steadily, "If you cannot resist."

She probably had no idea that there was a spark of hope in her eye. It made him almost obscenely confident, so that he had to bite his tongue from saying something that might ruin it. He just took a step back, reminisced privately about the taste of her as his fingers stroked over her wrist, and smiled wide. A moment after her eyes went to the dimple that appeared in his cheek, he dropped her hand and wished her a good day. The sigh that came out of her as he walked away was extremely promising.

It was hard to think of anything else in the days following. If she would insist on this game of relentless teasing, he'd play for as long as it took to win. Assuming his heart and various other organs could withstand the pressure.

Meanwhile, Freddy grumbled about the inconvenience of coming out from London once a week to retrieve drawings. He was further annoyed by Mason's lack of contribution beyond the illustrations. "You must have learned something at that manor that we can write about. What about that West Indian girl staying there?" he asked. "Why's Lady Huntingdon so close with her, eh? Could be something there."

But Mason lied and assured him there wasn't. Days later, the priggish Mr. Harner returned from an afternoon in London clutching the latest pamphlet and noted approvingly that it was far less scandalous.

"Why does he still not make their engagement public?" Marie-Anne hissed to Mason under her breath while she stared daggers at Harner. "There is no reason his disagreeable uncle should not approve."

Mason didn't answer, being too busy calculating how much money he and Freddy would lose if they failed to drum up a scandal. But he noticed how Marie-Anne unconsciously leaned closer than was necessary to whisper to him. Close enough for him to feel the heat of her. He wanted to touch the soft place behind her ear, framed in her honey-gold hair. But the room was filled with people, stifling and proper, and she was so entirely focused on taking care of others that she played this game and denied herself.

"You know I'll just keep resisting, don't you?" he murmured to her, and felt her stiffen in surprise. It was thrilling, this little hidden moment of whispering to her while all the others were unaware. "I'll keep resisting all the gossip – *and* you, day after day. Then the summer will end, and we'll go back to London, and there won't be any more secret passageways between our rooms."

He walked away before she responded, lightly trailing his hand across the small of her back as he did so. She gave a delicious shiver, and he felt her eyes on him for the rest of the day.

In the evening it rained, and they all sat in the drawing room after dinner exhausting their options for entertainment. St. James had left the party to return to London so there were fewer poetry readings, a blessed relief. Instead, Amy played the piano for them, though the music seemed to bore her, and she abandoned the instrument to ask Mason for tales of America. He had learned to be careful when asked for this sort of thing; he'd once mentioned, when asked, that he'd known some Shawnee and Phyllida had taken the opportunity to rhapsodize about the noble savage. There was only so much brainlessness he could endure.

He settled on telling them about the music he'd grown up with. "It's not anything like your elegant pianoforte," he said. "Those are rare so far outside of the cities. A ways out in the country, we'd be lucky to have more than a fiddle, and I never learned anything more complicated than the jaw harp."

"A jaw harp? Whatever is that?" asked Lady Huntingdon.

"I'm sure you know it," he began, but as he described it none of them seemed to recognize it. He supposed it was a low sort of music, not the kind of thing that would be found in a lady's drawing room. It almost made him laugh to think of hearing the twanging sound in a place like this.

"But how do you make music from it?" asked Marie-Anne, who looked up from embroidering a handkerchief. "It is very small, you say, and only a frame with one little string."

"It functions like a reed." He pressed his thumb and forefinger together lightly to form the approximate an oval shape that came to a point. "It's like a wire, here." He indicated the place where the pads of his finger and thumb met. "You put this part to your mouth, just inside your lips."

"And blow?"

He paused. "Yes. And suck. Among other things." She dropped her eyes and he knew she was, like him, struggling not to smile knowingly.

"But what other things?" Now it was Phyllida who asked, looking down at her own hand which she'd formed into the same shape. "How is it done?"

"The secret is to be very gentle," he explained, never looking away from Marie-Anne. "You can never bite down. You just hold it very gently between your lips in just the right way. At the tip of it," he tapped the tops of his joined fingers, "That's the magical spot. That's where the music is made."

Marie-Anne cleared her throat. She was refusing to

look up at him now, biting her lower lip and concentrating on her needlework while innocent Phyllida continued to ask questions.

"But how does the breath produce sound, if it is only a wire set across the mouth?"

"That's where your fingers come into play," he said to the top of Marie-Anne's head. "One finger just at the tip, to pluck at it gently. Or sometimes not so gently. Over and over again."

"As you would a harp string, I suppose," said Amy. "But how do you play the different notes? I cannot think how it is done."

"I'm sure you can," he assured her as he watched Marie-Anne's needle falter. "Can you guess, Marie-Anne?"

She blinked up at him with those very blue eyes. She gave him a quelling look but when he only raised his brows in response, she looked thoughtful. Dreamy, even. "You use your tongue?" she answered softly.

He nodded. "Yes, that's right."

She had a lovely light flush on her cheeks, and now she couldn't look at him at all.

"Are you very good at it?" asked Lady Huntingdon, who had a devilish gleam in her eye. "It sounds a difficult instrument to learn."

"I can hardly judge myself," he told her. "But I'm told I'm not half bad at it."

"What a shame we don't have one here," said Amy. "You could play it for us, if you would."

"Of course," he said while looking again at the top of Marie-Anne's head. "I'd never refuse a request." The light flush now spread to her décolletage, and she'd stopped her embroidery.

"Well, I'd much prefer to hear a proper harp, if you don't mind my saying so." Mr. Harner had been quietly waiting to suggest reading a sermon out of his book, but apparently would settle for a discussion of appropriate music. "We do very well to teach ladies the pianoforte, of course, but some variety would be not be amiss."

Phyllida argued that ladies would be better served by the study of philosophy, which sparked a debate among the guests about the merit of educating ladies at all. Marie-Anne fell silent rather than participating. She offered no witticisms that highlighted the absurdities of their arguments, or called attention to their hypocrisies. She just put her needlework aside as they chattered on, gave Mason a brief but direct look that he could not interpret, and said, very succinctly, "I am going to bed." She left without a word more.

Hours later he sat in his room at the desk, struggling to draw the delicate flush on her cheeks. The part of her hair, the curve of her ear, the light shining on her curls – these were easy now. But without color there was no way to show the soft rose that had suffused her face.

Without warning, the panel in the wall opened. She came through, pulling off her wine-colored dressing gown and dropping it to the floor as she walked with purpose. There was only the thin shift beneath. She went straight to the bed, never looking at him. She climbed onto it and, on hands and knees, with a saucy grin, looked back over her shoulder at where he sat stunned.

"Do not be slow," she advised him as she pulled the shift up around her hips, baring herself to him. "Or do you refuse my request?"

He was already out of his chair. There was nothing beneath her shift but skin, and the smell of her readiness. The barest touch, his hand to her thigh, and her whole body responded. She pressed back against his hand, that sweet hum deep in her throat as she stretched like a cat. He wasted no time sitting on the floor with his back to the bed and tugged at her ankles, prompting her to put her feet to the floor on either side of him, urging her down over his face.

"I take it this means that I win?" he asked before opening his mouth over her.

She pushed herself against his tongue, fingers of one hand gripping his hair as the taste of her flooded his mouth.

"*Mais non*," she gasped, in a voice slightly muffled by the counterpane. "I believe we both win."

He was not inclined to disagree.

꧁꧂

"Say it again." His voice was a sonorous rumble in his chest where her head rested against him, their naked legs entwined beneath the bedclothes.

"Rapscallion."

She purposely said it like it was a French word, and indeed it very easily could be, the way it rolled off the tongue. He laughed. He loved it, as he loved when she said *Kentucky*. It was wonderful – she had forgotten how wonderful it was, to have someone who loved every little thing about her, and who seemed not to want to change a thing.

"You make it sound like a vegetable. Or a sauce. Rapscallion en croûte. Or pâté de rapscallion."

"Rapscallion Provençal," she offered with a kiss

behind his ear. She caught his earlobe lightly between her teeth and relished the way he tried to pull her even closer. "I have known more than one rapscallion from Provence, so it fits very well."

"I don't think I like the idea of other *rapscallions* in your life." She burbled with laughter, because he said the word in a creditable French accent, mimicking her. His hand, large and warm, came up to hold her breast, and the laughter dissolved into a very different sound. He caught the peak between his fingers, teased her as he lowered his mouth to hers in a deep, deep kiss. "Your life before is your own business, of course." He was moving his mouth down her throat, little nipping kisses between his words. "But I sure do hope I'm enough scoundrel for you now."

His mouth had traveled down to her breast, where he sucked at her. He had the most marvelous way of reducing her to little more than whimpers. She was not used to this. She had never tolerated a selfish lover, but she had not dreamed a man could be like this. A lover who thought of her pleasure first, who was dedicated to it and excited by it, whose own pleasure depended utterly on it – this was new to her. She found it intoxicating.

"Mm, I *think* you are enough." She was beginning to lose all sense of herself. "But perhaps you must prove it."

He took this challenge immediately to heart, pressing his fingers inside her as his mouth worked at her breast. It was not long until she was gasping and shuddering, but he did not relent. It was the most exquisite torture, and he knew it. More than that, he knew how she loved it. She pushed against him, spread her legs, panted and bared her teeth – but he kept her there on the edge. It was unbearable. It was everything she wanted.

Finally she gasped, "I must beg?"

He took his hand away, smoothed it over her hip and the swell of her buttock as he held himself just an inch away from her. She could feel his heat all along her body, his chest grazing her nipples, their thighs almost touching. She was on fire.

"Yes," he said softly in her ear, the heat of his breath sending shivers through her. "Beg."

She did. She begged with abandon, with no idea if she was even managing to do it in English. It didn't matter. It was enough for him. He shoved himself inside her, heavy and hot, the only thing that could satisfy her. The way he groaned at the end, the little catch in his breath as she arched against him in release and he let himself go – oh, she could live on that moment for days, if she must.

And after, the sweet haze of coming back to herself and finding him there beside her, was just as satisfying. Even more satisfying, when he had that contented half-smile and the beginnings of an auburn beard dusted his jaw. She could feel him fending off sleep, as she did, because to be awake and alone together like this was so very sublime.

Tomorrow she would wonder if this was foolish. Or perhaps in a week. No, a month at least. What was the hurry in coming back down to earth? Reality was vastly overrated. Aurélie had used to say that the true foolishness was to invite the end of a dream to come any sooner than it must, and Marie-Anne had taken this view as her own, over the years.

It was true, what he had said. The summer would end and with it, the chance to be with him. If there was one lesson she had learned best in her life, it was that she must not squander the time she had with the people she cared for. She and Richard had thought they would have a lifetime instead of barely two years. But they had not wasted a minute of their time together and though their impulsiveness had come with a price, she had no regrets at all.

And just so, she should not waste any time she could have with Mason. An hour, a day, a few weeks left in a waning summer – she would take whatever was given, in a world so fickle. Here now in this bed with him, limp with lovemaking and giddy just with the memory of his laughter, she could not remember ever being more content. There was a weightlessness in the pit of her belly, the place inside her that wordlessly informed her she had fallen in love. Very much in love, and it was probably very foolish to love a man like him, but she would think of it tomorrow, or next week, or in a month.

She traced a finger down his breastbone and up again, then over the arc of muscle at his shoulder. It was remarkable to her, this body so hard and strong from work but with hands that could make art to steal her breath away.

"Tell me why you make money and run away," she said. "This is your custom, isn't it? But what is the money for?"

His breath stopped for a few moments. In the silence she said a little prayer – thick with dust, as her prayers tended to be – that she had not invited too much reality. But she wanted to know. She wanted more of him. More and more.

"It's what money's always for," he answered at last. "There's not some grand plan, if that's what you mean. I've always just done whatever honest work I can, to get by."

"But this is not honest, Mason, what you do here. You have lied very much."

She regretted saying it. It was better to make a joke, to tease so that he was excused from taking it seriously. But he only put a hand over hers to still the movement of her fingers across his skin, and looked at the ceiling as he answered her.

"What I come from, Marie-Anne... This is nothing. Small lies to trick fools into telling me the truths that they'd rather hide. When I was a boy..." He gave her hand a gentle squeeze. "This is nothing," he repeated.

"What is it you come from?" It was not just being poor, she was sure of it. She knew the smell of shame. "You cannot shock me, you know. I was raised by prostitutes." His head pulled sharply away and he turned surprised eyes on her. "Oh yes," she assured him. "I told you I have known many. The ones who were my closest friends, they were *les dames entretenues*. Women who are kept by rich men – well, their men were not always rich. I went to my cousin in Paris, and I found she had a very neat little *appartement*. A man had met her in a house of prostitutes and became her patron. There were two other women like her who lived in the same street. I was like their little pet. They took care of me, as much as they could."

"But you didn't – I mean, you weren't..."

"No, I was never a prostitute, or bought by a rich man." She smiled at his reluctance to ask it, as if she would be offended. "I thought I would be. It is not too terrible, if you can find a good patron. That is what I thought. But my friends, they wanted me to have a husband, or at least to try. They did not start out as prostitutes. They wanted better for me." She thought of them when they had met Richard, how Delphine's face had lit up with joy. "And I did find better. But before I did, I saw very bad things, and very bad people. This is why you cannot shock me."

There were questions in him. She could see them forming just behind his lips, but he did not ask them. What a pleasure, to see he was not dismayed. He only put his questions aside and then tensed as he prepared to tell her of his own life. It made her want to soothe him, to run her hands over him in a reassuring caress, an instinct that was tied to the weightlessness in her belly. But she made herself lie still and wait instead of touching him as she wanted to, until he finally spoke.

"I was kind of an orphan too. I didn't have a father, and my mother died before I ever knew her, so my uncle and cousin were all the family I had." He interlaced his fingers with hers and tucked her head close under his chin. It was very comfortable and warm, and a perfect way for him to not have to look at her as he said these things. "My uncle raised me to be a sort of thief. I don't know what else to call it. We lived on the river. The Ohio. People – settlers – they travelled along the river to go west. And our business was tricking them out of their money."

She remembered how he had handled the playing cards, so practiced and deft. "Do you mean gambling?"

"Sometimes. But it was cheating, not gambling. We worked up and down the river, wherever the new people came through. They were families, most of them, traveling with everything they owned in the world, looking to make some kind of life for themselves. Not rich people." She felt him hesitate. Her body tried to tell his not to fear, shifting so that she curled around him and gave all the warmth she had. "We had a system, different acts we put on. Different ways to fool them. Cheat at cards to take their last penny. Sell them a fake deed to land someone else owned. Convince them to trade their valuables for a sack of gunpowder that was mostly just dirt."

She listened to his heartbeat and wondered. Charlatans were everywhere in the world, and she had seen many in the streets of Paris. It did not seem so much more terrible to her than what he did now – lying and cheating – except for the kind of people who suffered from it. She said so, and felt him stiffen.

"You don't understand."

"Then you must explain," she urged him.

"I don't know how much you know about America, or Kentucky. But in lots of ways, it's not any better than here." He seemed to consider how best to make her understand. He took a deep breath and finally said, "We sold sugar water to dying people, and told them it was a miracle cure. My uncle struck a deal to help the local slavecatcher, do you understand?"

He paused as though he had guessed, correctly, that she needed to absorb this overlooked fact, this glaring reality of the far-off place she had incorrectly pictured. "That's what I mean when I tell you he didn't care who got hurt.

That's what I was taught – money from anyone we could get it from. The consequences didn't matter as long as we weren't the ones to suffer them."

Marie-Anne braced herself in case she might hear an answer that made her hate him. "How long ago did you do these things?"

"I was about thirteen years old before I really understood how bad it was. But I knew before that, that we were doing unforgivable things. I'd already started to see the truth."

She felt him rub a curl of her hair between her fingers. He was waiting for her to tell him he was unforgivable, but she would not. It was very young, thirteen – the age when a boy should begin to see these things but still too young to know what to do about them. "When did you stop?"

"Right about that time. One day I just saw... I just decided." His voice had taken on that slow rhythm, that way he had sometimes when he was relaxed and talking about this beautiful, brutal place he had lived. There must be more to such a decision, but she could feel how much he did not want to talk about that time. "It's an ugly world, Marie-Anne. It might be easier to see some places, or dressed up in pretty clothes other places, but I never went anywhere that didn't have some kind of ugliness at the center of it. And maybe you can't change it, but sometimes you get a moment. Just moments, where you can choose something. You can choose not to hurt people who don't deserve it, for one thing. That's what I mean when I say these gossip papers are nothing. Even if we ruin a reputation, it's always someone who can recover from it eventually. And it's never life and death, like it was back home. I make sure of that. I have some rules for myself. My uncle never did."

She had relaxed into him again. She could not like the gossip papers, but she knew, just as he did, that there were many varieties of cruelty in the world. And among them, his funny little drawings hardly signified.

"You wish to leave that life behind you?"

He pressed his lips to the top of her hair. "I aim never to be that bad again. I know I did shameful things, and nothing I do now will ever make it right."

"You were a boy."

"And a quick learner, and a valuable asset. I was good at looking innocent and wholesome. Me and my red hair and freckles – my uncle said they fooled as many people as my forgeries did." He played with a lock of hair that draped over her shoulder. "I could write out the letters with curls and embellishments, and everything looked official. It was the only use he had for my artistic aspirations."

"This is why you do not value your talent?" she asked. He stiffened, which meant she had been too blunt. She did not know how to be gentle, though, when it was such a terrible waste. She propped herself up on her elbow and faced him. "Someone has taught you that this art you make is not special. To me, this is unforgivable."

It was very hard not to kiss him, when he had that little wrinkle of concern between his brows. "The rest is forgivable, you mean?"

"You were a boy," she repeated. Confident he was no longer selling land he had no right to, she waved this aside and continued with her present concern. "Tell me about these artistic aspirations. It was your uncle who was the imbecile, to say your talent is not special?"

"Marie-Anne, it's just–" He seemed to search for words, a little exasperated. Very well, she was used to exasperating people. "No one had to tell me it's nothing special. I never studied it. I just fiddle around whenever I have paper. I never even saw anything that could be called real art until a few years ago, when I went to Boston."

Well, now he was exasperating her. He had taught himself this miraculous thing, with no examples to follow, and still he pretended it was nothing unusual! Little Phyllie with her stupid ideas about unspoiled nature would fall in love with Mason next, if she knew.

Marie-Anne tried very hard to be patient. "Did you not say to me that you wished to use color? To learn painting?"

"Yes, but." The purple flush began on his neck. Now she could see how it radiated down to his chest, too. "I can't."

"But why? You do not know where to find the paint?" He didn't answer, and the flush did not abate. "Why, this can't? Tell me what is to stop you."

"Because it's not *for* people like me," he said, like it was absurd that he had to explain something so simple. "You think they'd let someone like me into the Royal Academy? It's like this house, and these people. I'm not supposed to be here. They don't let people like me into places like this."

Marie-Anne took a breath, prepared to dispute this before she realized that she could not. She didn't know how anyone was let into the Royal Academy, but he was probably very right. Anything with "royal" in the title must, to her mind, be obscenely exclusive. It would be the same if he tried to learn from any worthwhile teacher. It always required introductions and the right connections. And money, of course.

She put her hand at the base of his throat, her fingers cool against his flushed skin. "You believe you are not good enough." She stopped abruptly to swallow down the sudden tears that pressed at the back of her throat. It was not his art he didn't think good enough – it was himself. He had not had, as she did, people who told him he deserved better. "But your talent is immense, that is what matters."

He raised his eyebrows, and she was pleased to see that the purple was starting to fade from his neck. "You really think that's all that matters?" His voice was heavy with skepticism.

"*Bien*. No, it matters who you know. But now you are friends with the Huntingdons, and Dahlia who will be a duchess, and Raven–"

"And I'll tell them I'm abandoning my thriving business in America to study painting, as a beginner and a pauper, in London." He smiled. At least she had succeeded in amusing him. "None of them are very sharp, so I suppose I could try it. But I'm not fond of that much risk. I'll get found out eventually, one way or another."

When he was found out, she knew, he would run away. She didn't want to think of it, because she suspected that when the moment came she might ask to run away with him.

His hand was sliding through her hair, and she must go to her own room before morning came. Later, she told herself. Later, she would devote time to considering how she had her own friends, and how she might convince them to be of some help in this.

For now, though, she wound her arms around him in the dark, and felt the beat of his heart against her bare chest. "They are not better than you, these people," she whispered into his ear. It was the secret to everything, if she could make him believe. "They are not better."

To waste time was to waste life. She intended to use every minute with him very well, and in every way available to her.

Chapter Fifteen

Fortunately, he seemed to have the same voracious appetite for her company as she did for his.

They tried out the hidden little alcove in the east salon the next day – a perfect place, since no one ever seemed to use that salon. The next afternoon Marie-Anne recalled the priest hole as they passed the north staircase, whereupon she tugged at his wrist and gave a meaningful look that confused him. But he, adventurous and clever as always, took her hint and met her there an hour later. After she pulled open the little hidden door to the small room and began unbuttoning his trousers, he wondered aloud if the people who'd built this house were smugglers. That was when she learned he was not at all religious and did not object to compromising her virtue in a place that once hid outlawed priests.

They made use of all the trysting spots that Joyce had told her about. It was a very pleasant way to pass the days – just as pleasant as the nights. Only once were they almost caught. It was in the hedge maze, and thankfully they had only been kissing when they heard Amy and Phyllida approach. Mason grabbed her hand before they were discovered and they ran like children, dashing off to the folly beyond the maze. It was overgrown with weeds and vines, left that way to seem like an abandoned Roman ruin which was most convenient as it meant no one else ever thought to venture inside.

She liked hiding there with him so much that she devoted much of her imagination to inventing ways to meet him there more often. One afternoon in the midst of her musing on how to arrange it again, Amy sought her out. She begged Marie-Anne to find some way to end Phyllie's infatuation with the hermit. Marie-Anne realized, rather to her chagrin, that she had completely forgotten her original reason for being here at all. She hadn't thought of it in days – weeks, even – because she was so preoccupied with her own romance.

According to Amy, things had progressed quickly now that Phyllida had broken with Mr. St. James and he had left to begin his studies. Now Phyllie was venturing out to see the hermit daily, dragging Amy along with her.

"Of course it's tedious, especially the way she sighs over him – over absolutely nothing, he barely says a word! But I worry she will do something untoward. Already the servants are talking. And Mr. Harner finds it unseemly."

"It will pass on its own," she assured Amy. "Does this tyrant uncle object to what he cannot even see? And why does he hesitate still to give the living to Mr. Harner? There is no excuse for it." She was warming to her theme. Amy's infatuation, if it could be called that, with this dreary vicar alarmed her far more than any of Phyllida's nonsense. Marie-Anne gave a little huff. "I think this uncle must object to Mr. Harner and not to you."

"Perhaps he does," said Amy. "But there is nothing in Mr. Harner that is objectionable, except for his choice in a bride."

She had tears in her eyes as she said it, and Marie-Anne was immediately awash in remorse. She bit her tongue against detailing the many objectionable things about Mr. Harner, and put an arm around Amy.

"Oh *ma petite*, you are a perfect bride in every way. I would say even *too* perfect. You are so busy in pleasing him with your perfection that you leave no room for yourself. No room at all."

She would have said more if Amy had not given her the strangest look. It seemed for a moment that she might actually burst into tears or shout at Marie-Anne. But then she gathered herself, quickly controlling every little thing inside, as she so often did. "That may be, but it is Phyllida who is my greater concern," she said. "I do worry about Phyll for her own sake, you know, and not just as her behavior reflects on me. But of course she is very headstrong. You've been such a help that I forget you cannot actually perform miracles."

She pulled away before Marie-Anne could point out that she'd done very little at all.

That night she stretched out in Mason's bed as he sat drawing at the desk, and told him she didn't like the idea of Amy marrying Mr. Harner, and could he think of some way to prevent it?

"Not any honest way." He barely looked up from

his work as he answered. He was making drawings to illustrate the latest rumors about the king's illegitimate son, according to Freddy's most recent communication. "And believe it or not, I have acquired some principles over the years. They don't include interfering in anyone's romance just because I don't like the fellow."

She was tempted to grumble at length about how it could hardly be called romance by her definition, but she was more interested in something else. "Where did you acquire them, these principles?"

"Oh here and there," he said vaguely, concentrating on his moving pencil. "I must've been born with a few or I wouldn't have run away. Then I picked up some more as time went on."

"You ran away from your uncle? When?"

"That same time as I told you about, when I was maybe thirteen years old. Ten years ago or so."

Her mildly stunned silence drew his eye from his paper. She tried to compose her face but it was no use. It was very simple math.

"But you are so much younger than me!" she blurted, and instantly regretted it.

She was thirty-one. When *he* turned thirty-one, she would be almost forty. When she turned fifty, he would be –

Well it didn't matter, she told herself sternly. She was not supposed to think past this summer. When she was fifty, he would most likely be a memory. A very beloved, favorite memory. A wave of melancholy washed over her when she pictured it. She would sit alone in her cottage in Bartle by the fire and remember this room and the way he always smiled at how she said the word *Kentucky*. She would remember the intense concentration on his face when he sketched, and what an excellent kisser he was, and how dismayed she was when he told her his age. It would be good, to have such memories. Well, not *good*. But at least it would not be so bad, if the village baker kept her in fresh bread.

"Is it that tragic?" He had abandoned the desk to come hover over her where she lay in the bed struggling to regain her good cheer. He had the dearest look of concern on his very young face. It was the freckles. She'd thought he only *looked* young, because of the freckles. "If it's any consolation, I'm guessing my age," he offered. "I don't know for sure."

"Then I will tell myself you are much older," she declared, determined not to sulk. "And I will tell you I am much younger." He smiled, displaying the dimple among the freckles that had so misled her. "But it is very young, thirteen, to run so far from your home. How did you get by?"

His hand was pulling the sheet from her, revealing her nakedness. "Can we talk about my sordid past another time? I'm a little distracted right now."

"Young people are so easily distracted," she sighed with a welcoming smile. "*Dieu merci.*" She pulled him to her and didn't ask again about this past that pained him.

The question of what she should do about Amy's engagement to Mr. Harner still haunted her, though, and she spent several days trying to think what dear Richard would have wanted for his sister. To be safe and cared for, that was the answer – but would he have disapproved of this Harner? Richard had cared more for the immediate, material well-being of those he loved than anything as ephemeral as happiness. But that was, as he had said to her once, a reason why he had loved Marie-Anne so much: she always concerned herself over whether a soul was nourished as well as the body that housed it. He habitually overlooked such intangible things.

She finally convinced herself that Richard would want her to act on her concerns. She was still trying to think of what she might do or say make Amy see she was choosing an unhappy future, when a most unlikely intervention occurred.

It began when Mr. St. James unexpectedly returned one rainy afternoon. Marie-Anne was with the Shipley girls in the library, of all places. They had strewn every surface with bits of the Lady's Magazine, sent by Dahlia in a plea to aid her in narrowing her choices as she planned her trousseau. Just as they were agreeing that it would be best to plan a trip to London to visit Dahlia, the door opened and Lady Huntingdon appeared.

"Oh yes, here you are, my dears." Joyce seemed politely befuddled. She gestured to the gentlemen who followed her inside the library. "As you see, Mr. St. James has returned to us and brought a visitor. Mr. Nigel Harner is uncle to our own Mr. Harner, who I had thought to find here with you. Your nephew is so often in the library," she said warmly to the older gentleman. "He is quite devoted to his theological studies."

"It's no surprise to me, none at all," said the cheerful man. He spoke loudly, as if he was hard of hearing. Or from the look of him, perhaps he was more accustomed to shouting hunting cries from horseback. "I've told him since he was in short trousers that his nose will be stained permanently black from the ink if he doesn't take it out of the books from time to time. But do you know what he says to me? Eh? He says it would be a mark of honor, and how do you like that?"

"I like it very well indeed." Joyce beamed at him. She had always just adored jovial old gentlemen like this, especially when they sported such impressive whiskers. "I shall leave you and Mr. St. James to wait here while I go and see if I can find your nephew, shall I?"

There was an awkward silence when she left. Mr. St. James seemed both nervous and grim, which was such an odd mixture of emotions that it captured Marie-Anne's attention entirely. Though to be fair, it was also because she had forgotten how ridiculously good-looking he was.

"I happened to meet Mr. Harner in London," he said, his eyes skittering over each of the ladies in turn before settling on Amy. "I explained to him that I'd recently been a guest with his nephew here, and in due course learned he had not yet had the honor of meeting you, Miss Shipley."

"Yes, and this fine young man offered to introduce me!" He clapped a hand on St. James' back. "Been trying for months now to get a glimpse of this girl my nephew has his eye on. Now which one of you is it?"

Poor Amy looked like she might be ill. She patted her hair nervously and then snatched her hands away. She swallowed several times and finally said, "I am Miss Amarantha Shipley, sir." This was accompanied by an uncharacteristically clumsy curtsy. She managed to stutter out introductions, and was clearly praying that Phyllida would not say anything to mortify her.

In the few moments where the old gentleman looked her over, Marie-Anne saw St. James give a somewhat apologetic look to Phyllie, who for once did not seem at all inclined to her usual dramatics. She only nodded at her former beau in a very friendly way, and looked quite pensive.

"Well I must say I don't see why Charles has hidden you away from me," the older man bellowed with a genial grin. He leaned in confidentially, but still spoke at a volume that could probably be heard several rooms away. "I don't think I'm supposed to know about you at all. I had my suspicions, but he's never said a word! And I keep away in the country, you know – don't like all this society bosh."

Amy was momentarily speechless with confusion, a polite smile frozen on her face. This account was contrary to the situation as Mr. Harner had painted it. This strict uncle was not strict at all. He did not seem remotely superior and didn't care one whit for society's opinion. And he could not possibly be withholding approval of an intended bride when he had not even been told there *was* one.

Fearing that Amy would not confront the kindly gentleman with these facts, Marie-Anne opened her mouth, prepared to do so with gusto. But just then Joyce reappeared with the nephew in question. At the sight of him, Marie-Anne blurted something entirely different than what she'd intended.

"Are you quite all right?"

The younger Mr. Harner was alarmingly flustered and his neck was a brilliant red. It was impossible to say what emotion caused it, but he truly looked like he might have an apoplexy. His wild-eyed glance hit Marie-Anne for an instant before moving on, but he said nothing.

"Charles! There you are, my boy, and you see I've met Miss Jibney, you can't keep her a secret anymore."

"Shipley. It's Miss Shipley," said Mr. St. James reflexively, as if he'd made the same correction many times. He was looking at Harner now, and he was angry. "Sir, I must congratulate you. Your uncle tells me that he has had the pleasure of granting you, immediately upon your ordination, the living of a parish."

Marie-Anne was so thoroughly absorbed in the way the two young men glared at each other (while the older man was pleasantly oblivious) that the significance of this statement did not immediately register. It was only when Phyllie gasped loudly that she realized.

Amy was staring very fixedly at absolutely nothing. "But Mr. Harner was ordained last year." Nothing but silence answered her until she looked at her fiancé and asked, "Is it true? Charles?"

His failure to reply, along with his inability to look at her, supplied all the answer that was needed.

"I see." Amy spoke just barely above a whisper. Her sister, however, was incapable of such a hesitant response in the face of this treachery.

"*Oh,* you…" Phyllida was breathing fire, pointing at Mr. Harner like she would put a curse on him. "Oh…*you!*"

She would begin screeching at him soon enough, if she did not go immediately for his eyes. Marie-Anne rushed to put herself between Phyllie and the gentlemen.

"Lady Huntingdon!" she said very loudly, and gave

Joyce her most desperate and pleading look. "Perhaps Mr. Harner's uncle would like to see... He could see the grounds?"

And say what she might about the stifling politeness of the upper classes: it had its uses. Everyone who had been a moment away from shouting – Phyllie, young Mr. Harner, and St. James – immediately clamped their mouths shut and waited in silence while the elder Mr. Harner pretended to want nothing more than to see the Huntingdon estate. Joyce hurried off with him, pulling the door closed behind them. Marie-Anne quickly suggested, with a significant look at Phyllie and Mr. St. James, that they join her for a walk in the garden.

"It's raining," replied St. James flatly, still glaring at Mr. Harner.

Marie-Anne resisted the urge to grumble about his sudden appreciation for reality. She reach for Phyllie's hand so that they might leave, but Amy stopped her with a word.

"Please stay, Marie-Anne."

"You would not like some privacy?" she asked.

Amy shook her head. "You are as much entitled to an explanation as I am. When I think that you came here," her voice was gaining strength now, "That you returned to London after so many years and endured the insults of my parents – only because I asked it of you, and only in the hopes of preserving..." She looked at Mr. Harner, who did not meet her eye. "Did you ever plan to marry me, sir?"

"Of course!" He had the audacity to look affronted. "What do you think I am?"

"I think you are a liar and a cad," she replied, impressively calm. "I should only like to know why you tormented me so."

"Tormented! My dear Miss Shipley, I only ever sought to improve your situation. You will recall how you expressed regret that you were not better suited to the role of a clergyman's wife, and the behavior of your sisters has caused you great distress–"

"You see, Miss Shipley, it is as I've told you." Mr. St. James had not taken his eyes from the red-faced Mr. Harner. "Even now he faults you, as though you are responsible for his deceit. There can be no reason to pretend that his future depended upon the approval of his uncle, except as a means to restrain your conduct and suffocate your spirit."

"Oh!" Phyllida had a look of discovery on her face. "That was the inspiration for the poem about the goldfinch, wasn't it? With its xanthic plumage muted 'neath Albion's leaden heritage?"

This was met with a brief and uncertain silence, during which Marie-Anne tried, reflexively and fruitlessly, to decipher Mr. St. James' tortured verse. Thank heavens he had turned his effort to law. Xanthic plumage indeed.

"But you!" Phyllida rounded on Mr. Harner now, no longer thinking of goldfinches. "Despicable man! That you dared to lecture me on my behavior, to appeal to my love for my sister and hopes for her future! You vile hypocrite! A liar and a cad indeed! Feet of clay!"

"Well said, Phyllie, another poet is born." Marie-Anne patted the girl's arm in hopes of calming her, worried that her shouting would upset Amy further. "But me, I would like to hear what this terrible Harner has to say for himself now."

She turned to him expectantly and, when he did

not speak, prompted, "That is you. Your uncle is the agreeable Harner and you are the terrible Harner."

He gave her the pursed-lip look he so often did, which cheered her enormously. It was a pleasure to annoy someone so deserving. The sight was disappointingly short-lived, though, as he turned to speak to Amy.

"I have suspected since you invited this...person" – he made a vague gesture in Marie-Anne's direction – "back into your life that your doubts were not unfounded. That is, your doubts that you might be unequal to the demands that will be placed upon you as my wife. But I persevered, as you know, in helping you to prepare for such a role despite your obvious deficiencies."

"What a saint you are," observed Marie-Anne drily, but it was lost under Mr. St. James' "*Her* deficiencies!" and Phyllie's heartfelt "Swine!"

"*Nevertheless*," Harner continued, doggedly refusing to acknowledge the others, "I can see now that my efforts have been misplaced. It saddens me to say it, but I fear we will not suit."

Amy had been looking very pale throughout this entire ordeal, but now her cheeks began to grow pink. She blinked rapidly, frowning in concentration as though she were translating his words from some unknown language.

"I agree with you, sir," she finally said. It seemed for a moment that she would remain composed, her usual decorous self – until Harner gave an excessively pleased smile that clearly incensed her. Her cool façade dropped away and suddenly she was nearly as loud as her sister. "We are not suited because you are a liar! And you seek to blame me for it all, as you always do, but I tell you, sir, that it is not *you* who has decided to end this connection, it is me. I would not have you if you begged me on your knees to be your wife, not for all the...the tea in India, do you understand me?"

The terrible Harner looked appalled at this absolutely delightful eruption of emotion, but he did nothing. He only stood there with his pursed lips and his general air of long-suffering patience until Amy burst out at him again.

"There! The door is there!" She shouted, raising her arm and gesturing heatedly at the exit. "Why do you tarry? You are not welcome – not in this room or in this house, sir!"

She veritably chased him out the door, and actually slammed it behind him. She turned back to them, breathing hard and pushing her curls away where they bounced in her face. Then she ruined her coiffure by giving a vicious yank at the ribbon that was wound around her upswept hair and flinging it away with a sound of disgust.

Marie-Anne reflected that the Shipley sisters really did provide far more entertainment than even she had anticipated all those weeks ago when she had received Amy's letter. But how splendid it was to see Amy become more like her old self again, animated and full of opinions. The dear girl seemed slightly astonished at herself.

"You didn't just happen to meet Mr. Harner's uncle, did you?" Phyllida asked, looking in sudden comprehension at Mr. St. James. "You sought him out."

Mr. St. James did not reply. He had truly never looked more handsome, though he seemed to have exchanged his fashionable clothes for a more severe suit and his hair was not artfully windswept. He looked rather boyish, standing very still and stealing uncertain glances at Amy.

Amy looked up at him, and then to Phyllida, back and forth between the two as though trying to understand something. "Did you?" she asked him. "Did you seek him out?"

He spoke haltingly. "I thought to – I took the liberty…that is, my suspicions…" He stopped and took a very deep breath, and then met Amy's look fully. His heart was in his exceedingly beautiful eyes. "I could not bear to see you treated so."

Marie-Anne gaped at him, prepared to settle in for a very good show indeed. But Phyllida grasped her arm and began hauling her toward the door while the other two looked at each other, captivated. "A walk in the garden, Marie-Anne!" she proclaimed enthusiastically. "It will be so refreshing, won't it? Such a lovely day!" she called over her shoulder as they exited.

The last thing Marie-Anne saw before the door closed was Amy was throwing herself into his arms, and the beginning of a thrillingly passionate kiss.

Phyllida urged a stunned Marie-Anne through the short portrait gallery until they reached the empty music room. When they stopped, Marie-Anne turned to her and found the girl wore a brilliant smile.

"I'm sorry to pull at you, but Amy is so circumspect I feared she might turn shy if we were there to watch." She took a deep breath. "Isn't it wonderful? Oh, say you think it's wonderful, Marie-Anne!"

Marie-Anne was still trying to get over the shock.

It wasn't caused by the sudden knowledge that Amy and St. James might have fallen in love, nor even that Phyllida seemed thrilled at the idea. It was that she herself had been completely and utterly unaware.

"But when did this happen? I thought she disliked Mr. St. James very much!"

"Too much," agreed Phyllida, rather smugly. "I didn't see it until after I broke with him, but then she defended him to me – long past the point that I even cared. And then I caught them talking once, in private in the hedge maze, and the way they looked!" She smiled broadly, delighted.

"You amaze me," said Marie-Anne. "You were so taken with him that I would think you could not stand to see him with your sister."

Phyllida crinkled her face in distaste. "Oh but that was ages ago. And I'd grown a bit disenchanted with him even before he decided to abandon a life of poetry. There was always a bit of the lawyer in him, under the veneer of poetry – and how can a man of law hold any appeal for me, or inspire any woman to jealousy! But it is *perfect* for Amy. And did you see how she looked at him?" She gave a deep, dreamy sigh. "He is exactly what she needs. Just a touch of passion."

Marie-Anne found herself staring at the girl as though she had sprouted an extra head. It had never occurred to her that Phyllie could be right in any matter concerning love. And yet here they were. "Is this possible? She has become passionate and you have become practical. And there is a romance under my nose that I do not even see! Now the pigs will fly and the chicken will have teeth, the world is upside down."

Phyllie laughed. "I am not as brainless as everyone thinks, you know. I hold true passion in the highest esteem, and so it does not escape my notice. I daresay it is also why *you* failed to see what was between Amy and St. James."

"I missed it because I do not hold passion in high esteem?" asked Marie-Anne, mystified.

"Not that." She had the most impish grin. "It's because you have been too occupied in falling in love with Mr. Mason."

"Have I?"

"Yes, and what's more, he's terribly busy falling in love with you too."

Marie-Anne felt suddenly very hot. It seemed every pore had opened in unison to flood her with perspiration. "Now you speak nonsense," she said, and heard the irrepressible note of hopefulness in her voice. "We are only friends, he and I."

"Falling love is not nonsense." Phyllie's smile was replaced with an expression of great earnestness. "There is nothing more foolish than to ignore one's heart. Surely you must know I learned that from you and Richard. It was one of the greatest privileges of my life, to witness how my brother looked at you, and it is *not* nonsense to say that Mr. Mason looks at you in that same way. I do hope you will act on it." She smiled again. "And that you will tell me all about it when you do!"

Marie-Anne threw up her hands. "Impertinent little hussy!" she said with affection, sliding an arm around Phyllie's waist and giving her a faint squeeze.

"I shall take that as the greatest compliment," giggled Phyllida, and said no more about it.

Chapter Sixteen

Freddy was getting anxious, and rightly so. The only reason for Mason to be at this gathering of fine people was to glean material for the pamphlets. Without that, his presence here was a purposeless inconvenience that made the exchange of instructions and drawings an ordeal and forced Freddy to operate alone in London. Worse by far was that they were starting to lose money now that there was nothing to distinguish their publication from others that shared the same stale gossip.

It was fake wealthy businessman Mr. Mason, not Freddy, who got invited to the parties, who was in a position to overhear all sorts of useful information. And they could not take advantage of that if he stayed here in the country listening to secrets he couldn't use. So of course Freddy wanted him to come back to London.

As an added temptation, some of these nabobs (as Freddy called them) were seeking Mason out. They wanted to hear more about investing jaw-dropping sums of money in the virgin forests of America and the blindingly successful, utterly fictional timber business. Mason had only thrown that lure out there in the beginning as a way to test the waters, and then again just a few weeks ago to Ravenclyffe – but mostly because he couldn't resist toying with a cretin who judged a man by his skull shape and gave far too many lingering looks to Marie-Anne's bosom.

He had no plans to go through with the swindle. He hadn't needed to resort to that kind of fraud for years, but there was no denying that it held a lot of appeal at the moment. Men like Ravenclyffe had more money than they could spend in ten lifetimes, and they hadn't exactly come by it honestly themselves. Only stubborn pride stopped Mason from doing it, the determination not to revert to what his family had taught him to be.

He could avoid it, if the drawings were profitable enough. They just needed to keep making money from the gossip papers, and to do that he'd have to go back to London soon. There was no reason to stay here, whiling away the hours in idleness and splendor, while the business lost all the ground they'd gained.

No reason except that Marie-Anne was here. Delectable Marie-Anne, who ravished him nightly and did indescribable things to his body, to say nothing about what she invited him to do to hers. Marie-Anne, who regularly made him laugh a dozen times before breakfast without even trying. Who looked with reverent eyes at his feeble artistic efforts – the ones closest to his heart, that he had never dared to show anyone – and detailed all the ways they were wonderful. Who told him he should see the art in

Paris, that perhaps he might take a trip to Holland as she'd heard the Dutch had many beautiful paintings, and that he must go to Italy above all.

That was ridiculous. He knew it was. No matter what she said, he knew it was just an absurd dream – so absurd that he'd never even bothered to consider dreaming it. But she put it in his mind now, for the first time. She talked about finding a patron, someone to introduce him to the right people so he could find an apprenticeship. She wondered idly what the costs might be, and where he might find lodgings. Always with the tone of curiosity, like it was an interesting question to ponder from time to time. And that's how she made him ponder it too. He knew it was what she was doing, and it still worked.

"The portrait of the old man," she said as they lingered in the silly little building made to look like a Roman ruin. She sat astride him in the aftermath of lovemaking, satisfied for the moment, her arms curled around his head and her fingers playing with the hair at his temple. His legs were beginning to fall asleep and anyone might stumble upon them here, but he didn't care. "And the one of Charlotte reading, and the hands of the hermit – the people are the most fascinating of your drawings. I wonder which would be best to assemble. To show to someone more experienced, I mean. In Paris I knew an artist who could tell us. Delphine posed for him."

"Marie-Anne, stop." There was no way to explain to her the way it made him feel, to think about it as something he could actually do: assemble some pages covered in his scribbles, hand them to a professional, ask to be considered and evaluated. Terrifying only began to describe it. He'd even had a nightmare about it, for god sakes.

And she knew it, he was sure. That's why she very agreeably kissed the top of his head and spread her fingers through his hair as she shifted in his lap and changed the subject in that playful way. "Stop? How can you wish me to stop this, hm?" Her hips curled up against him, both of them bare beneath her skirt. She turned his head up and gave his lips the lightest peck. He kissed her back until she was breathless.

"Mmm, not a stop," she smiled against his lips. "Only perhaps a pause. Until tonight."

But she had put it in his head, no matter how laughable, and now he found himself thinking through every page already drawn and what else he might still put down on paper, and which would be good enough to be shown to someone who knew art. He wouldn't, of course. But he thought of it. Then he made the mistake of mentioning some he hadn't shown her – his cousin singing in front of the fire, the view of the Ohio River as he remembered it from their house – and she smiled and said she wanted to see them. He said he would dig them up and show her sometime, and that should have been the end of it. But it was only the beginning of something else.

He fell asleep with her beside him one night, which only happened because he'd been up so late preparing sketches for Freddy the night before. Every few nights the lack of sleep caught up with him, and he'd wake up in the full light of morning with Marie-Anne long returned to her room. But this night, after he'd drifted off, something woke him long before dawn.

He opened his eyes to find her there in the candlelight. She sat beside him on his bed wearing only her thin shift, looking down at him. It was a wonderful but worrisome look, full of affection and an unusual gravity that filled him with apprehension. Maybe it was just that she was so beautiful in the candlelight. Even in the dead of night, wearing only a chemise and her hair spilling down her back, she looked too good for him. Lovely and worldly and wise, used to wearing silks and instructing servants, despite what she came from. Even barely clothed, she was like a fashion plate of a real lady, the kind he used to glimpse when he turned the pages of old magazines with his dirty pilfering fingers.

"Is something wrong?" He asked it as casually as he could manage.

She smiled faintly, her soft mouth softening further, warmth radiating out from her as always. He only noticed the hint of reserve because it was so uncharacteristic.

"There is something I must say to you." He tensed, and she traced a finger down the line of his jaw, and then over his hand where it lay on the bed between them. "You know that I loved Richard. So very much. When he died, I thought…" She gave the slightest shrug. "I thought, well, that is all for me. I have had more love than anyone can ask in life, just in that short time with him, and I do not need more of it. I was filled up, like when you eat so much that another bite is impossible. You know?"

He watched her fingers move softly across his wrist, and bit his tongue against asking her why she had woken him in the night to tell him about her love for another man. He could hear the hint of tears in her voice, and he was doing his best not to hate a ghost for making her sad.

"I knew I would not love again in that way," she continued. "I was very sure. It cannot be possible. But then...you came. You." He held his breath and looked up at her. She seemed to glow in the candlelight, perfect blue eyes fixed on him in absolute sincerity. "I am falling in love with you. No – already I have fallen." She gave the barest shake of her head, wonder and disbelief together in her face. Her lips moved in a tremulous smile. "I know love, you understand? And I am in it, with you. I love you very much, Mason."

Before he could say anything, she pulled her hand away and shifted her weight just barely. It called his attention to the paper she had put beside her, lower down on the bed. He lifted his head to see it, and felt his heart drop out of his body. It was the forgotten sketch of her friend Helen, playing the coquette whore to radical revolutionaries.

Marie-Anne tented a hand over the page, her fingertips barely touching the surface as she looked at it and spoke very calmly, very gently.

"If you hurt my friend, I will never speak to you again." She blinked, and there were tears there. It was not a ghost that made her sad. It was him. "It will break my heart to do it, and I will not hesitate for an instant. Even with this very great love for you inside me. Do you understand?"

He was afraid to move. One wrong word could blow everything apart, and for once there was no thrill in the danger of it. At least a few times in his life, he'd felt as miserable as this – but it had been a very long time ago, and it had never come with quite the same flavor of despair.

"I understand."

And he did. He knew nothing about her friendship with Helen or why harming her reputation should be more unforgivable than anything else, but he knew she meant it. She meant all of it, including the miraculous fact that she loved him.

Marie-Anne nodded once, then blinked rapidly to clear the tears from her eyes.

"Burn it," he said. "Put the candle to it. Or rip it to pieces."

She made a sound like laughter, but there was no humor in it. "Oh yes, and I will break your fingers too? You can always make another. I cannot stop you."

"You have stopped me. I'm stopped. Right now, no more, never again. One word from you, that's all it took." She didn't answer, and still didn't look at him. "I wasn't going to publish it. I forgot it was even there."

She grimaced and looked across the room to where his traveling case was open. There were neat piles of things she'd pulled out of it to get at the false bottom where he kept his sketches. The folder that held other drawings he'd put far away and forgotten was open on the desk. Careless idiot that he was, he'd told her weeks ago that she was welcome to look at any of his work. She knew where he kept it.

"I wanted to put together all of your best work. So I dug very deep, as you see." She took a breath, looking at the open case thoughtfully. "Now I am wondering where are the other things you do not wish me to see, and how many they are."

He took her hand, glad that she let him. "I'm not trying to hide anything from you. Not that, or anything else. There's plenty I'd prefer you don't see, but it's…just details. From before. Nothing now."

She looked at him a very long time, like she would be able to see any lies on him. He fought against the urge to put on his most innocent face, that guileless look he'd perfected as a boy. That look would be a lie, and he wasn't lying. It was strange and wonderful and terrifying, to let someone see who he really was, with no pretending. To think that she loved who he really was.

Finally her expression lightened a little, the unmistakable air of decision and her usual determination to move on to happier topics.

"Well, you are hiding your very great talent from the world. And you hide this naked Frenchwoman in your room every night."

That made him smile and bring her hand to his mouth for a kiss. "I know how you feel about the talent, but I thought you approved of the Frenchwoman."

She didn't give an answering smile, or lean down to kiss him. Instead she fixed her eyes on his hand where it held hers.

"I am so sorry I must be serious again," she said. Her lashes lowered, and he saw something on her face that was almost shame. "But I have been reminded of my friend, and I cannot pretend to myself anymore. I think we must stop this, you and I." She disregarded his sound of protest, and only gave a sigh. "You do not understand this world, so I must explain. Hélène and her husband, they have used their reputation to tell all of their acquaintance that I am respectable. Stephen most of all – Lord Summerdale, he is so spotless and so respected that if he says someone is clean then everyone must believe.

267

So he has told them I am clean – *et voilà*."

He could feel her holding herself back from him, how she wanted to lean down and stretch her body against his, but resisted. It was a little invisible barrier between them, put there by someone else's idea of what was right and wrong. She took a breath and continued.

"If we are discovered, you and I, then I am a terrible harlot again. I do not mind for me, but it is Hélène who will be treated badly. To have a friend like me, who behaves so, it reflects onto her and reminds everyone of her own past. They can be so cruel. I have been very selfish, not to think of this. But now I do think of it, and the risk is too great. So I think we must stop."

Her fingertip moved idly over the sheet and he watched it, the half-moon at the base of the nail bed, the curve of her palm. He had memorized the geometry of this woman – her nails, her hands, her navel, the arc of her cheek. The angles of her were in everything he saw, awake and asleep. She had become the shape of his world.

"If we were married," he heard himself say, "It wouldn't be improper."

He felt her shrug. "No, it would be… Oh."

The silence was horrible. Her tiny caress had stopped, and he stared at her still fingers poised near his hand.

"I'm sorry to be so serious myself," he said. "But you didn't give me a chance to say I'm in love with you too."

"Oh."

He waited. It was a very specific kind of hell. One in which he began to wonder how one would go about cutting out his own tongue or, even more tortuous, if there were any bits of Aloysius St. James' poetry that might be of some use in this situation. If she didn't answer soon, he'd start turning purple. He stayed frozen, wondering just who the hell he thought he was, to say such a thing, until she put a hand to his chin and turned his face up to her.

"It is true? You love me?"

"From the first moment you called me a cad," he confirmed. "No, sooner than that. From the moment you said kangaroo."

"Oh, I am *very* glad," she said with great earnestness. Relief rolled through him as her most dazzling smile burst onto her face. "It is so obvious to say, I know. But it is all I can think. You have made me simpleminded. You love me."

"I love you." Her smile grew impossibly, and his matched it. It felt so good to say. It must be joy, this thing unfurling in his chest. "And you love me."

She nodded vigorously, sending a sheaf of her hair forward over her shoulder and into his face. He pushed it out of his eyes and mouth while she fussed and laughed and apologized. When he emerged from the mass, she pulled it back and raked her fingers through it. She stopped in the midst of gathering the golden strands with an arrested look on her face. The smile was fading.

"What?"

"To be married." She bit her lip. "I don't... You will think it strange, maybe, but this is something I have not been wanting."

That very effectively killed his smile, too. What a way to say no. Maybe it was politeness that made her so clumsy with the words.

"Not strange," he mumbled, wishing to God he wasn't naked beneath this sheet, or that they were in her room and not his, so that he could say good night and leave. Walk into the sea. That sounded like a terrific plan. How far to the sea from here?

"Oh! Oh no!" Her hands were fluttering an inch from his chest, fanning him. "I did not mean *you*. Oh please, Mason, I said you made my mind simple. Now you see how simple!"

She pressed her cool fingers against the skin at the base of his throat, like she could stop the flush in its tracks. He reached up and caught her hands, held them flat against his heart. It beat hard against her palms, but he supposed he was far past the point of hiding anything of what he felt for her.

"I meant – I only meant that I thought of myself as Richard's wife and…" It would probably haunt him his whole life, the way she looked at him with such kindness. "When there was no more chance to be married to him, I stopped thinking of being married. To anyone."

He let his hands slide away from hers. "It doesn't matter." He reached across to the far side of the bed, where his shirt had fallen earlier in the night. He sat up and pulled it over his head. "Really. It was just a thought."

A rash thought. An impulsive thought. A thought that became, at the moment he said it, exactly what he wanted. Even though he had no business thinking it or wanting it, it was there now. Damn it.

He got up to retrieve his trousers from where they lay on the floor, and hastily buttoned them over his nakedness. At the desk, he began stacking the pages she had set out, trying to preserve the order she had made before closing them up in folders. He'd want to know, later, which ones she'd grouped together as her favorites. He could torture himself with it.

"Why do you say it does not matter?" she asked from somewhere behind him. "I think it matters very much or you would not put on clothes in the middle of the night."

He couldn't fault her logic, and he didn't feel like explaining that it was hard to feel dignified without trousers on. He just carried the folders to the traveling case and began replacing the few items that she'd taken out, that were only there to conceal the false bottom. "You meant it, though. That we have to stop." He set a book that he'd never read in the corner of the case. "Seems like clothes are a good idea."

At first he thought the rustling he heard was her putting on her dressing gown, until he remembered she hadn't been wearing it tonight. He turned to see her pulling on his jacket over her chemise. As though in any possible world, that made her *less* tempting.

"I will not be like these so proper ladies who say 'Oh it does not matter' and then bite my tongue until it bleeds," she declared with a mutinous scowl. "Say to me what you are thinking."

"For God's sake, Marie-Anne, you wake me in the dead of night and tell me you love me, then threaten never to speak to me again, then say we can't be together. And I told you I love you and proposed *marriage* – which I promise you was nowhere in my plans for the evening – and you say no." He closed the lid to the case with a little too much force, and dropped his voice to a whisper for fear he'd shout and wake the household. "It's a lot for one night, and now you're standing there looking irresistible but we're not going to do anything about it, and you're asking me what I'm *thinking*? Give me a goddamn minute to think, that's what I'm thinking."

Her scowl deepened. She wanted to argue more, it was plain to see, but she only clamped her jaw tight shut and kept her arms folded across her chest. After a while she gave a resentful little huff. Poor long-suffering Marie-Anne, who had suffered for all of thirty seconds so far.

"I hope it doesn't bleed," he said. She looked up at him sharply. "Your tongue."

She glared for a moment. But then she took a deep breath and gave a terse nod at him, an acknowledgement. With stilted movements, she took off his jacket and folded it carefully over the desk chair. He still wanted to shout, but he held his breath as she passed him on her way to the panel that led to her room. He wondered if she'd ever come through it again.

When she reached the wall, she paused. "I did not say no." She looked over her shoulder at him. "Maybe I need a… a *goddamn* minute to think, too."

She opened the panel and stepped through. He didn't watch as she closed it behind her. He looked at the bed instead. The empty, rapidly cooling bed.

He hurried to the wall and spoke to the place where she'd disappeared.

"You can have more than one minute. You can have however many you need." There was nothing but silence. She was probably already in her own bed. "Marie-Anne?"

He leaned against the wall, his ear to the crack, because he was a lovesick ass. It was a good thing, too, because after a minute he heard her soft, "I will think, *mon amour.* I will. Good night."

Chapter Seventeen

Marie-Anne did think. She thought all night and did not sleep. Why had she never imagined that she would fall in love again, and when had her mind decided that there was no such thing as marriage for her unless it was with Richard?

She thought about what it would mean to marry Mason. She thought about how she could not lie to her friends about how he made his money, and wondered if he would quit it to do something else. Would he want to come to Bartle and, if not, would she want to leave it? She thought about how long the little inheritance from her uncle might sustain both of them, and about whether or not it really mattered – and how much – that he was so much younger than she was. She thought until her head ached.

The sun was beginning to rise and she was finally drifting off to sleep when she had the thought that it was too impulsive to marry someone she had known for barely two months. But that forced her to think about how she had agreed to marry Richard only two weeks after she had met him. She was not hesitant by nature, or indecisive.

Yet here she was hesitating, lying awake in indecision. Oh, love was very troublesome.

Sleep only came at last when she took refuge in thinking about the placid life of Bartle, and of the smell that came from the bakery on Saturdays when Mr. Higgins kept the ovens going past mid-morning. It was a delight to dream about fresh butter melting into hot bread, but it made her unusually bad-tempered when she finally woke. It was late. She was no closer to knowing what to do about Mason, and now she had missed breakfast too.

"Lucy, will you tell the cook that I will pray the rosary for him if he will send up bread toasted with very much butter?"

"I don't think it will move him, madame," replied the maid. "He don't hold with popish manners, beggin' your pardon. But I'll tell him it's you who wants it and he'll send up as much as you can eat, see if he don't."

"One compliment to his custard tart and he is devoted to me, the darling man." She put a hand over her eyes, feeling a headache coming on. "I want to be very rude today, and hide here with bread and tea."

Lucy was very happy to aid her in this endeavor, explaining that the other guests had gone on a ramble to see the ruins of a nearby abbey – a real one – and would not return for hours. This would allow Marie-Anne to hide until the evening meal, which suited her very well. She spent the afternoon chewing steadily through a stack of toasted bread slices until she nearly made herself sick with it. Then she added jam for variety. It was proving to be very difficult to gather her thoughts, so she just let them float by. By the time the maid returned to help her dress for dinner, the only thing she knew for sure was that she still loved Mason, and that she wanted him to have a different and better life than this one he was living – even if she could not quite see where she fit into it.

When she came downstairs for dinner, he was talking with the insufferable Poetess in a corner of the drawing room. The searching way he looked at Marie-Anne was too obvious, but only Phyllida seemed to notice. She came to stand beside Marie-Anne, who was studiously avoiding Mason's eyes, and tell her all about the lovely long walk they'd taken today.

Amy talked about it too. She was seated next to Marie-Anne during the meal and, after observing that Marie-Anne looked rather pale, made everything a little worse by recounting how The Poetess had rhapsodized over the ruins and how much Mason had enjoyed her effusive descriptions of the scene.

"He kept encouraging her," Amy said low while the soup was served. "I think he is quite entertained by how very absurd – Marie-Anne?" She looked worried. "Whatever did I say? I thought it would amuse you, but you look as though you would like to drown me in the consommé."

Marie-Anne was in fact trying to decide between Mason and The Poetess as drowning victims, which she knew was very stupid. Mason loved her. He did not even like The Poetess. She was being very irrational, but somehow she could not stop herself. "No, it is only that I ate too much butter and jam today," she said to Amy. "My delicate digestion, you know."

Amy looked askance as Marie-Anne took several healthy swallows of wine, but did not challenge this blatant falsehood. "I do hope it's not the beginning of an illness, or anything that would interfere with our visit to London. Dahlia is depending on us, and she has promised that Mama will not be there so it will be a perfectly pleasant afternoon."

Marie-Anne had half-forgotten that they were to spend a day with Dahlia and her dressmaker in London. It sounded exhausting, but the planned visit was in a few days when hopefully she would be feeling her usual, sociable self. And how very kind of the girls, to ensure that Marie-Anne would not have to encounter their mother again. Lady Shipley, as Amy reported it, had been "entirely shocked" to learn of the events that had resulted in Amy's sudden engagement to Mr. St. James, but neither parent had objected to the match. Now that they had a daughter in line to become a duchess, they weren't very likely to object to anything. What a blessed relief.

When the meal was over, Marie-Anne decided she could not endure an evening in the drawing room, playing cards and attempting conversation while Mason sent her questioning looks. And she could hardly make a decision about marriage while having passionate fantasies of stuffing a stocking in The Poetess' mouth. She pleaded a headache, which was not entirely fiction, and ran back to her room.

It wanted a good night of sleep for everything to seem clearer, that was all. If only she could fall asleep instead of playing over the previous night's conversation with Mason. She had never really seen him angry before, and to her surprise she got a bit of a belated thrill, thinking about it. He did not bluster and intimidate like so many men. But he *was* very commanding. It reminded her of the time when he had bent her over the desk, then gleefully pounded into her and made her scream with pleasure. That had been wonderful.

Oh, really. Now she was flushed and lustful, and not thinking about serious things as she was supposed to be. She exasperated herself.

Almost as though he knew where her mind was, a very soft tapping came at the wall. It took a moment for her to recognize what it was but when she did, she was caught between excitement and annoyance.

"Leave me alone," she said to the ceiling, knowing he could not hear her from this distance. She did not want to get out of bed despite the lascivious thoughts that had recently come to her. "Go away, *mon amour*. I really must think without you."

There was a long silence, during which she thought very affectionately of the freckles on his forehead. The soft tap came again.

She was out of bed and pulling open the panel on her side before she even thought. Thankfully, she stopped herself before lifting the latch and shoving open panel on his side. She just spat words at the barely visible seam in the wall. "Oh, what is it, you said I could have many minutes to think, I am trying to sleep, what do you *want?*"

Perhaps it was better sometimes to bite one's tongue, even if it bled. He was probably bewildered at her vehemence. She was certain she would be bewildered at it too, later. Right now she didn't have time for bewilderment, she was too busy being annoyed.

"I just wanted to give this to you," came his

whisper. A corner of paper poked through the seam, but it was too narrow to allow more than that. "I didn't want to trust it to a servant."

She frowned at it for a moment, debating. It was probably a drawing. Something beautiful and surprising and perfect, like all the art he made, and it would melt her completely. This was a very unfair thing to do. But curiosity got the better of her, as it always did, so she fortified herself with visions of him listening intently as The Poetess droned on, and lifted the latch. She only opened the panel a bare inch. Enough to see a sliver of his very dear face. The paper was folded into an envelope.

She opened it and found the tiny torn pieces of the odious sketch of Helen. He had ripped it to bits.

"Thank you." She said it begrudgingly even though she was inexplicably moved by the gesture. It was only right he should destroy it, after all.

He was looking at her hopefully, waiting. She scowled at him and closed the panel swiftly. Even after she latched it, she could still hear him waiting on the other side.

"And stop flirting with the horrible poetess," she hissed at the wall.

"I'm not flirting!" He was incredulous. After a little silence, he asked with an unmistakable note of hope, "Are you jealous?"

"I hate this stupid panel!" she cried, because it seemed like an excellent rejoinder. "I would like to find the one who made it and scratch his eyes out, *espèce de connard!*" Then she hastily secured it shut on her side, flung herself into her bed, and commenced weeping like a complete idiot.

It all made perfect sense when she woke in the

morning to find her monthly courses had begun in the night. Of course.

No wonder she couldn't think. No wonder that she was so irrationally angry and petulant, an ogre shouting at his sweet, hopeful face. Poor Mason!

The sun was barely up and she had time before the maid came, but she didn't know how early a servant might come to Mason's room. She put her ear to the panel to listen and after many minutes of hearing only a deep silence, she opened it just a crack. He was sitting up in the bed, looking at the exact place in the wall where she appeared. Dear man, he was probably sitting there all night.

"No, do not get up," she said, putting up a staying hand. "I am here for just a moment, to tell you that I am sorry to be disagreeable. I am only a little unwell, but it will pass, you understand? And then we will talk."

He looked alarmed. "Unwell? What do you mean?"

There was a bit of panic in his face. He probably worried she was pregnant, which almost made her laugh even though there was nothing humorous about it. How to tell him what it was? She didn't know whether he'd understand it if she was vulgar and told him *the English have landed*, so she hoped he could get the general idea from less explicit words.

She settled on saying, "It is only what happens every month." Thank heaven, he understood that. She could tell by the slight mortification. "I just – I do not want you to take my silence for an answer."

"Right."

The dark flush started creeping up his neck, which made her irrationally angry again. Or perhaps it was only that she wanted to be back in bed. Alone. She quickly bid him a good day and retreated, only to hear him call softly after her. "Is there anything I can do? To help, I mean?"

"Just leave me alone," she sighed. "I am sorry, it is inconvenient this happens now. We will talk when I am well."

She latched the panel and then threw herself back into the bed. She always felt most wretched on the first day, so she decided the best thing to do was just stay beneath the coverlet until she felt like moving again. Sweet man, asking if he could help. She supposed it meant something, that she had not hesitated to tell him. Like they were already an old married couple.

༄

In the afternoon Joyce entered with the maid, who carried a tray. Marie-Anne sat up hopefully.

"Is that cake?"

"Yes, and cook has made a creditable attempt at Bath buns. Thank you, Lucy, I'll pour," said Joyce as the maid set the tray down carefully. Once she was gone, Joyce continued in a confidential tone. "Mr. Mason found his way to the kitchen, if you can believe it, and was trying to persuade the cook to make any number of cakes for you. But I daresay I know your tastes better than either of them, so here are the buns and some sweet chocolate to drink with them."

"Joyce, if you were not married, I would make passionate love to you," declared Marie-Anne through a mouthful of bun. It was perfect.

"Mm, Charlotte would have something to say about that." She uncovered a dish of absolutely beautiful clotted cream and then began pouring steaming chocolate into a cup. "But then it's often difficult to have a care for convention – or discretion – when one is indulging a passion, isn't it, my dear."

She gave a subtle look toward the panel in the wall as she handed the cup to Marie-Anne.

"Oh." Marie-Anne felt rather like a child who'd been caught out, clutching her sugary bun and beginning to blush.

"I must say – purely as a matter of conjecture, of course – that I believe Lucy would perjure herself in defending you against the suspicions of the laundress with her last breath. She is very fond of you." She patted Marie-Anne's hand reassuringly. "And I am silent as the sphinx. Or I mean to say I would be, if there were anything to tell. Which of course there is not. I do hope you'll feel yourself again soon. Enjoy the cake, dear."

She closed the door gently behind her. It was a very friendly warning to be more careful, given with great kindness, and confirming to Marie-Anne that she was right to have told Mason they must stop. To which he'd replied that there would be no problem if they were married. She sipped at the chocolate and wondered if he had only said it to keep her in his bed.

Well, so what if he had? He did not take the words back. And she wanted to be with him in the bed and out of it, too. Maybe she even wanted children. Oh, to be a mother would be such a wonderful, unexpected delight. The vision of a sweet little red-haired baby rose up in her mind and, as it caused her to actually coo aloud to her chocolate, she quickly thrust the thought away. It was entirely too overwhelming. One could not make a rational decision when faced with the prospect of a redheaded baby. She was only human.

Marie-Anne was much more herself the next day and though she was fairly certain of her answer, still she could not quite commit to it. It did not seem strange anymore, to imagine herself as his wife. She might have talked to him if she could have found a moment alone with him. But it proved impossible all day, and she did not want to risk using the secret door between their rooms any more.

The following day, she was determined to find a moment of privacy to speak with him. She would say yes. She was sure she would, but only after she could ask him a few very simple questions about his plans for his future. How very responsible of her! Her reputation for recklessness would suffer quite a blow when she told Helen about this.

Just as she began looking for Mason, the butler approached her. "Mr. Meeks to see you, madame," he said in hushed tones. "I've taken the liberty of putting him in library again."

"Again?" She blinked at him.

They were only a few steps from the library, which gave her very little time to wonder who this Meeks person was before the door opened and the square-faced secretary to Lord Summerdale was greeting her. She'd completely forgotten him.

"I hope I do not inconvenience you by coming unannounced," he said. "But in the interest of both expediency and discretion, we deemed it best that I should come in person immediately."

This sounded very ominous. Oh, she did not like

this at all.

"It is not inconvenient for me, Mr. Meeks, but I will come to London in only two days for a visit. I could have saved you the trouble."

"No trouble at all, I assure you. Acting with haste in this matter is far more important." He gestured to a chair and she lowered herself into it, hoping this was only courtesy and not an indication that she should sit down for what he had to say. "First I must ask, madame, if there is perhaps anything further about the character of Mr. Mason – or shall I say, the man who calls himself by that name – well, any further troubling facts you may have discovered about him?"

"No." She said it so quickly that anyone could tell it was a lie. But why should she tell this secretary about Mason's gossip pamphlets? It could not matter.

"Anything you might tell me will of course be held in strictest confidence." He waited, but she only bit her lip and kept her silence. "Yes. Well. My own investigations have continued, and I have come here to tell you what we have learned."

"We? Who is this we?"

"I beg your pardon, madame, I should have said that I am here at the request of Lord Summerdale. Being uncertain as to the nature of your present acquaintance with Mr. Mason, he thought it best to proceed with some delicacy."

All these careful words made her frown at him. "What is this you are saying, that Stephen gave instruction for you to tell me something?"

"Indeed, madame. In the normal course of things, Lord Summerdale would simply take action as he sees fit. But in this instance, he should like to know your feelings on the matter before he acts publicly in any way."

She clutched her hands together and took a breath, stealing herself. "Then you must tell me what this matter is. It is to do with Mr. Mason?"

"Yes. You already know the suspicions about his timber business. I must tell you that they are no longer suspicions, but have been confirmed as fact. There is no timber business. There would also appear to be no Mr. Mason."

The falseness of his business was not new to her, so she let her breath out in an exasperated sigh. "But of course there *is* a Mr. Mason. He is here in this house."

"He calls himself Mr. Spencer Mason, but it is not his name. In New York, it would seem he went by the name of Mr. Mason Hawes. When he was not Mason Hawes, he was Mason Hagman, or Samuel Irby Mason, or Mason Hardin, or in one memorable instance, a Mr. Beauregard Shearn."

She could not seem to look away from his mouth as he dropped this string of absurd names. "I see."

"In Boston, we believe he called himself Mason Fawcett for a time, and Bartholomew Mason. In Philadelphia, it was Mason Hancock and Clover-"

"Please stop." She wanted to stand. She thought it might be very good to pace energetically about the room. But her legs felt as if they were made of lead, and she could think of nothing more to say than just, "Stop."

He did. But after a long moment, he continued. "It is possible there are more names he has used, in other cities, but it is doubtful we will ever uncover his true identity. Furthermore, there can no longer be any doubt that he has a habit of engaging in criminal enterprise."

"When?" she asked. He had said he'd made political drawings in New York. That was why he had run to London – because he had made powerful men angry, not because he was a criminal. "It is long ago, I think, this crime he commits."

"We cannot be sure of that, madame. Lord Summerdale does not entirely trust the motives of the men from New York who have provided much of this information. I pass along to you only those facts about which we have little or no doubt." Just as she began to feel a little relieved, he spoke again. "But it must be said that his continued efforts to persuade several gentlemen to give their money to him under the guise of investment–"

"He has taken their money?"

The secretary seemed startled. Probably he did not expect her to care about the particulars, asking so many questions and challenging him. She was supposed to swoon and call Mason infamous and let the men decide what should be done while she smelled salts and fluttered in a corner. How very bad of Stephen, not to warn this secretary about her.

He recovered his aplomb, though. "As yet, it is difficult to know with any certainty. But it was less than a month ago that he invited the Duke of Ravenclyffe to invest. In the last week, Ravenclyffe has persuaded several peers to join him in the investment and he is even now preparing to hand over a very large sum. All the gentlemen are."

"How large?"

"Just among those few gentlemen who are willing to confide the sum to Lord Summerdale, Mr. Mason can expect twelve thousand pounds."

Marie-Anne, who had been expecting to hear nothing greater than one thousand – and even that was an impossibly large number – could only stare at him. It took a very long time for her mind to think past it. When it did, she gradually realized that she should not be so surprised to hear this news. This secretary had told her of this investment scheme before, in this very room. He had mentioned it on his first visit. It was the only reason to look into Mason's background in the first place.

She had ignored it completely. Because she was in love. Well, and because she was distracted by learning about the gossip papers. But mostly because she loved him.

"What will happen to Mr. Mason if..." Her voice died as she remembered his name was not Mr. Mason. She tried to gather her thoughts. What was it this Meeks had said about Stephen acting publicly?

The secretary cleared his throat. "Lord Summerdale has not indicated what actions he might take, except of course to prevent anyone from being defrauded if it comes to that point, as it seems likely to. But as I have said, madame, his immediate concern is for your welfare." He seemed caught between concern and slight embarrassment. "He believes it possible that you may have developed an attachment to Mr. Mason. If that is the case, Lord Summerdale would take pains to act with very great discretion."

He'd run Mason out of town quietly, that's what it meant. So civilized and neat, that was the way of Society – and Stephen's way. Well, not entirely. Marie-Anne remembered with a smile, how he had invited her to break as many hearts as she liked.

"It must be a very loud rumor, my fondness for Mr. Mason, if it is heard all the way in Norway."

"I could not say, madame. Lord Summerdale learned of it upon his return recently, and you can be assured that it is not commonly known–"

"They've returned?" Mr. Meeks nodded, and she rather wanted to shake him. "But why did you not tell me! They were not to be back for another month! And why does he send you here and not come himself to say these things?"

"They have only just arrived in London. Upon learning of this...situation, Lord Summerdale wished above all to act with the utmost discretion. He has shared this information with no one but myself, and now you. He has not come himself so as not to arouse Lady Summerdale's curiosity, as she would naturally wish to know why he must speak to you so urgently."

"Oh, well!" This made her equal parts angry and affectionate. "You may tell him from me that he can tell my secrets to his wife. I would tell her myself if I knew she was in the country!"

She was too busy being happy she would soon see Helen to notice the expectant look Mr. Meeks gave her. After a moment, he cleared his throat again.

"I shall be happy to convey that message to him, madame. As Lord Summerdale greatly values your opinion in the other matter, he eagerly awaits any word you might care to send as regards Mr. Mason's character."

Marie-Anne had no ready response. It was so unexpected that Stephen wanted her opinion – especially when all she wanted was *his* opinion. How could she possibly think clearly about Mason?

Minutes ago she had been preparing to accept his marriage proposal. Minutes ago, she had thought he was not a criminal – and that his name was Mason.

Oh, men were very disappointing.

"You must tell him that I am still making my opinion," she said as she stood up. "And when it is ready, I will deliver it myself – straight to his door in London. They are in London, yes?"

"At present, yes. I believe they will remove to the country in a week's time."

"I will be there long before that. You must tell them so."

She thanked him for coming and then chose a comfortable chair in an isolated corner of the library where she could sort her thoughts. It did not take terribly long, so when Mason entered not long after, she was as ready as she could hope to be.

Chapter Eighteen

"Amy was looking for you," he said when he saw her rise from the chair. "Are you hiding, or should I go tell her where to find you?"

He looked so very respectable in his well-made clothes, with his shoes polished to a high shine and not a hair out of place – yet still, somehow, possessing an air of lightly disheveled elegance. She wondered how long he had studied the men he meant to emulate before he'd perfected their look. Not long at all, she imagined, since he had a lifetime of experience at it.

He crinkled his freckled brow at her. "Marie-Anne?"

She considered declaring him a cad once more, or a terrible fraud, in that flippant way she employed so often. But she must be even more in love than she'd realized, if she did not feel like being the least bit flippant.

"No, I do not want to talk with her. I want to talk with you."

He closed the door behind him, his pleasant look dissolving into uncertainty and faint anxiety. She could see he held his breath. He thought she would give him her answer, and was bracing himself for rejection. The familiar impulse came to her – to go to him, cross the carpet in a few steps to be within touching distance so she might soothe him. But she stayed where she was.

"First I must ask you what I should call you," she finally said. "What is your name?"

"My name?" He seemed genuinely confused by the question. She only looked at him expectantly until he answered. "What do you mean? Why would you call me anything other than Mason?"

"Because perhaps you are really Clayton or Samuel or… oh, what is the ridiculous one – Bartholomew."

He was motionless, staring at her. It felt like a very long time until he took a deep breath and began, "Marie-Anne, just–"

"No, it was Beauregard! This is the most absurd, you look nothing like a Beauregard." She was surprised to find that she was not angry at him, really. It all seemed like a game. A very bad game that she did not want to play. "But you do not look like a liar, either. It is like you said, the very innocent face you have. It serves you well in this business you do."

He had taken a step toward her but stopped in his tracks. She could see his mind working, which was new. He was normally so very good at hiding whatever calculations went on behind his eyes. But now he was not calculating, he was only trying to understand what was happening.

"Is it Summerdale?" he asked. "Is that who told you all these names?"

"What does it matter? I know these names now. It is very inconvenient, to think I might want to be Mrs. Mason and then learn there is no Mr. Mason. I do not want to be Mrs. Bartholomew Beauregard, or whatever name you will think of next." Her voice was rising. Very well, she was a little angry. "That is what you do, *non*? You must make a new name when it is time to run away with the money. All the money these wealthy men will give you for a business that does not exist."

He closed his eyes briefly. "Shit."

"Yes, it is shit," she agreed. "It is very much shit."

"Will you let me explain?" he asked, and then plowed on without waiting for her to answer. "I wasn't going to take their money. It was never supposed to go that far, it was just something I said months ago to some idiot and now he won't shut up about the brilliant American investment scheme. And now other people are talking about it—"

"Because you told Ravenclyffe. That was not months ago."

His lips pressed together, his eyes fixed on her hands where she clutched them together before her. There was no sign of the purple flush. She wondered what that meant. Probably, she realized with a sinking sensation, it meant that he was not ashamed.

"What do you want me to say?" he asked her quietly.

More than anything the secretary had told her about him, this made her want to weep. "Whatever I want to hear, that is what you will say? There is no truth for you, there is only what gets you what you want."

"Fine, the truth." He was a little angry too. "You've known for weeks I'm a fake. And you know where I came from. What do you think my first instinct was, when I found all these superior gentlemen with more money than sense? It's what I *know*. I hadn't planned on using it unless I had to. In case the honest work dries up, there has to be something else. I do it without even thinking. It's like a bad habit."

She gave an incredulous laugh. "A bad habit! Yes, it is a very bad habit, to steal thousands of pounds."

"Well obviously I haven't managed to habitually get that kind of money, have I? And I haven't taken it now even when they're trying to give it to me. No, I've been drawing little pictures instead of taking their money – and I haven't hidden *that* from you. I told you what I am. You just heard what you wanted to hear."

It was true. She had deceived herself a little. He had told her that he could be doing things much worse than the gossip papers. When she'd wondered what else he had tried to keep hidden, he had said – what? That there were only harmless things which he preferred she did not see, from before. Just details, he had called it. Such easy audacity, to think of stealing thousands of pounds as just a detail.

It didn't matter, though. She didn't really care about the money or the stealing. She had already decided that. She knew very well what wicked, malicious men were like, and he was not that. He only did not know a different way to be.

She felt like she could not breathe in the sudden quiet after so many heavy words. It was horrible, that they were such friends and that she loved him so much, and yet there was this sudden distance and silence between them.

"Tell me your true name."

Now the purple came up his throat, swift and vivid. It caused a terrible little twist of her heart to see it.

"Mason is all I know. It's either the name my mother gave me before she died or it was my father's name. Or maybe my uncle just gave it to me. I guess I could have taken his name when I left, but I never wanted to. So I'm just Mason. It's as true a name as I'll ever have." He moved his eyes over her, the same look as he gave to the oil paintings at the exhibition – like he was memorizing her, taking in every stroke and every line. "I'm a fool, aren't I? Thinking I could marry you when I don't even have a name. But I thought... I thought I'd like to just stop. Just be me. With you."

Oh, he had stumbled onto it – the exact thing she wanted to hear. But there was a reason why she had hesitated, why she had not immediately said yes to him, even if she had not understood it until now.

"I would like that too. But you cannot continue this way. You call them honest work, the pamphlets, but for me they mean I must lie to my friends. This cannot be your work if we are together. Over and over, to turn around and find some new lie you have invented – I will not live like this. And *you* should not live like this." She took a step toward him, to make him hear her, to make him look at her and understand. "You are meant to be a true artist. To study with masters, like I have said. Why do you turn from it? This is the honest life you must make."

It was so obvious to her, but he looked at her like she had suggested something unthinkable. She could feel the stubbornness coming into her face. He would act like he always did – like this idea was so impossible and his talent was so small and she was so silly to think this way.

Already he was giving her that skeptical look. "It's just that easy, is it?"

"Who has said easy? It will not be easy. It will be very hard and it is even possible you will fail." She dismissed that with a wave of her hand. "You will *not* fail, but it is possible. This way you live now, always running and always lying – that is the failure. Do you not see, *mon amour*? You are in the wrong life."

He was looking away from her, his mouth tight and his jaw clenched. She prepared herself for more of his disputing, more denials that he could not be what she knew he was supposed to be. But when he finally answered, he did not say any of that. He took a deep breath and asked, "What if I don't want to? What if I just got some other kind of work – I don't know, driving a carriage or something? As long as it's safe and respectable, would that be enough?"

Her mouth dropped open in mild disbelief. She walked to him and gave a little push to his shoulder. "What is this? I am supposed to think you make these pages and pages of beautiful things because you want to hide them? I see your face when you show them to me. I do not believe you if you say you do not want it."

His face was full of caution and reserve, and she hated it. She had not fallen in love with some careful, sensible man. She had fallen in love with Mason, who said risqué things to make her laugh and never bowed and drew pornographic flowers and pulled her into a hidden niche so he could have his way with her while genteel ladies played whist in the next room.

"You should not be in this small and shabby life," she insisted. "There is very much more in you."

He let out a scoffing breath. "You're telling me to get out of my small life? You?"

"Yes, me." She scowled. "Why should it not be me?"

"What have you been planning to do with *your* life, Marie-Anne? Same as you've done for years, I bet. Same as you'll want to do after this. Hide away in your village."

"I like my village!"

She meant it, but even to her own ears it sounded like a thoughtless reflex, a child's defensive response. He was looking at her differently, like she had said something very stupid and he was determined to set her straight.

"You listen to me, now. You lived your whole life in adventure until Richard died. Learning English as a child so you could come here, and when that plan was dashed, you took yourself to Paris. Even there you made the best of it, and when some wealthy English lord invited you to run away with him, you did." He looked at her like he could not believe she'd called his own life small. "Now you just sit still in your little village for years. Is that who you're meant to be?"

"I am very happy in my little life." It came out mechanically, like she had said it a hundred times to herself, because she had. She had always believed it.

"Right." His voice was heavy with irony. "You're happy."

There was a horrible, pressing feeling in her chest.

She did not like this, any of it. They were not supposed to be talking about her. He was supposed to say he loved her enough to change everything, to chase a dream and hope for more. He was not supposed to point at the smallness of her own life, and make her see how she had kept it small on purpose.

She was still looking for words when the door to the library opened. She took a step away from Mason to see that it was Amy, who looked startled to find them both there with such serious looks. Joyce was behind her, but lingered just outside the door.

"Marie-Anne, there you are." Amy hovered at the threshold, obviously uncertain of her welcome. "I'm so sorry to intrude. Have you spoken with Phyllida today?"

"No," she said faintly, suddenly overcome with a terrible sadness. These fresh, young Shipley girls and their romances – how well it had all worked out for them. Why could it not be as easy for her?

"It's only that after luncheon, I went to our room and found some of her belongings are gone. It looks as if she's packed a bag, but no one has seen her leave. No one has seen her at all since breakfast."

"She is not with her hermit?"

Joyce's gently exasperated voice filtered in from the corridor. "We have no hermit, dearest!"

"Lady Huntingdon believes it is Mr. Hill who often comes to the hermit's cottage. He is a farmer."

"Aha!" Marie-Anne could not resist a little burst of triumph. "I said he was a farmer! And so did Mason, didn't you?"

She glanced to see him give a nod, but he did not speak. He was looking at her in that way again, like she was framed in a gallery and he must drink in every detail before it was time to leave.

"Regardless of who he is, Phyllie isn't there." Amy chewed her lip. "We argued and she *did* threaten to go back to London. I worry she might have taken herself there, but I can't imagine how."

Normally Marie-Anne would have asked what they'd argued about, purely for the entertainment. Now, she did not care at all. She wanted them to go away, all of them, and take all of their silly problems and bad poetry and questionable philosophy – and hermits and farmers and manners and money and all their utter nonsense with them. And for once she did not wish she could run to Bartle and be left in peace there. She only wanted to be left with Mason.

"I am sure she will appear," she said to Amy, not bothering to hide her impatience. "I need only two minutes, and then I will help you to look."

"Oh, of course! Pardon me, I'll go now." Amy hastily backed out of the room.

But when she was left alone with Mason again, she found she did not know what to say. She only looked at his hands where they hung at his sides. They did not look how she imagined an artist's hands should look – not fine-boned and elegant and smooth. Mason's hands were large and a little rough, the hands of a workman. There were freckles on the back of them, and tiny golden hairs.

She picked one up and lifted it to her mouth to press a kiss against it. "You are afraid," she whispered to the warm skin beneath her mouth. "Oh, my Mason – will you not find a little courage, to be with me?"

He didn't answer for what felt like an eternity. The pulse in his wrist sped up, and she could feel him turning warmer. "Marie-Anne." She looked up, hopeful, but there was an apology in his face. "I can't be that. I don't know how. Can't you understand?"

She couldn't. Not really. She only understood that he would never leave his old life behind him, as long as he refused to choose a new one. It was too much of a habit, like he said.

She let go his hand and sighed.

"I do not want to be with a thief and a liar. Or with a man who pretends to be a simple working man, and lies to himself about what he is meant to be. Maybe I can learn to do it. It is possible, because I love you very much." She shrugged. "But I do not want it."

She turned and walked to the door. He didn't try to stop her. Even when she hesitated, even when she closed the door and waited on the other side, he didn't say a word to call her back. Moments and choices, he had said. This was a moment, and this is what he chose.

Coward. He was a coward and a cad and a scoundrel, and she loved him anyway.

෴

For an embarrassingly long time, she stood in her room and did nothing but stare at her feet. "I think we may be finished with each other," she said to her toes. Were they finished? Probably they were. It would explain why she felt so wretched.

A memory of her old friend Aurélie came to her, one of the unhappy memories near the end of her life. She had spent her last hours in her sparse little room in the heart of Paris, dying slowly of a sickness that the doctor said her lover had given her. She had been abandoned by a faithless man who had tired of keeping her, but still Aurélie loved him. Until her last breath, she believed he would come to her.

It had been an important lesson for Marie-Anne, to learn that love could bring such great joy and still be so very cruel. "Oh *ma chérie*," her friend had smiled. "It is my greatest hope for you, that you will know what it is to love like this one day." But for Marie-Anne, her greatest hope was not that she would love anyone so completely; it was that she would *be* loved, as well and as much as she deserved, by whomever she gave her heart to.

She could not stay in this room. Without consciously deciding to do it, she found she had begun to gather her things. It was very haphazard, and she stopped her aimless movements to sit on the bed with some stockings and her comb in one hand and her bonnet in the other. She was avoiding looking at the wall with the panel.

Maybe this person she loved was not real. Maybe he had invented it, as he had invented so many versions of himself – a custom-made lover.

What a terrible thought. Oh, this was the worst part of coming out of a love-induced fog: the doubting. She would like to go back to Bartle, and sit in her little cottage with a loaf fresh from the bakery and Helen beside her, neatly listing all the facts and applying reason to the problem as though it were a theoretical matter.

"Oh, I am very stupid!" she said aloud to the room. Helen was in London. Marie-Anne had completely forgotten. She did not have to wish for her friend, she could simply go to her. It would not take two hours to get there, and before she had finished the thought Marie-Anne was ringing for the maid. If she left now, she could be there by nightfall.

As the maid packed a few things, Marie-Anne scribbled a note to Amy explaining that she would send word if silly Phyllida had run to London, and would see the sisters at Dahlia's dressmaker in a few days, as planned.

Dear Joyce looked concerned but hastily instructed the coachman to prepare for the journey at once, and in very short order Marie-Anne was standing in the drive saying a quiet farewell.

"You need only send word that you would like the rest of your baggage sent on, and I shall see to it, my dear. I know how devoted you are to Helen, and the summer is almost at an end."

Marie-Anne nodded, afraid she might burst into tears if she tried to say how grateful she was for her friend's understanding. "I might come back. I do not know," she said. Oh, and now the tears were threatening anyway. She pressed her fingertips under her eyes in an effort to hold them in by force. "I do not seem to know anything anymore."

"I daresay you know a few things with certainty." Joyce patted her arm comfortingly. "Perhaps you should dwell on those, and the certainty will spread."

In the carriage, she tried to do just that. It didn't work at all, because her first thought was how she was certain Mason was a very great artist, and that made her angry at him for not believing in himself – which led her to be angry at everyone who ever bought a gossip pamphlet, and even more angry at his uncle, and the entire state of Kentucky, and quite possibly all of America. After that she spent the journey mired in resentment and misery, which brought her no certainty at all. It only exhausted her.

By the time they reached Summerdale House, the sun was almost down and she felt like she hadn't slept in a month. A surprised Collins met her at the door, and told her that the Summerdales had only just left for a dinner engagement and would not be back for several hours.

"But your room is ready for you, madame, if you would like to retire early. Shall I have a tray sent up?"

She stared at him, mystified. "How can my room be ready? Even me, I did not know I would come here!"

"Lord Summerdale confided to me that you might visit, madame, and instructed me to have a room prepared. I've had Cook make the seedcake you favor in anticipation of your arrival, if you care for some refreshment?"

This orchestrated solicitude proved entirely too much for her. "Oh Collins," she said with a trembling lip. "I am going to be very improper now."

And she put her head on his shoulder and burst into tears. Consummate professional that he was, he showed no surprise or dismay at all. He only patted her shoulder in a fatherly way and offered a handkerchief, while quietly instructing a footman to carry her things up to her room.

Money did not buy everything, but it could provide very great comforts when one's spirits were low. She had hot tea and a hot bath and a hot brick in her bed. A maid brushed her hair and the cook kept sending up more little treats to try to tempt her to eat. Really, Marie-Anne reflected, if she could have one magical wish, it would be to give this level of pampering to everyone when their heart was broken. It should be required by law, in fact.

In the end, she could not keep her eyes open and fell asleep before Helen and Stephen came home. She had very strange dreams that she did not care to interpret, all about flowers as big as her head with petals the color of Mason's hair. Perhaps she should have eaten something. When she woke in the morning, it took her a moment to remember where she was. As soon as she did, she threw on her clothes – the old dress she had worn in Bartle, because it was the kind that did not require a maid's help. She ran down the stairs with slippers on her feet but her hair trailing down her back, because she did not care at all how she looked. She only wanted her friends.

She found them in the dining room, sipping coffee.

"Marie-Anne!" Helen was joyous at the sight of her, and stood from the table to come to her. "You're the best kind of surprise, whatever are you doing here?" Marie-Anne was already embracing her with a kind of fierce desperation. "My goodness, I've never seen you dressed so carelessly. Collins said you arrived just after we left and Stephen pretends he knows nothing but—"

"Oh Hélène, everything is dreadful and I missed you terribly and I will hate Norway forever!" She could feel Helen laughing at this passionate declaration, even as her friend squeezed her with an almost equal enthusiasm. "Has your husband told you nothing about Mason?"

Helen pulled back to look at Marie-Anne's face. "Told me what about Mr. Mason?"

"I did not wish to worry her unduly," Stephen

said. He was standing behind Helen now, a worried look on his face.

Helen made a tart remark about how she was not made of glass, then kept hold of Marie-Anne's hand as they sat down and she demanded to know exactly what was going on. Not eager to explain it all, Marie-Anne was happy for Stephen to recount the facts as he had come to know them – and he seemed to know everything. He even made some remarks that made her think the gossip pamphlets were not a mystery to him. But then of course he would know, he was very clever about learning these things. He could print his own gossip papers and put the others out of business, if he wanted.

It took quite a long time, with Helen asking many questions and Stephen taking great pains to be as thorough as he could be. As he talked, Marie-Anne managed to eat some toast and eggs. It was done more out of a sense of duty to Helen, who cast concerned looks at Marie-Anne's full plate, than any kind of appetite. But after an hour or so she did feel better, and more able to listen to Stephen dispassionately listing Mason's deceptions.

"But have you taken any action against him?" Helen asked, when she had begun to grasp it. "Ravenclyffe mentioned some American investment last night at the dinner party, surely you must warn him."

"I don't feel particularly obliged to save Ravenclyffe from making an ass of himself," said Stephen, but he was looking at Marie-Anne now. "I did suggest to him and other interested parties that it was best to wait, and fortunately my suggestions are seldom disregarded in business matters. But I saw no need to entirely ruin Mr. Mason's reputation, unless Marie-Anne should wish it."

"But why should Marie-Anne *not* wish – oh!"

She was looking at Marie-Anne with sudden comprehension and, just as compassion began to creep across her features, Marie-Anne dropped her eyes. She could not quite bear to see it.

"Well," she said with an effort at what her friend would call a very Gallic shrug, "You did hope I would meet someone to put stars in my eyes, if you remember."

"Oh, the blackguard," Helen seethed. "The beastly *cad*. The – he – oh–" She gave up in English and, bless her, let loose a string of obscenities in French. Marie-Anne had taught them to her a long time ago, and was greatly cheered to see how well the lesson had been remembered.

"He is not a cad, *mon amie*," she explained once Helen had finished. "Well I suppose he *is*, but you may trust me when I say he is not a bad man. And he has not treated me with dishonor." She looked to Stephen. "I would not like to see him ruined. He will not make trouble. I think he will probably just... go away."

Then she had to stop, because she really did not want to begin weeping again. She listened as Stephen assured her he would be very discreet. He spent some time apologizing to his wife for not telling her immediately, insisting that he feared she would make herself ill with worry for Marie-Anne. Helen was very cross to hear this, but Marie-Anne privately thought Stephen had done right – Helen did tend to overreact when faced with deceptive men, and she might easily have made herself sick with fear for Marie-Anne. But now that she could see her friend was perfectly safe and well, Helen only grumbled a bit and pressed Marie-Anne's hand in sympathy.

"There is more to tell you about Mason," Marie-Anne said to her. "But it is nothing to do with money or false names. I must tell you how he is a very great artist who squanders his talent, and he asked me to marry him, but maybe we are finished now and I do not know what to do because I am terribly in love. Do you have some mysterious and important business affairs you can attend to, Stephen? I would like to steal your wife, and probably some wine. I would like to drink very much, I think."

"Oh, my." Helen was standing, and leading the way to the morning room. "It's hardly noon, Marie-Anne."

"Ah, you are right. If we want to be properly shocking we should have the whisky."

Chapter Nineteen

The thing about falling in love with someone like Marie-Anne, Mason reminded himself, was that she was indisputably worth the risk. Any risk. He wasn't sure if he'd leave the Earl of Summerdale's office in shackles or in triumph – or just deeply humiliated – but he was sure that he wouldn't regret trying.

So despite his uncertainty as to the outcome, detailing his sins to an actual lord of the manor was an improvement over the vast oceans of regret he'd been feeling from the moment he'd let Marie-Anne walk away. Admittedly, it wasn't even a whole day, but it had felt like a lifetime of misery. He didn't know for certain if she was in this house – perhaps she had gone off to her little village already – but just thinking she might be nearby made him feel more like himself. More like he could *be* himself, and not give in to the impulse to invent someone new to get himself out of trouble.

"There were no other gentlemen you told about the scheme directly, then?" asked Lord Summerdale. He was polite and distant, like they were talking of something as inconsequential as the coal delivery. "Just Whipple and Ravenclyffe?"

"Taney asked me about it. I think he got it from Whipple. I did tell them both to keep it under their hats. Doesn't seem like it did much good."

"On the contrary, they were both impressively tight-lipped. It was Ravenclyffe who told anyone who would listen. He began a very small frenzy."

"Well, at least it's small. It'll die out sooner that way. Even sooner if I have a word with him."

"You needn't worry. It's been seen to. Discreetly."

"You told them I'm a fraud?"

"It wasn't necessary."

Mason just looked at him, dumb, as he absorbed the meaning of this. He hadn't ever been face to face with this kind of power before. It took some adjustment. The Earl of Summerdale had seen to it, discreetly. He'd said a few chosen words to a few people, who believed him without question when he said that – what? It was a bad investment, he'd probably say, and that would kill it on the spot. It was nothing but the flick of a wrist to him, and he presented it with as much ceremony as that. There wasn't even the tiniest hint of disdain in his face to betray what he thought. Nothing.

"Why discreetly?" Mason asked. He could not imagine why his name should be spared, especially given that it was a fake name.

"I thought it best."

That was all he was going to get out of him, it was clear. Mason made a mental note never to play cards against the man. "Even Ravenclyffe will stop talking about it?"

"Especially Ravenclyffe. It seems he wants to give himself a reputation as a shrewd investor. He advocated loudly for this investment, in an effort to demonstrate his superior intellect and acumen. Now that I've let him know he'll only look a fool if he keeps it up, he's been eager to rescind his former endorsement, to show how very knowledgeable he is. I understand he spent last night at his club talking of little else."

"Well, that's convenient. Can I ask how you found all this out if you haven't even been in the country?"

"I left instruction for my secretary, who is very adept."

There seemed to be little more to say on the topic. He could feel the earl watching him, and Mason forced himself to meet his eyes. "There's something else. Like I said, I never planned to go through with it. I didn't come to London to trick people out of their money."

He reached into the smaller folder he had brought and pulled out three pamphlets. He'd gone through them all and chosen these specifically because they were the only ones where Freddy had written anything about Summerdale and his wife. It was just the usual imbecilic society chatter, nothing cruel: speculation as to the worth of her diamond choker, rumors that his mother was not a cherished guest in their home, that sort of thing. He waited, palms sweating and heart pounding, as Summerdale looked through the pamphlets. But Summerdale showed no surprise, and his glance only barely lingered over the page where his name was mentioned.

"This is why I came here, and why I told everyone...what I told them."

Mason held his breath as Summerdale took in the drawing of the marquess caught in bed with his mistress. It could easily be a friend of his. All these people he'd spent months ruthlessly mocking – these were Summerdale's people.

"It's how I've made my money," he explained, and set the small folder filled with all the other pamphlets he'd drawn on the desk between them. "They're all here."

Well, there it was, all his offenses laid out in front of a man who could throw him on a prison barge without batting an eye. But it was not as hard as he'd thought it would be. It was for Marie-Anne, and the new life she wanted. And that meant not hiding from any of it, no matter the consequences.

Summerdale pulled out a pamphlet that featured a drawing of Ravenclyffe. He held it up. "Ravenclyffe was most keen to get people talking about his ingenious investment in the hopes that it might deflect from less flattering stories that are circulating about him." His mouth twitched. "He's unamused by his sudden, wide reputation for depravity."

Well, no surprise – beware of tangled webs and hoisted petards, he and his cousin used to warn each other. They were an occupational hazard. There was some kind of balance, at least, in Ravenclyffe trying to improve a fabricated reputation by using a fabricated business venture, and exposing Mason to the earl's increased scrutiny in the process.

"Is it too hopeful to think the reputation I gave him will last longer than his talk about my brilliant investment opportunity?"

"Not at all. He was always a lecherous rogue, but it was never considered noteworthy. Your pamphlets changed that. Now that it's become a favorite joke, not just to his immediate acquaintance but to all of London, I doubt he'll ever disassociate himself from it."

Mason experienced a small burst of satisfaction at this news. He really should have dedicated himself to dragging down more of these hateful people, it was such a rewarding feeling. It'd teach him to be even more discerning in the future. If he had a future.

Summerdale was sifting through the papers. "I am very fond of the one where he's helplessly enchanted by the voluptuous curve of a horse's derriere."

Mason gave a light snort and leaned forward to put his elbows on his knees. "That one was Marie-Anne's idea."

The earl's eyebrows lifted for a moment, and then he verifiably grinned. It was quick and almost immediately suppressed, but there was no mistaking it, or the lingering amusement in his face. "I must remember to tell her that it's become one of the most popular prints the shop has ever sold, according to the printer. You have exceptional talent."

It took far too long for Mason to say "thank you." It seemed to be a genuine compliment, and he had to fight against his natural inclination to contradict it. But he managed to spit it out, and then gripped the larger folder still in his lap in an effort not to fidget. He didn't know how to do this next part, especially since he wasn't sure if they were done with this part. Surely, Summerdale would have more questions about the pack of lies Mason had strewn about England. Or maybe not – he seemed to know everything anyway.

Including how well the prints had sold, for God's sake. He took a deep breath and made himself speak.

"I'm hoping to make something of it. As a profession. In a more honest fashion, I mean. Here, if I can. I want to draw…not like I did for the papers." God, this was torture. He was so ignorant he didn't even have the words to describe what he meant. "To make real art, I mean."

Summerdale considered him for a long time. Mason could only endure it by keeping Marie-Anne firmly in mind. She had asked him to find the courage, because she didn't know – she couldn't know, what it was like to open this part of himself to strangers and let them look and judge him. She was right to call him afraid. Just the thought of it made him queasy with fear.

But in the early hours of this morning he'd caught himself thinking *nothing's worth going through that,* and it finally woke him up from the sullen misery that had held him for hours. Because Marie-Anne was worth it. There was no question. And among all the myriad reasons why she was worth it was this one: because she knew that, deep down in the most secret corner of his heart, he wanted this.

He didn't have much courage, but he could try. You have to try, Aloysius St. James had told him, if you want a thing so badly, if you love it like it's a part of yourself. *What else can matter?* he'd asked. And Mason was fairly sure he was better at art than St. James had ever been at poetry.

"You surprise me," Summerdale said, watching him closely. "I thought you'd slip away quietly, given the opportunity. You prefer to stay in England to live as an artist?"

"If I can. I don't know what I'd have to do. I don't even know where to start."

Summerdale rose from his chair and came around to the front of the desk. He leaned against it and folded his arms, looking down at Mason. It could have been an intimidating pose, but it wasn't. He seemed slightly less guarded, and vastly more human. "I presume you've had no formal study? There is the Royal Academy, of course – unless you prefer to begin taking commissions immediately."

Taking commissions. Right.

"I don't..." He was going to be purple soon, better to spit out what he could and have it over with. "I might have to start somewhere smaller, sir, I don't even know if I'm good enough for the Academy."

Summerdale shrugged. "That's the point of the Academy, it's open to all. May I?" He indicated the large folder in Mason's lap. "I'm no great judge, of course. Just curious."

Mason took a deep breath and handed it over. Now more than just his palms were sweating. Rather than watch Summerdale flip through the pages, he looked down at his own hands where they rested on his knees. He concentrated on breathing very calmly, to combat the flush that wanted to creep up his throat and the fear that wanted to suffocate him, and thought of Marie-Anne. She was worth this. Absolutely.

He did look up, finally, when he heard Summerdale say, "That's my wife." He wasn't angry. He just did as Marie-Anne had done, a soft look on his face as he let his fingers hover over the page.

"You can touch it," Mason told him. "It's just graphite." It showed Lady Summerdale leaning close to Marie-Anne's ear, as though to share a secret. He had drawn it only a week ago, intending to surprise Marie-Anne with it. "Her face is hard to capture."

"And yet you've managed to capture it. Even though you only saw her once, at a distance."

He didn't think the Earl of Summerdale would like to hear that his wife left quite an impression. He just kept his mouth shut and waited until the man was ready to say something else.

"You've said you wish to leave your former life behind. It is an admirable sentiment, but I hope you will forgive me my doubts. After all, you have only ended this charade because you've been discovered. You've lied to everyone you've met for months, with great ease."

Mason nodded, unsure how to defend himself. How to explain his life to someone who grew up in a house like this one? No – many houses, and bigger than this one. He probably had a castle somewhere. This man had never known deprivation or uncertainty for a day in his life.

"It's what I know how to do. It's what I grew up with, the way you grew up being a lord. But if it's what I really wanted, I wouldn't have left Kentucky." He'd already told him a little about how he was raised and everything about what he'd done here in London. He should have rehearsed it in his head more, the right things to say to convince him he wanted to leave it all behind. But he was used to practicing lies, not truth, so here he was at a loss for words.

"I know it's not honorable, the things I've done here," he finally said. "And I know you all set a lot of store by honor. But I did my best to make sure no one was ever really harmed by anything I did. The most that was ever at stake was reputation or money, and only from people who had plenty to spare."

Summerdale didn't respond to this. He only looked at him for a long moment, then returned to his seat at the desk. He opened the large folder again and went through the handful of drawings, lingering over the portrait of his wife before turning to one that showed Marie-Anne and Phyllida arranging flowers. That one wasn't quite as good – he should have chosen easier flowers.

"Marie-Anne de Vauteuil is one of the best people I have ever known," Summerdale announced. "It is one of the greatest honors of my life that she calls me friend, and an even greater privilege that I can call her the same." He closed the folder but did not hand it back. "I don't know that I've ever met anyone who is a superior judge of character. And she has said, only hours ago, that you are a good man."

"She did?"

"Well, not a bad man – those were her exact words, and it's a useful distinction. Regardless, she believes you are worth the effort it might take to establish you in some sort of honest life. She also declared her affection for you, and described you as a great talent." He actually smiled. "I see no reason to disbelieve any of her assertions."

He was sure Summerdale had all sorts of reservations about him, but it didn't matter. Nothing much mattered to Mason at all except for the tentative relief that began to trickle through him, and the knowledge that Marie-Anne had been here only hours ago.

"Is she still here?"

The earl smiled a little more broadly. "One thing at a time."

༄༅

At the height of her inebriation, Marie-Anne had confided in a very loud whisper, "He has a miraculous mouth, Hélène. No matter where he puts it!"

"Marie-Anne, *please*."

"Do not worry your blushes, I will not say more to shock you. This is another way to for me to know it is love, because I do not want to tell you every detail to make you turn red. I do not want to share things like that about my Mason, even to mortify you."

"Excellent, thank you. Shall I call for tea now?"

"Mm tea. It *is* excellent. If I were rich I would build a monument to it. Not the tea, his mouth. To commemorate its great feats." She began to giggle. "An obelisk. Just the right size, you know, not too—"

"Marie-*Anne!*" Helen had squealed, and they had both laughed so hard that Marie-Anne put down her glass of whisky and began to slowly sober up. She had managed to tell her friend just about everything and had finally gotten to how Mason had proposed. Now she sat back on the divan and recounted how hesitant she had been to say yes, while she waited for her head to stop its gentle spinning.

She spent such a long time moaning about her heartache that her head had stopped spinning and begun to ache with the aftereffects of drink by the time she finished. Helen was very good and did not interrupt, even though it was obvious several times that she wanted to.

"Now I do not know what to think, or if I am

right," a sober Marie-Anne at last concluded. She had closed her eyes against the little headache. "Tell me what is your advice, please."

When Helen did not answer, Marie-Anne opened her eyes to see her friend was a little startled.

"I don't believe you've ever asked my advice before, Marie-Anne! I hardly know what to say. It's always me who needs setting right, not you. Whether it's a matter of fashion or a matter of the heart, you always seem to know. It's so rare to see you doubt yourself."

Marie-Anne sighed. "Yes. I do not like it. It is very vexing!"

"I suppose it is noteworthy that you do not seem to doubt *him*, though, in spite of his duplicity."

"This is true. I trust in his love for me, and I trust his intentions are good."

"His intentions seem especially important—"

"But it is that he does not trust in himself!" she burst out, which caused her head to throb. She rubbed her temple, and vowed to confine her future drinking to a single glass of wine in the evenings. "It is this that confuses, that I am not happy to have him come back to Bartle with me. It makes me angry to think of it! My Mason should be in Paris or Florence. Or even here in London, but not hiding his talent in little Bartle-on-the-Glen."

"I must say, Marie-Anne, that I do not find it confusing at all." Helen got up and spoke as she crossed to the bell pull. "I cannot imagine you would respect anyone who would be so cowardly that they would not even try to pursue their dreams. You have always scorned self-denial in every way, and that's what it would be, isn't it? Oh yes, Collins," she said, turning to the butler who had appeared. "Tea, please."

She came back to sit on the divan beside Marie-Anne, and very gently said, "But perhaps he needs time to accustom himself to the idea, if it is such a very new one. We do not all throw ourselves into new experiences with good cheer and enthusiasm, as you do."

Helen was very diplomatically saying that Marie-Anne was too impatient, and she was not wrong. Marie-Anne gave a very heavy sigh, and eased herself down until she lay on the divan with her head on Helen's lap. She pulled her feet up too, and noticed distantly that she'd lost a slipper somehow.

"Was it right, what he said to me?" she asked. "Do I hide myself in my little village, and away from living?"

"I think you needed to, as I did, for a while. Only you can say whether you need to hide anymore." Helen stroked her aching forehead. It felt very nice. "But you are built for adventure, Marie-Anne, he's right about that. Built for adventure and impulse and all kinds of untidy, human things."

Startled by this insight, Marie-Anne's eyes snapped open. This was so true that it was disturbing she had ever questioned it. She had even tried to tell herself to be responsible, of all the ridiculous things. "*Mon dieu.* You are right," she said. "And now I am thinking also that Richard would hate that I sit in Bartle alone for the rest of my life."

"Well, what would you like to do instead?"

She sighed. "Have little babies with red hair. But I am trying not to think of that."

Helen looked down at her. Even from below at

this unflattering angle, she was very lovely. "You asked my advice, Marie-Anne, so I'll tell you I think you should be with this Mason. You love him far more than you even realize. Do you know why I am so sure?"

Marie-Anne shook her head. "Why?"

"Because you've mentioned Richard more than once today. Just Richard, not 'my Richard'. In all the years I've known you, he was always *your* Richard. Surely that means something." She smiled. "And if that wasn't telling enough, there is an entire plate of cakes right there that you haven't touched in all this time."

Well, there was no disputing either point. She would always love Richard, and cherish everything he had been to her. But it was Mason's heart that was in her care now. Or at least she hoped it was. She supposed she must go claim it for herself, just as soon as she could sit upright without her head splitting open. Perhaps a bit of cake would help.

Helen's nearly untouched glass of whisky sat on the little table near her, and the sight of it made Marie-Anne feel too queasy to eat. "You are a terrible friend, to let me drink so much by myself. And why do you only take a little swallow? The whisky from Scotland is your favorite."

Helen gave a telling pause before saying, "It will upset my digestion. Everything seems to do lately, I had a terrible time with the fish in Norway."

"Oh! I am a very bad friend!" Marie-Anne sat up too suddenly and clutched her aching head. "I have not even asked why you came back so soon! Are you ill?"

Helen was trying not to laugh at Marie-Anne's

wincing. "No, not ill. Not truly. Oh dear, I should have asked Collins to bring you a cold cloth for your head."

But now Marie-Anne was smiling wide enough that her face hurt too. "Hélène! Is it true? Tell me!"

Helen shrugged, still holding back a laugh. "You are trying not to think of babies, I thought."

"Oh!"

Marie-Anne was unequal to saying anything more comprehensible than that for some time. She merely threw her arms around her friend and let herself think of nothing but the joy of it. What happy, happy news. She quite forgot her own troubles for a few minutes.

When Collins entered with the tea, she was almost giddy. "Don't you think Marie-Anne is a perfect name for a girl, Collins?" she asked over Helen's laughter. "But of course it is only a suggestion, Hélène, you may name her anything you like. What about Marie? Or Anne? So many choices!"

"All excellent choices, madame," was the butler's sedate reply. He cleared his throat and addressed Helen. "Lord Summerdale wished you to know that he will be going out this afternoon, my lady, but he anticipates returning in time for dinner."

"Going out? How very odd, he said nothing about an engagement. Did he say where he is going?"

The butler slid an impassive look toward Marie-Anne. "I believe he will be accompanying Mr. Mason to pay a call upon Lady Whitemarsh."

Helen's curious "Lady Whitemarsh?" competed with Marie-Anne's yelp of "Mason!" Collins, unflappable, looked at each of them in turn and said simply, "Yes."

"But is Mr. Mason here?" Helen was asking.

Marie-Anne was already on her feet – entirely too quickly, causing the ache in her skull to swell and her stomach to make dire threats.

"He is," Collins was saying behind her. She was rushing to the door, not stopping to find the slipper that had fallen off. She stood in the entrance hall and turned a circle, looking up the elegant staircase, wondering where he could be.

Just as she decided it must be Stephen's office and began to make her way toward it, the door opened and the men emerged. Oh, his wonderful red hair and his glorious freckles, she had missed them terribly. One little day – one ghastly, miserable whole day – and she never wanted to pass another one without him.

He caught sight of her and stopped, arrested, gazing at her. How long had he been here while she drank too much and moaned about him to her friend? He didn't say anything, or move nearer, and she suddenly realized that he may not have come here for her at all. Oh, what an awful thought.

"Mason?" She looked at Stephen and then back to Mason. "What are you doing here?"

"I just – we're going to..." He clearly had no idea what to say, and her heart began to sink, thinking he must once again be caught in some lie. Thoroughly caught, if he faltered so obviously. "I was going to tell you after we arranged it. Nothing's settled yet."

"Arrange what?" she asked, but she had noticed the large folder in Stephen's hand. They were his drawings. He had brought his drawings to Stephen.

"Lady Whitemarsh's cousin is presently staying with her," Stephen explained. "He is a very accomplished artist of considerable standing. Trained in portraiture, I believe. I'm given to understand he accepts students if they are sufficiently talented."

"He is," said Marie-Anne promptly, never taking her eyes off Mason. "You are." She took a few steps toward him, but he stayed where he was. He seemed frozen, and she recognized a kind of faint panic in him. "Oh *mon coeur*, he will love your work, I promise you. You are very frightened?"

He swallowed. "Terrified. I might vomit on this very fine carpet." A smile began to pull at his lips, though. "You?"

"I drank too much," she said, in case standing before him with loose, bedraggled hair and one bare foot did not make this obvious. She beamed at him. "My head is splitting."

His smile grew to reflect hers, and suddenly everything was perfect. They just stood, smiling at each other for a long moment in which Marie-Anne thought her face might crack, until he took a step toward her and she threw herself at him. His arms around her were absolutely what she wanted, but when he immediately began to whirl her about, she beat at his shoulders and protested that he would make her ill. He laughed and put her down, but did not let her go. That was good. She never wanted him to let her go again.

She pulled back a little to see him, and his face so full of joy made her feel like he *had* spun her about. She was dizzy with happiness.

"Oh," she said, suddenly a little anxious, her hands holding his face as she looked for signs of misgiving. "But it is what you want? I should not push, it is very bad of me to be so impatient! You must want it for yourself, Mason."

"I like you impatient." He curled his fingers in her tangled mass of hair. "I want it. And I want you. It seems crazy to think I can have both, all at once." He gave a disbelieving laugh. "It's an embarrassment of riches. And I'm not used to any kind of riches."

She smiled again, elated. "You will get used to it. It will be a new habit."

"Will it?" he grinned, and she nodded.

She was interrupted in her intention to kiss him because she became conscious of some kind of mild commotion behind her. As she didn't have any desire to take her arms from around Mason, she didn't turn around. Instead, she pulled him a little, shuffling their feet as they still embraced, until they could both see what it was.

"Under no circumstances will you allow her entrance, Collins," Helen was saying to the butler. Amy and Dahlia had appeared in the entrance hall, and Collins held the front door open at barely a crack. "Lady Shipley is not welcome in my home, nor will she ever be. Her husband as well."

A squawk, rather like an outraged chicken, came from outside the door where presumably Lady Shipley was being made to cool her heels. Marie-Anne snorted with laughter as Collins closed the door firmly and Helen assured the girls they were most welcome, unlike their mother. It was as Mason had said – an embarrassment of riches, to have such a loyal friend by her side and such a man in her arms.

"Marie-Anne, it's the most dreadful thing!" Dahlia was very pale. "Phyllida has run off!"

Marie-Anne felt a little twinge of guilt. She'd completely forgotten she had promised to look for Phyllida – though really, she'd only ever planned to call in at the Shipley's townhouse to see if she was there, and obviously she wasn't.

"She left a note. We only found it this morning." Amy clutched the paper in her hands and looked like she was also a candidate for being ill on the very fine carpet. "She's gone off with the hermit. She says they are to be married."

"But he's not a hermit at all, as though that weren't bad enough. He's a farmer!" Dahlia looked appalled. "He raises pigs!"

Marie-Anne was too supremely happy to be anything but delighted at this news. "How lovely! Will we be invited to the wedding?" Dahlia looked stricken. "Oh, I am so sorry to be rude! I forgot, dear Dahlia. Do you mind if I marry Mason?" She turned her face back up to him. "We are very much in love."

"I can't see – Marie-Anne, you – well no, of course I don't object in the least!" Dahlia spluttered, clearly thinking this was far from relevant.

"You want to marry me?" Mason asked. "You're sure?"

"Oh, very sure. Can I marry you twice? Three times, for luck."

"I'm very happy for you both, truly, but there is little time." Amy sounded a little frantic. "Mr. St. James believes he knows where they are, and if you can come with us I'm sure you can persuade Phyllida–"

"I'm not going to persuade Phyllida." Marie-Anne didn't look away from Mason, because he was the only thing she really wanted to see. "Phyllie is in love with her farmer. She follows her heart, as you have both done. Good for her."

"But my sister cannot be allowed to marry a pig

farmer!" Dahlia protested.

Marie-Anne's only reply to this was a concise, "Pfft." It made Mason laugh. Delightful, perfect sound, this laughter she would get to hear every day now.

"But Marie-Anne!" Amy was using her most practical tone. "You know she will come to regret it. It is a terrible match, you can't think she'll be happy."

"Oh, it is probably a very bad idea," Marie-Anne agreed. "You may tell her from me that to be a farmer's wife is much less romantic than she has considered. After that, if she marries him, then I will only wish her joy. As you should." She moved her hands up to the back of Mason's neck so she could feel his hair against her fingertips. "Now go away. We are going to be very improper."

"Just what I wanted to hear," said Mason as he bent his head to kiss her.

It was very passionate – very deep and very long, as he had long ago promised his kisses would be. She held on to his shoulders as his hands gripped her bottom and lifted her closer to him, as tight as they could be. Really, why would anyone ever want to be less than shocking? All the best things were a little scandalous, like the way her hips fit against his and that little hint of a groan at the back of his throat.

She thought she heard Helen invite the girls into the morning room for tea, but only came up for air after she heard Amy reluctantly say that they should not leave their mama on the front step. Then Collins announced to Stephen that the carriage was ready. Marie-Anne sighed against Mason's lips, which were blessedly still near hers for the moment, and told herself he would be back very soon. She could make herself presentable while he was gone, even though she had a burning desire to be extremely unpresentable.

He pulled his face back from hers a little. "Lord Summerdale," he called to Stephen, still looking into Marie-Anne's eyes. "Can we postpone this interview until tomorrow? I have a headache to cure."

"Yes, I will show him to his room," Marie-Anne laughed.

"That is easily arranged," said Stephen, trying and failing to suppress his amusement. "Helen, shall we call on Lady Whitemarsh? We'll meet this cousin."

Mason lifted off Marie-Anne off her feet and made his way toward the stairs with her.

"It's very nice to meet you, Mr. Mason!" Helen called after them, as they headed up the stairs. "We'll be back at dinner, and I shall thank you properly for putting stars in her eyes again."

Mason paused on the stair. "It's my pleasure, ma'am," he said over his shoulder. He grinned at Marie-Anne. "Quite a lot of pleasure."

Marie-Anne pulled at his hand, giggling like a girl. A girl who had temporarily forgotten that she was indeed built for adventure, and messy love affairs, and impulsive acts. But she remembered now. She could hear the Shipley girls tittering, and imagined her friend's blushes.

"I will be a married woman soon, Hélène," she shouted down the stairs. "I do not promise anymore that I will not be outrageous!"

After all, if he was to become who he was always meant to be, then so would she. And it was her true nature to be a little shocking. What a wonderful thing, that she enjoyed it so well.

Epilogue

Mason had fully intended to arrange his day differently, so that he might actually be able to help Marie-Anne for once. But instead of coaxing a child to sleep in the middle of the day, somehow he was hunched over a table on the little terrace, carefully mixing pigment in the shade with the Italian sunlight warm on his back.

"I'm sorry." He called it softly over his shoulder when he heard her step behind him. The children were probably already asleep and it took a lot more than a shout to wake them, but better to be safe than sorry. "I was working on the Bronzino all morning and I lost track of time."

Marie-Anne snorted. "He will not be happy even if you spend a year at it. If he did not pay you so well, I would tell him his face is very ordinary and it does not deserve so much attention."

Mason smiled to himself. Her exasperation with Signore Bronzino was no different from her impatience with anyone else who paid him to paint them. She couldn't think of Mason as a beginner still, so he had given up trying to get her to understand. Like everyone, Bronzino saw himself one way and Mason saw him another way, and the job was to make something the paying customer wanted. Marie-Anne saw every requested change as a slight to his talent; Mason saw every new iteration as a chance to learn – so much so that he had moments where he questioned whether this was actually honest work, getting paid to learn.

His unreasonably adorable wife had come up behind him to kiss his neck. "But what is this?" she asked. "You made two different blue paints this morning. Already you need more?"

"I do," he said, quickly pressing an answering kiss to her temple before returning to the work. "This morning I made one to match your eyes when you are tired and another to match them when they look at Rebecca."

"They are always the same blue, my mad *artiste*."

"They're not. This one will be the blue of you looking at Aurélien, which has more gold in it, like his hair. And these," he pointed at the other pigments he'd already made up, "are your happy blue eyes, and then angry, and this is how they looked in England. The light's different there, you know."

"*Pazzo*," she replied. She had developed a deep affection for the Italian language and, despite this assertion that he was crazy, fortunately still had affection for him too, even after four years, two countries, and a set of exhausting twins. "Will you ever finish this portrait? Francesca says there is another who thinks to commission you, if you have the time."

"I plan to finish very soon, but I don't think I'm interested in that commission." He finished with the pigment at hand, made a mental note to buy more linseed oil, and prepared to have what he hoped would eventually be a very happy conversation. Right now, though, his wife was scowling.

"But you have not even heard who it is! You remember Francesca worked for that merchant's wife, to take care of her baby?" Francesca was the indispensable nursemaid who made their life with a pair of two-year-olds bearable. "Now the baby is grown and they would like her to be painted. It is perfect!"

"I found something better," he assured her.

"Better! What is better? She is still so young, she will not be like these others who always demand more and more because they do not have eyes in their heads to see how perfect you paint them."

He laughed at that. She still loved his sketches best, because they were always truest to what he saw. At least, the first set of sketches were truest, until he showed them to the subject who inevitably wanted to look more noble or intelligent or delicate as a flower. For him, it was the best of both worlds – he got to make what he saw as well as what someone else saw. And he kept the sketches.

"What if I told you I had a letter from Stephen?"

She looked sharply at him. "Hélène's Stephen? Summerdale?"

"That's the one." He wound an arm around her waist and pulled her into his lap. Thankfully she wore the dress of many stains, as he had named it – or as she called it, her most avante-garde gown, custom designed – and another smear was never amiss.

"Why would he write to you?"

She seemed more concerned than anything else, though he could not imagine what there was to be concerned about. It had proven a miraculous advantage, to have someone like the Earl of Summerdale as his ally. He had made sure all of London knew the fabulously wealthy American businessman in their midst had quietly sold his company to an undisclosed buyer, and deflected any curious questions with suggestions of other, more promising business ventures. If that weren't enough, he'd introduced Mason to his first art teacher, and his first art dealer, and his first paid commission. And now this.

"Summerdale wants a family portrait done, and he'd like to hire me to do it."

"But – they are not coming here, Hélène would have written to me. They cannot, she will have the new baby in a few months!"

"Yes, and it must be a boy so that Rebecca can marry him," he recited, having heard this little dream of hers many times. "Just like our little Aurélien will marry their Margaret. And they'll all be best friends, no matter how unlikely I think it is that I could have children who'll marry lords and ladies. I know."

She narrowed her eyes at him. "If you do not tell me how you will paint them when they are in England and you are in Italy, I will refuse to kiss you for an entire hour."

That would not do at all.

"We'll move back to England," he said promptly, and kissed her. He could feel all the energy bubble up in her, all the questions, how half of her wanted to pull away and demand answers. But being Marie-Anne, she never passed up the opportunity to kiss him, and she only opened her mouth wider and pulled herself even closer in a fervent embrace.

When she finally let him breathe, he explained Summerdale's proposal. It had been long enough that very few people were likely even to remember Mason, but if they did, they would simply be told the truth: yes, he had used to be a businessman but now he was an artist. Nobility and foreigners were allowed these little eccentricities, Stephen had explained. Helen would happily give them the use of the large dower house she had inherited, which had a room that would serve perfectly as a studio, and was only a few miles from the Summerdale country estate in Herefordshire.

"Oh!" gasped Marie-Anne in delight. "But it is just outside of Bartle! I can eat Mr. Higgins' bread every day again, and little Agnes Turner will want to steal the red curls right off our babies' heads."

"I kept her from stealing mine, I think we can stop her from doing any damage." They had visited Bartle in the months before leaving England, and he understood why Marie-Anne had stayed there so long. It was a very peaceful place, full of people who clearly cared for her. Now she put her excitement at the idea aside and began to fret. Didn't he want to stay in Italy to learn more, was he sure he wanted to go back to England, what about when the commission was done and he must find new work?

But he wasn't worried about any of it. Italy was wonderful, but so was England. So was anywhere that she was. There would be more than just one commission in England – there had been a showing in London that included his work, and already he was becoming more well-known. And he could always teach, as audacious and improbable as it seemed that he not only had an actual skill, but knowledge that people might pay for.

They would make it work, he told her. They had made it work these past several years, after all, and it had been far easier than he'd ever thought it could be. As Marie-Anne was fond of reminding him, everything was easier when you let yourself be who you're meant to be. Besides, he reminded her, didn't she also want to take all these thrilling fashions and fabrics back to England? She'd have her own commissions soon enough. She'd already had him make dozens of sketches of dresses and jackets and hats to her specifications, only to have the dressmakers of Milan turn green with envy.

"I will make the villagers look very smart," she giggled. "And I will put a cravat on John Turner's goat, who is very handsome. He will eat it immediately, of course, but this will amuse the children."

"Then it's settled." He kissed her nose and picked her up as he stood. "Now when will the little monsters wake up so we can tell them?"

"We have time for you to ravage me first, I think. You see how I am very clever, I keep track of time much better than you do."

"I think you mean ravish, but I won't quibble over words."

She was kissing his neck as he carried her, saying something about how it sounded too much like radishes and she wondered what the Italian word for it was. He paused and set her down as he passed the room where the twins were sleeping, sprawled on the bed and snoring. Rebecca's long red curls tangled with her brother's strawberry blond hair.

"Are you sure?" Marie-Anne whispered to him as they both gazed at the children. "If we go now, you will make your career in England, and a whole life. They will grow up there. You are sure you want to make it your home?"

He took her hand and tucked a stray lock of her hair behind her ear. He watched her toes curl against the floor. She loved to go barefoot in the house and watch the Italian nurse suck in her breath and scold her for exposing herself to dangerous draughts. Marie-Anne teased that it was one of the few shocking things left to her, and laughed at every scold.

His wife. His thrilling, beautiful, perfect, priceless wife. It still seemed like a dream, every day, that he'd wound up here, with her.

"I already have a home," he told her. "It's wherever you are, and they are."

She looked at him and smiled. "Well, if one day you do not like it there, we will leave. Our home is you, too, my Mason." She leaned against him and wrapped her arms around him, and added, "My true home with my true Mason. It is a very great wealth, like you said. An embarrassment of riches."

THE END

ꞋꞋ

Acknowledgements

Do you always read my acknowledgements, dear readers? If so, you already know who I'm going to mention: Susanna Malcolm, the best reader ever (beta, alpha, omega, you name it – she gets it at every stage) and believe it or not, an even better friend. In keeping with this book's refrain about an embarrassment of riches, I must also thank Laura Kinsale from the bottom of my heart for being as good a reader as Susanna. Who the heck gets TWO amazing critique partners/editors/dear friends? I might have made some Faustian bargain years ago and totally forgotten, because I truly don't deserve that much awesomeness. And if that weren't enough, I also have to thank Candy Tan (and also Canby Tan, forever buying flowers) for her timely, generous, and invaluable input. All three of these incredibly smart, thoughtful, patient women pushed me to make this a better book and, in turn, to make me a better writer. I can't thank you enough, and am very glad you accept payment in donuts.

And even though it's maybe cheesy or seems like pandering or whatever to include My Readers in the acknowledgements, the truth is you guys are so great and you've kept me writing. If you ever sent a note or a tweet, or even just liked a Facebook post or mentioned my books to another human being: seriously, I cannot thank you enough. You guys never fail to give me a second – and third and fourth and fiftieth – wind in the midst of the marathon that is novel-writing. Thank you so much, please treat yourself to the baked good of your choice, I will arrange it with the cosmos so that it has no calories whatsoever.